THE MONEY MASTER

BY

GILBERT PARKER

The Money Master

CHAPTER I. THE GRAND TOUR OF JEAN JACQUES BARBILLE

"Peace and plenty, peace and plenty"—that was the phrase M. Jean Jacques Barbille, miller and moneymaster, applied to his home-scene, when he was at the height of his career. Both winter and summer the place had a look of content and comfort, even a kind of opulence. There is nothing like a grove of pines to give a sense of warmth in winter and an air of coolness in summer, so does the slightest breeze make the pine-needles swish like the freshening sea. But to this scene, where pines made a friendly background, there were added oak, ash, and hickory trees, though in less quantity on the side of the river where were Jean Jacques Barbille's house and mills. They flourished chiefly on the opposite side of the Beau Cheval, whose waters flowed so waywardly—now with a rush, now silently away through long reaches of country. Here the land was rugged and bold, while farther on it became gentle and spacious, and was flecked or striped with farms on which low, white houses with dormer-windows and big stoops flashed to the passer-by the message of the pioneer, "It is mine. I triumph."

At the Manor Cartier, not far from the town of Vilray, where Jean Jacques was master, and above it and below it, there had been battles and the ravages of war. At the time of the Conquest the stubborn habitants, refusing to accept the yielding of Quebec as the end of French power in their proud province, had remained in arms and active, and had only yielded when the musket and the torch had done their work, and smoking ruins marked the places where homes had been. They took their fortune with something of the heroic calm of men to whom an idea was more than aught else. Jean Jacques' father, grandfather, and great-great-grandfather had lived here, no one of them rising far, but none worthless or unnoticeable. They all had had "a way of their own," as their neighbours said, and had been provident on the whole. Thus it was that when Jean Jacques' father died, and he came into his own, he found himself at thirty a man of substance, unmarried, who "could have had the pick of the province." This was what the Old Cure said in despair, when Jean Jacques did the incomprehensible thing, and married l'Espagnole, or "the Spanische," as the lady was always called in the English of the habitant.

When she came it was spring-time, and all the world was budding, exuding joy and hope, with the sun dancing over all. It was the time between the sowing and the hay-time, and there was a feeling of alertness in everything that had life, while even the rocks and solid earth seemed to stir. The air was filled with the long happy drone of the mill-stones as they ground the grain; and from farther away came the soft, stinging cry of a saw-mill. Its keen buzzing complaint was harmonious with the grumble of the mill-stones, as though a supreme maker of music had tuned it. So said a master-musician and his friend, a philosopher from Nantes, who came to St. Saviour's in the summer just before the marriage, and lodged with Jean Jacques. Jean Jacques, having spent a year at Laval University at Quebec, had almost a gift of thought, or thinking; and he never ceased to ply the visiting philosopher and musician with questions which he proceeded to answer himself before they could do so; his quaint, sentimental, meretricious observations on life saddening while they amused his guests. They saddened the musician more than the other because he knew life, while the philosopher only thought it and saw it.

But even the musician would probably have smiled in hope that day when the young "Spanische" came driving up the river-road from the steamboat-landing miles away. She arrived just when the clock struck noon in the big living-room of the Manor. As she reached the open doorway and the wide windows of the house which gaped with shady coolness, she heard the bell summoning the workers in the mills and on the farm—yes, M. Barbille was a farmer, too—for the welcome home to "M'sieu' Jean Jacques," as he was called by everyone.

That the wedding had taken place far down in Gaspe and not in St. Saviour's was a reproach and almost a scandal; and certainly it was unpatriotic. It was bad enough to marry the Spanische, but to marry outside one's own parish, and so deprive that parish and its young people of the week's gaiety, which a wedding and the consequent procession and tour through the parish brings, was little less than treason. But there it was; and Jean Jacques was a man who had power to hurt, to hinder, or to help; for the miller and the baker are nearer to the hearthstone of every man than any other, and credit is a good thing when the oven is empty and hard times are abroad. The wedding in Gaspe had not been attended by the usual functions, for it had all been hurriedly arranged, as the romantic circumstances of the wooing required. Romance indeed it was; so remarkable that the master-musician might easily have found a theme for a comedy—or tragedy—and the philosopher would have shaken his head at the defiance it offered to the logic of things.

Now this is the true narrative, though in the parish of St. Saviour's it is more highly decorated and has many legends hanging to it like tassels to a curtain. Even the Cure of to-day, who ought to know all the truth, finds it hard to present it in its bare elements; for the history of Jean Jacques Barbille affected the history of many a man in St. Saviour's; and all that befel him, whether of good or evil, ran through the parish in a thousand invisible threads.

What had happened was this. After the visit of the musician and the philosopher, Jean Jacques, to sustain his reputation and to increase it, had decided to visit that Normandy from which his people had come at the time of Frontenac. He set forth with much 'eclat' and a little innocent posturing and ritual, in which a cornet and a violin figured, together with a farewell oration by the Cure.

In Paris Jean Jacques had found himself bewildered and engulfed. He had no idea that life could be so overbearing, and he was inclined to resent his own insignificance. However, in Normandy, when he read the names on the tombstones and saw the records in the baptismal register of other Jean Jacques Barbilles, who had come and gone generations before, his self-respect was somewhat restored. This pleasure was dashed, however, by the quizzical attitude of the natives of his ancestral parish, who walked round about inspecting him as though he were a zoological specimen, and who criticized his accent—he who had been at Laval for one whole term; who had had special instruction before that time from the Old Cure and a Jesuit brother; and who had been the friend of musicians and philosophers!

His cheerful, kindly self-assurance stood the test with difficulty, but it became a kind of ceremonial with him, whenever he was discomfited, to read some pages of a little dun-coloured book of philosophy, picked up on the quay at Quebec just before he sailed, and called, "Meditations in Philosophy." He had been warned by the bookseller that the Church had no love for philosophy; but while at Laval he had met the independent minds that, at eighteen to twenty-two, frequent academic groves; and he was not to be put off by the pious bookseller—had he not also had a philosopher in his house the year before, and was he not going to Nantes to see this same savant before returning to his beloved St. Saviour's parish.

But Paris and Nantes and Rouen and Havre abashed and discomfited him, played havoc with his self-esteem, confused his brain, and vexed him by formality, and, more than all, by their indifference to himself. He admired, yet he wished to be admired; he was humble, but he wished all people and things to be humble with him. When he halted he wanted the world to halt; when he entered a cathedral—Notre Dame or any other; or a great building—the Law Courts at Rouen or any other; he simply wanted people to say, wanted the cathedral, or at least the cloister, to whisper to itself, "Here comes Jean Jacques Barbille."

That was all he wanted, and that would have sufficed. He would not have had them whisper about his philosophy and his intellect, or the mills and the ash-factory which he meant to build, the lime-kilns he had started even before he left, and the general store he intended to open when he returned to St. Saviour's. Not even his modesty was recognized; and, in his grand tour, no one was impressed by all that he was, except once. An ancestor, a grandmother of his, had come from the Basque country; and so down to St. Jean Pied de Port he went; for he came of a race who set great store by mothers and grandmothers. At St. Jean Pied de Port he was more at home. He was, in a sense, a foreigner among foreigners there, and the people were not quizzical, since he was an outsider in any case and not a native returned, as he had been in Normandy. He learned to play pelota, the Basque game taken from the Spaniards, and he even allowed himself a little of that oratory which, as they say, has its habitat chiefly in Gascony. And because he had found an audience at last, he became a liberal host, and spent freely of his dollars, as he had never done either in Normandy, Paris, or elsewhere. So freely did he spend, that when he again embarked at Bordeaux for Quebec, he had only enough cash left to see him through the remainder of his journey in the great world. Yet he left France with his self-respect restored, and he even waved her a fond adieu, as the creaking Antoine broke heavily into the waters of the Bay of Biscay, while he cried:

"My little ship,

It bears me far

From lights of home

To alien star.

O vierge Marie,

Pour moi priez Dieu!

Adieu, dear land,

Provence, adieu."

Then a further wave of sentiment swept over him, and he was vaguely conscious of a desire to share the pains of parting which he saw in labour around him—children from parents, lovers from loved. He could not imagine the parting from a parent, for both of his were in the bosom of heaven, having followed his five brothers, all of whom had died in infancy, to his good fortune, for otherwise his estate would now be only one-sixth of what it was. But he could imagine a parting with some sweet daughter of France, and he added another verse to the thrilling of the heart of Casimir Delavigne:

"Beloved Isaure,

Her hand makes sign—

No more, no more,

To rest in mine.

O vierge Marie,

Pour moi priez Dieu!

Adieu, dear land,

Isaure, adieu!"

As he murmured with limpid eye the last words, he saw in the forecastle not far from him a girl looking at him. There was unmistakable sadness in her glance of interest. In truth she was thinking of just such a man as Jean Jacques, whom she could never see any more, for he had paid with his life the penalty of the conspiracy in which her father, standing now behind her on the leaky Antoine, had been a tool, and an evil tool. Here in Jean Jacques was the same ruddy brown face, black restless eye, and young, silken, brown beard. Also there was an air of certainty and universal comprehension, and though assertion and vanity were apparent, there was no self-consciousness. The girl's dead and gone conspirator had not the same honesty of face, the same curve of the ideal in the broad forehead, the same poetry of rich wavy brown hair, the same goodness of mind and body so characteristic of Jean Jacques—he was but Jean Jacques gone wrong at the start; but the girl was of a nature that could see little difference between things which were alike superficially, and in the young provincial she only saw one who looked like the man she had loved. True, his moustaches did not curl upwards at the ends as did those of Carvillho Gonzales, and he did not look out of the corner of his eyes and smoke black cigarettes; but there he was, her Carvillho with a difference—only such a difference that made him to her Carvillho II., and not the ghost of Carvillho I.

She was a maiden who might have been as good as need be for all life, so far as appearances went. She had a wonderful skin, a smooth, velvety cheek, where faint red roses came and went, as it might seem at will; with a deep brown eye; and eh, but she was grandly tall—so Jean Jacques thought, while he drew himself up to his full five feet, six and a half with a determined air. Even at his best, however, Jean Jacques could not reach within three inches of her height.

Yet he did not regard her as at all overdone because of that. He thought her hair very fine, as it waved away from her low forehead in a grace which reminded him of the pictures of the Empress Eugenie, and of the sister of that monsieur le duc who had come fishing to St. Saviour's a few years before. He thought that if her hair was let down it would probably reach to her waist, and maybe to her ankles. She had none of the plump, mellow softness of the beauties he had seen in the Basque country. She was a slim and long limbed Diana, with fine lines and a bosom of extreme youth, though she must have been twenty-one her last birthday. The gown she wore was a dark green well-worn velvet, which seemed of too good a make and quality for her class; and there was no decoration about her anywhere, save at the ears, where two drops of gold hung on little links an inch and a half long.

Jean Jacques Barbille's eyes took it all in with that observation of which he was so proud and confident, and rested finally on the drops of gold at her ears. Instinctively he fingered the heavy gold watch-chain he had bought in Paris to replace the silver chain with a little crucifix dangling, which his father and even his great-grandfather had worn before him. He had kept the watch, however—the great fat-bellied thing which had never run down in a hundred years. It was his mascot. To lose that watch would be like losing his share in the promises of the Church. So his fingers ran along the new gold-fourteen-carat-chain, to the watch at the end of it; and he took it out a little ostentatiously, since he saw that the eyes of the girl were on him. Involuntarily he wished to impress her.

He might have saved himself the trouble. She was impressed. It was quite another matter however, whether he would have been pleased to know that the impression was due to his resemblance to a Spanish conspirator, whose object was to destroy the Monarchy and the Church, as had been the object of the middle-aged conspirator—the girl's father—who had the good fortune to escape from justice. It is probable that if Jean Jacques had known these facts, his story would never have been written, and he would have died in course of time with twenty children and a seat in the legislature; for, in spite of his ardent devotion to philosophy and its accompanying rationalism, he was a devout monarchist and a child of the Church.

Sad enough it was that, as he shifted his glance from the watch, which ticked loud enough to wake a farmhand in the middle of the day, he found those Spanish eyes which had been so lost in studying him. In the glow and glisten of the evening sun setting on the shores of Bordeaux, and flashing reflected golden light to the girl's face, he saw that they were shining with tears, and though looking at him, appeared not to see him. In that moment the scrutiny of the little man's mind was volatilized, and the Spanische, as she was ultimately called, began her career in the life of the money-master of St. Saviour's.

It began by his immediately resenting the fact that she should be travelling in the forecastle. His mind imagined misfortune and a lost home through political troubles, for he quickly came to know that the girl and her father were Spanish; and to him, Spain was a place of martyrs and criminals. Criminals these could not be—one had but to look at the girl's face; while the face of her worthless father might have been that of a friend of Philip IV. in the Escorial, so quiet and oppressed it seemed. Nobility was written on the placid, apathetic countenance, except when it was not under observation, and then the look of Cain took its place. Jean Jacques, however, was not likely to see that look; since Sebastian Dolores—that was his name—had observed from the first how the master-miller was impressed by his daughter, and he was set to turn it to account.

Not that the father entered into an understanding with the girl. He knew her too well for that. He had a wholesome respect, not to say fear, of her; for when all else had failed, it was she who had arranged his escape from Spain, and who almost saved Carvillho Gonzales from being shot. She could have saved Gonzales, might have saved him, would have saved him, had she not been obliged to save her father. In the circumstances she could not save both.

Before the week was out Jean Jacques was possessed of as fine a tale of political persecution as mind could conceive, and, told as it was by Sebastian Dolores, his daughter did not seek to alter it, for she had her own purposes, and they were mixed. These refugees needed a friend, for they would land in Canada with only a few dollars, and Carmen Dolores loved her father well enough not to wish to see him again in such distress as he had endured in Cadiz. Also, Jean Jacques, the young, verdant, impressionable French Catholic, was like her Carvillho Gonzales, and she had loved her Carvillho in her own way very passionately, and—this much to her credit— quite chastely. So that she had no compunction in drawing the young money-master to her side, and keeping him there by such arts as such a woman possesses. These are remarkable after their kind. They are combined of a frankness as to the emotions, and such outer concessions to physical sensations, as make a painful combination against a mere man's caution; even when that caution has a Norman origin.

More than once Jean Jacques was moved to tears, as the Ananias of Cadiz told his stories of persecution.

So that one day, in sudden generosity, he paid the captain the necessary sum to transfer the refugees from the forecastle to his own select portion of the steamer, where he was so conspicuous a figure among a handful of lower-level merchant folk and others of little mark who were going to Quebec. To these latter Jean Jacques was a gift of heaven, for he knew so much, and seemed to know so much more, and could give them the information they desired. His importance lured him to pose as a seigneur, though he had no claim to the title. He did not call himself Seigneur in so many words, but when others referred to him as the Seigneur, and it came to his ears, he did not correct it; and when he was addressed as such he did not reprove.

Thus, when he brought the two refugees from the forecastle and assured his fellow-passengers that they were Spanish folk of good family exiled by persecution, his generosity was acclaimed, even while all saw he was enamoured of Carmen. Once among the first-class passengers, father and daughter maintained reserve, and though there were a few who saw that they were not very far removed above peasants, still the dress of the girl, which was good—she had been a maid in a great nobleman's family—was evidence in favour of the father's story. Sebastian Dolores explained his own workman's dress as having been necessary for his escape.

Only one person gave Jean Jacques any warning. This was the captain of the Antoine. He was a Basque, he knew the Spanish people well—the types, the character, the idiosyncrasies; and he was sure that Sebastian Dolores and his daughter belonged to the lower clerical or higher working class, and he greatly inclined towards the former. In that he was right, because Dolores, and his father before him, had been employed in the office of a great commercial firm in Cadiz, and had repaid much consideration by stirring up strife and disloyalty in the establishment. But before the anarchist subtracted himself from his occupation, he had appropriated certain sums of money, and these had helped to carry him on, when he attached himself to the revolutionaries. It was on his daughter's savings that he was now travelling, with the only thing he had saved from the downfall, which was his head. It was of sufficient personal value to make him quite cheerful as the Antoine plunged and shivered on her way to the country where he could have no steady work as a revolutionist.

With reserve and caution the Basque captain felt it his duty to tell Jean Jacques of his suspicions, warning him that the Spaniards were the choicest liars in the world, and were not ashamed of it; but had the same pride in it as had their greatest rivals, the Arabs and the Egyptians.

His discreet confidences, however, were of no avail; he was not discreet enough. If he had challenged the bona fides of Sebastian Dolores only, he might have been convincing, but he used the word "they" constantly, and that roused the chivalry of Jean Jacques. That the comely, careful Carmen should be party to an imposture was intolerable. Everything about her gave it the lie. Her body was so perfect and complete, so finely contrived and balanced, so cunningly curved with every line filled in; her eye was so full of lustre and half-melancholy too; her voice had such a melodious monotone; her mouth was so ripe and yet so distant in its luxury, that imposture was out of the question.

Ah, but Jean Jacques was a champion worth while! He did nothing by halves. He was of the breed of men who grow more intense, more convinced, more thorough, as they talk. One adjective begets another, one warm allusion gives birth to a warmer, one flashing impulse evokes a brighter confidence, till the atmosphere is flaming with conviction. If Jean Jacques started with faint doubt regarding anything, and allowed himself betimes the flush of a declaration of belief, there could be but one end. He gathered fire as he moved, impulse expanded into momentum, and momentum became an Ariel fleeing before the dark. He would start by offering a finger to be pricked, and would end by presenting his own head on a charger. He was of those who hypnotize themselves, who glow with self-creation, who flower and bloom without pollen.

His rejection of the captain's confidence even had a dignity. He took out his watch which represented so many laborious hours of other Barbilles, and with a decision in which the strong pulse of chivalry was beating hard, he said:

"I can never speak well till I have ate. That is my hobby. Well, so it is. And I like good company. So that is why I sit beside Senor and Senorita Dolores at table—the one on the right, the other on the left, myself between, like this, like that. It is dinner-time now here, and my friends—my dear friends of Cadiz—they wait me. Have you heard the Senorita sing the song of Spain, m'sieu'? What it must be with the guitar, I know not; but with voice alone it is ravishing. I have learned it also. The Senorita has taught me. It is a song of Aragon. It is sung in high places. It belongs to the nobility. Ah, then, you have not heard it—but it is not too late! The Senorita, the unhappy ma'm'selle, driven from her ancestral home by persecution, she will sing it to you as she has sung it to me. It is your due. You are the master of the ship. But, yes, she shall of her kindness and of her grace sing it to you. You do not know how it runs? Well, it is like this—listen and tell me if it does not speak of things that belong to the old regime, the ancient noblesse—listen, m'sieu' le captainne, how it runs:

"Have you not heard of mad Murcie?

Granada gay and And'lousie?

There's where you'll see the joyous rout,

When patios pour their beauties out;

Come, children, come, the night gains fast,

And Time's a jade too fair to last.

My flower of Spain, my Juanetta,

Away, away to gay Jota!

Come forth, my sweet, away, my queen,

Though daybreak scorns, the night's between.

The Fete's afoot—ah! ah! ah! ah!

De la Jota Ar'gonesa.

Ah! ah! ah! ah! ah! ah! ah! ah!

De la Jota Ar'gonesa."

Before he had finished, the captain was more than ready to go, for he had no patience with such credulity, simplicity and sentimentalism. He was Basque, and to be Basque is to lack sentiment and feel none, to play ever for the safe thing, to get without giving, and to mind your own business. It had only been an excessive sense of duty which had made the captain move in this, for he liked Jean Jacques as everyone aboard his Antoine did; and he was convinced that the Spaniards would play the "Seigneur" to the brink of disaster at least, though it would have been hard to detect any element of intrigue or coquetry in Carmen Dolores.

That was due partly to the fact that she was still in grief for her Gonzales, whose heart had been perforated by almost as many bullets as the arrows of Cupid had perforated it in his short, gay life of adventure and anarchy; also partly because there was no coquetry needed to interest Jean Jacques. If he was interested it was not necessary to interest anyone else, nor was it expedient to do so, for the biggest fish in the net on the Antoine was the money-master of St. Saviour's.

Carmen had made up her mind from the first to marry Jean Jacques, and she deported herself accordingly—with modesty, circumspection and skill. It would be the easiest way out of all their difficulties. Since her heart, such as it was, fluttered, a mournful ghost, over the Place d'Armes, where her Gonzales was shot, it might better go to Jean Jacques than anyone else; for he was a man of parts, of money, and of looks, and she loved these all; and to her credit she loved his looks better than all the rest. She had no real cupidity, and she was not greatly enamoured of brains. She had some real philosophy of life learned in a hard school; and it was infinitely better founded than the smattering of conventional philosophy got by Jean Jacques from his compendium picked up on the quay at Quebec.

Yet Jean Jacques' cruiser of life was not wholly unarmed. From his Norman forebears he had, beneath all, a shrewdness and an elementary alertness not submerged by his vain, kind nature. He was quite a good business man, and had proved himself so before his father died—very quick to see a chance, and even quicker to see where the distant, sharp corners in the road were; though not so quick to see the pitfalls, for his head was ever in the air. And here on the Antoine, there crossed his mind often the vision of Carmen Dolores and himself in the parish of St. Saviour's, with the daily life of the Beau Cheval revolving about him. Flashes of danger warned him now and then, just at the beginning of the journey, as it were; just before he had found it necessary to become her champion against the captain and his calumnies; but they were of the instant only. But champion as he became, and worshipping as his manner seemed, it all might easily have been put down to a warm, chivalrous, and spontaneous nature, which had not been bitted or bridled, and he might have landed at Quebec without committing himself, were it not for the fact that he was not to land at Quebec.

That was the fact which controlled his destiny. He had spent many, many hours with the Dona Dolores, talking, talking, as he loved to talk, and only saving himself from the betise of boring her by the fact that his enthusiasm had in it so fresh a quality, and because he was so like her Gonzales that she could always endure him. Besides, quick of intelligence as she was, she was by nature more material than she looked, and there was certainly something physically attractive in him—some curious magnetism. She had a well of sensuousness which might one day become sensuality; she had a richness of feeling and a contour in harmony with it, which might expand into voluptuousness, if given too much sun, or if untamed by the normal restraints of a happy married life. There was an earthquake zone in her being which might shake down the whole structure of her existence. She was unsafe, not because she was deceiving Jean Jacques now as to her origin and as to her feelings for him; she was unsafe because of the natural strain of the light of love in her, joined to a passion for comfort and warmth and to a natural self-indulgence. She was determined to make Jean Jacques offer himself before they landed at Quebec.

But they did not land at Quebec.

CHAPTER II. "THE REST OF THE STORY TO-MORROW"

The journey wore on to the coast of Canada. Gaspe was not far off when, still held back by the constitutional tendency of the Norman not to close a bargain till compelled to do so, Jean Jacques sat with Carmen far forward on the deck, where the groaning Antoine broke the waters into sullen foam. There they silently watched the sunset, golden, purple and splendid—and ominous, as the captain knew.

"Look, the end of life—like that!" said Jean Jacques oratorically with a wave of the hand towards the prismatic radiance.

"All the way round, the whole circle—no, it would be too much," Carmen replied sadly. "Better to go at noon—or soon after. Then the only memory of life would be of the gallop. No crawling into the night for me, if I can help it. Mother of Heaven, no! Let me go at the top of the flight."

"It is all the same to me," responded Jean Jacques, "I want to know it all—to gallop, to trot, to walk, to crawl. Me, I'm a philosopher. I wait."

"But I thought you were a Catholic," she replied, with a kindly, lurking smile, which might easily have hardened into scoffing.

"First and last," he answered firmly.

"A Catholic and a philosopher—together in one?" She shrugged a shoulder to incite him to argument, for he was interesting when excited; when spurting out little geysers of other people's cheap wisdom and philosophy, poured through the kind distortion of his own intelligence.

He gave a toss of his head. "Ah, that is my hobby—I reconcile, I unite, I adapt! It is all the nature of the mind, the far-look, the all-round sight of the man. I have it all. I see."

He gazed eloquently into the sunset, he swept the horizon with his hand. "I have the all-round look. I say the Man of Calvary, He is before all, the sun; but I say Socrates, Plato, Jean Jacques—that is my name, and it is not for nothing, that—Jean Jacques Rousseau, Descartes, Locke, they are stars that go round the sun. It is the same light, but not the same sound. I reconcile. In me all comes together like the spokes to the hub of a wheel. Me—I am a Christian, I am philosophe, also. In St. Saviour's, my home in Quebec, if the crops are good, what do men say? 'C'est le bon Dieu—it is the good God,' that is what they say. If the crops are bad, what do they say? 'It is the good God'—that is what they say. It is the good God that makes crops good or bad, and it is the good God that makes men say, 'C'est le bon Dieu.' The good God makes the philosophy. It is all one."

She appeared to grow agitated, and her voice shook as she spoke. "Tsh, it is only a fool that says the good God does it, when the thing that is done breaks you or that which you love all to pieces. No, no, no, it is not religion, it is not philosophy that makes one raise the head when the heart is bowed down, when everything is snatched away that was all in all. That the good God does it is a lie. Santa Maria, what a lie!"

"Why 'Santa Maria,' then, if it is a lie?" he asked triumphantly. He did not observe how her breast was heaving, how her hands were clenched; for she was really busy with thoughts of her dead Carvillho Gonzales; but for the moment he could only see the point of an argument.

She made a gesture of despair. "So—that's it. Habit in us is so strong. It comes through the veins of our mothers to us. We say that God is a lie one minute, and then the next minute we say, 'God guard you!' Always—always calling to something, for something outside ourselves. That is why I said Santa Maria, why I ask her to pray for the soul of my friend, to pray to the God that breaks me and mine, and sends us over the seas, beggars without a home."

Now she had him back out of the vanities of his philosophy. He was up, inflamed, looking at her with an excitement on which she depended for her future. She knew the caution of his nature, she realized how he would take one step forward and another step back, and maybe get nowhere in the end, and she wanted him—for a home, for her father's sake, for what he could do for them both. She had no compunctions. She thought herself too good for him, in a way, for in her day men of place and mark had taken notice of her; and if it had not been for her Gonzales she would no doubt have listened to one of them sometime or another. She knew she had ability, even though she was indolent, and she thought she could do as much for him as any other girl. If she gave him a handsome wife and handsome children, and made men envious of him, and filled him with good things, for she could cook more than tortillas-she felt he would have no right to complain. She meant him to marry her—and Quebec was very near!

"A beggar in a strange land, without a home, without a friend—oh, my broken life!" she whispered wistfully to the sunset.

It was not all acting, for the past reached out and swept over her, throwing waves of its troubles upon the future. She was that saddest of human beings, a victim of dual forces which so fought for mastery with each other that, while the struggle went on, the soul had no firm foothold anywhere. That, indeed, was why her Carvillho Gonzales, who also had been dual in nature, said to himself so often, "I am a devil," and nearly as often, "I have the heart of an angel."

"Tell me all about your life, my friend," Jean Jacques said eagerly. Now his eyes no longer hurried here and there, but fastened on hers and stayed thereabouts—ah, her face surely was like pictures he had seen in the Louvre that day when he had ambled through the aisles of great men's glories with the feeling that he could not see too much for nothing in an hour.

"My life? Ah, m'sieu', has not my father told you of it?" she asked.

He waved a hand in explanation, he cocked his head quizzically. "Scraps—like the buttons on a coat here and there—that's all," he answered. "Born in Andalusia, lived in Cadiz, plenty of money, a beautiful home,"—Carmen's eyes drooped, and her face flushed slightly—"no brothers or sisters—visits to Madrid on political business—you at school—then the going of your mother, and you at home at the head of the house. So much on the young shoulders, the kitchen, the parlour, the market, the shop, society—and so on. That is the way it was, so he said, except in the last sad times, when your father, for the sake of Don Carlos and his rights, near lost his life—ah, I can understand that: to stand by the thing you have sworn to! France is a republic, but I would give my life to put a Napoleon or a Bourbon on the throne. It is my hobby to stand by the old ship, not sign on to a new captain every port."

She raised her head and looked at him calmly now. The flush had gone from her face, and a light of determination was in her eyes. To that was added suddenly a certain tinge of recklessness and abandon in carriage and manner, as one flings the body loose from the restraints of clothes, and it expands in a free, careless, defiant joy.

Jean Jacques' recital of her father's tale had confused her for a moment, it was so true yet so untrue, so full of lies and yet so solid in fact. "The head of the house—visits to Madrid on political business—the parlour, the market, society—all that!" It suggested the picture of the life of a child of a great house; it made her a lady, and not a superior servant as she had been; it adorned her with a credit which was not hers; and for a moment she was ashamed. Yet from the first she had lent herself to the general imposture that they had fled from Spain for political reasons, having lost all and suffered greatly; and it was true while yet it was a lie. She had suffered, both her father and herself had suffered; she had been in danger, in agony, in sorrow, in despair—it was only untrue that they were of good birth and blood, and had had position and comfort and much money. Well, what harm did that do anybody? What harm did it do this little brown seigneur from Quebec? Perhaps he too had made himself out to be more than he was. Perhaps he was no seigneur at all, she thought. When one is in distant seas and in danger of his life, one will hoist any flag, sail to any port, pay homage to any king. So would she. Anyhow, she was as good as this provincial, with his ancient silver watch, his plump little hands, and his book of philosophy.

What did it matter, so all came right in the end! She would justify herself, if she had the chance. She was sick of conspiracy, and danger, and chicanery—and blood. She wanted her chance. She had been badly shaken in the last days in Spain, and she shrank from more worry and misery. She wanted to have a home and not to wander. And here was a chance—how good a chance she was not sure; but it was a chance. She would not hesitate to make it hers. After all, self-preservation was the thing which mattered. She wanted a bright fire, a good table, a horse, a cow, and all such simple things. She wanted a roof over her and a warm bed at night. She wanted a warm bed at night—but a warm bed at night alone. It was the price she would have to pay for her imposture, that if she had all these things, she could not be alone in the sleep-time. She had not thought of this in the days when she looked forward to a home with her Gonzales. To be near him was everything; but that was all dead and done for; and now—it was at this point that, shrinking, she suddenly threw off all restraining thoughts. With abandon of the mind came a recklessness of body, which gave her, all at once, a voluptuousness more in keeping with the typical maid of Andalusia. It got into the eyes and senses of Jean Jacques, in a way which had nothing to do with the philosophy of Descartes, or Kant, or Aristotle, or Hegel.

"It was beautiful in much—my childhood," she said in a low voice, dropping her eyes before his ardent gaze, "as my father said. My mother was lovely to see, but not bigger than I was at twelve—so petite, and yet so perfect in form—like a lark or a canary. Yes, and she could sing—anything. Not like me with a voice which has the note of a drum or an organ—"

"Of a flute, bright Senorita," interposed Jean Jacques.

"But high, and with the trills in the skies, and all like a laugh with a tear in it. When she went to the river to wash—"

She was going to say "wash the clothes," but she stopped in time and said instead, "wash her spaniel and her pony"—her face was flushed again with shame, for to lie about one's mother is a sickening thing, and her mother never had a spaniel or a pony—"the women on the shore wringing their clothes, used to beg her to sing. To the hum of the river she would make the music which they loved—"

"La Manola and such?" interjected Jean Jacques eagerly. "That's a fine song as you sing it."

"Not La Manola, but others of a different sort—The Love of Isabella, The Flight of Bobadil, Saragosse, My Little Banderillero, and so on, and all so sweet that the women used to cry. Always, always she was singing till the time when my father became a rebel. Then she used to cry too; and she would sing no more; and when my father was put against a wall to be shot, and fell in the dust when the rifles rang out, she came at the moment, and seeing him lying there, she threw up her hands, and fell down beside him dead—"

"The poor little senora, dead too—"

"Not dead too—that was the pity of it. You see my father was not dead. The officer"—she did not say sergeant—"who commanded the firing squad, he was what is called a compadre of my father—"

"Yes, I understand—a made-brother, sealed with an oath, which binds closer than a blood-brother. It is that, is it not?"

"So—like that. Well, the compadre had put blank cartridges in their rifles, and my father pretended to fall dead; and the soldiers were marched away; and my father, with my mother, was carried to his home, still pretending to be dead. It had been all arranged except the awful thing, my mother's death. Who could foresee that? She ought to have been told; but who could guess that she would hear of it all, and come at the moment like that? So, that was the way she went, and I was left alone with my father." She had told the truth in all, except in conveying that her mother was not of the lower orders, and that she went to the river to wash her spaniel and her pony instead of her clothes.

"Your father—did they not arrest him again? Did they not know?"

She shrugged her shoulders. "That is not the way in Spain. He was shot, as the orders were, with his back to the wall by a squad of soldiers with regulation bullets. If he chose to come to life again, that was his own affair. The Government would take no notice of him after he was dead. He could bury himself, or he could come alive—it was all the same to them. So he came alive again."

"That is a story which would make a man's name if he wrote it down," said Jean Jacques eloquently. "And the poor little senora, but my heart bleeds for her! To go like that in such pain, and not to know—If she had been my wife I think I would have gone after her to tell her it was all right, and to be with her—"

He paused confused, for that seemed like a reflection on her father's chivalry, and for a man who had risked his life for his banished king—what would he have thought if he had been told that Sebastian Dolores was an anarchist who loathed kings!—it was an insult to suggest that he did not know the right thing to do, or, knowing, had not done it.

She saw the weakness of his case at once. "There was his duty to the living," she said indignantly.

"Ah, forgive me—what a fool I am!" Jean Jacques said repentantly at once. "There was his little girl, his beloved child, his Carmen Dolores, so beautiful, with the voice like a flute, and—"

He drew nearer to her, his hand was outstretched to take hers; his eyes were full of the passion of the moment; pity was drowning all caution, all the Norman shrewdness in him, when the Antoine suddenly stopped almost dead with a sudden jolt and shock, then plunged sideways, jerked, and trembled.

"We've struck a sunk iceberg—the rest of the story to-morrow, Senorita," he cried, as they both sprang to their feet.

"The rest of the story to-morrow," she repeated, angry at the stroke of fate which had so interrupted the course of her fortune. She said it with a voice also charged with fear; for she was by nature a landfarer, not a sea-farer, though on the rivers of Spain she had lived almost as much as on land, and she was a good swimmer.

"The rest to-morrow," she repeated, controlling herself.

CHAPTER III. "TO-MORROW"

The rest came to-morrow. When the Antoine struck the sunken iceberg she was not more than one hundred and twenty miles from the coast of Gaspe. She had not struck it full on, or she would have crumpled up, but had struck and glanced, mounting the berg, and sliding away with a small gaping wound in her side, broken internally where she had been weakest. Her condition was one of extreme danger, and the captain was by no means sure that he could make the land. If a storm or a heavy sea came on, they were doomed.

As it was, with all hands at the pumps the water gained on her, and she moaned and creaked and ached her way into the night with no surety that she would show a funnel to the light of another day. Passengers and crew alike worked, and the few boats were got ready to lower away when the worst should come to the worst. Below, with the crew, the little moneymaster of St. Saviour's worked with an energy which had behind it some generations of hardy qualities; and all the time he refused to be downcast. There was something in his nature or in his philosophy after all. He had not much of a voice, but it was lusty and full of good feeling; and when cursing began, when a sailor even dared to curse his baptism—the crime of crimes to a Catholic mind—Jean Jacques began to sing a cheery song with which the habitants make vocal their labours or their playtimes:

"A Saint-Malo, beau port de mer,

Trois gros navir's sont arrives,

Trois gros navir's sont arrives

Charges d'avoin', charges de ble.

Charges d'avoin', charges de ble:

Trois dam's s'en vont les marchander."

And so on through many verses, with a heartiness that was a good antidote to melancholy, even though it was no specific for a shipwreck. It played its part, however; and when Jean Jacques finished it, he plunged into that other outburst of the habitant's gay spirits, 'Bal chez Boule':

"Bal chez Boule, bal chez Boule,

The vespers o'er, we'll away to that;

With our hearts so light, and our feet so gay,

We'll dance to the tune of 'The Cardinal's Hat'

The better the deed, the better the day

Bal chez Boule, bal chez Boule!"

And while Jean Jacques worked "like a little French pony," as they say in Canada of every man with the courage to do hard things in him, he did not stop to think that the scanty life-belts had all been taken, and that he was a very poor swimmer indeed: for, as a child, he had been subject to cramp, and so had made the Beau Cheval River less his friend than would have been useful now.

He realized it, however, soon after daybreak, when, within a few hundred yards of the shores of Gaspe, to which the good Basque captain had been slowly driving the Antoine all night, there came the cry, "All hands on deck!" and "Lower the boats!" for the Antoine's time had come, and within a hand-reach of shore almost she found the end of her rickety life. Not more than three-fourths of the passengers and crew were got into the boats. Jean Jacques was not one of these; but he saw Carmen Dolores and her father safely bestowed, though in different boats. To the girl's appeal to him to come he gave a nod of assent, and said he would get in at the last moment; but this he did not do, pushing into the boat instead a crying lad of fifteen, who said he was afraid to die.

So it was that Jean Jacques took to the water side by side with the Basque captain, when the Antoine groaned and shook, and then grew still, and presently, with some dignity, dipped her nose into the shallow sea and went down.

"The rest of the story to-morrow," Jean Jacques had said when the vessel struck the iceberg the night before; and so it was.

The boat in which Carmen had been placed was swamped not far from shore, but she managed to lay hold of a piece of drifting wreckage, and began to fight steadily and easily landward. Presently she was aware, however, of a man struggling hard some little distance away to the left of her, and from the tousled hair shaking in the water she was sure that it was Jean Jacques.

So it proved to be; and thus it was that, at his last gasp almost, when he felt he could keep up no longer, the wooden seat to which Carmen clung came to his hand, and a word of cheer from her drew his head up with what was almost a laugh.

"To think of this!" he said presently when he was safe, with her swimming beside him without support, for the wooden seat would not sustain the weight of two. "To think that it is you who saves me!" he again declared eloquently, as they made the shore in comparative ease, for she was a fine swimmer.

"It is the rest of the story," he said with great cheerfulness and aplomb as they stood on the shore in the morning sun, shoeless, coatless, but safe: and she understood.

There was nothing else for him to do. The usual process of romance had been reversed. He had not saved her life, she had saved his. The least that he could do was to give her shelter at the Manor Cartier yonder at St. Saviour's, her and, if need be, her father. Human gratitude must have play. It was so strong in this case that it alone could have overcome the Norman caution of Jean Jacques, and all his worldly wisdom (so much in his own eyes). Added thereto was the thing which had been greatly stirred in him at the instant the Antoine struck; and now he kept picturing Carmen in the big living-room and the big bedroom of the house by the mill, where was the comfortable four-poster which had come from the mansion of the last Baron of Beaugard down by St. Laurent.

Three days after the shipwreck of the Antoine, and as soon as sufficient finery could be got in Quebec, it was accomplished, the fate of Jean Jacques. How proud he was to open his cheque-book before the young Spanish maid, and write in cramped, characteristic hand a cheque for a hundred dollars or so at a time! A moiety of this money was given to Sebastian Dolores, who could scarcely believe his good fortune. A situation was got for him by the help of a good abbe at Quebec, who was touched by the tale of the wreck of the Antoine, and by the no less wonderful tale of the refugees of Spain, who naturally belonged to the true faith which "feared God and honoured the King." Sebastian Dolores was grateful for the post offered him, though he would rather have gone to St. Saviour's with his daughter, for he had lost the gift of work, and he desired peace after war. In other words, he had that fatal trait of those who strive to make the world better by talk and violence, the vice of indolence.

But when Jean Jacques and his handsome bride started for St. Saviour's, the new father-in-law did not despair of following soon. He would greatly have enjoyed the festivities which, after all, did follow the home-coming of Jean Jacques Barbille and his Spanische; for while they lacked enthusiasm because Carmen was a foreigner, the romance of the story gave the whole proceedings a spirit and interest which spread into adjoining parishes: so that people came to mass from forty miles away to see the pair who had been saved from the sea.

And when the Quebec newspapers found their way into the parish, with a thrilling account of the last hours of the Antoine; and of Jean Jacques' chivalrous act in refusing to enter a boat to save himself, though he was such a bad swimmer and was in danger of cramp; and how he sang Bal chez Boule while the men worked at the pumps; they permitted the apres noces of M'sieu' and Madame Jean Jacques Barbille to be as brilliant as could be, with the help of lively improvisation. Even speech-making occurred again in an address of welcome some days later. This was followed by a feast of Spanish cakes and meats made by the hands of Carmen Dolores, "the lady saved from the sea"—as they called her; not knowing that she had saved herself, and saved Jean Jacques as well. It was not quite to Jean Jacques' credit that he did not set this error right, and tell the world the whole exact truth.

CHAPTER IV. THIRTEEN YEARS AFTER AND THE CLERK OF THE COURT TELLS A STORY

It was hard to say which was the more important person in the parish, the New Cure or M'sieu' Jean Jacques Barbille. When the Old Cure was alive Jean Jacques was a lesser light, and he accepted his degree of illumination with content. But when Pere Langon was gathered to his fathers, and thousands had turned away from the graveyard, where he who had baptised them, confirmed them, blessed them, comforted them, and firmly led them was laid to rest, they did not turn at once to his successor with confidence and affection. The new cure, M. Savry, was young; the Old Cure had lived to be eighty-five, bearing wherever he went a lamp of wisdom at which the people lighted their small souls. The New Cure could command their obedience, but he could not command their love and confidence until he had earned them.

So it was that, for a time, Jean Jacques took the place of the Old Cure in the human side of the life of the district, though in a vastly lesser degree. Up to the death of M. Langon, Jean Jacques had done very well in life, as things go in out-of-the-way places of the world. His mill, which ground good flour, brought him increasing pence; his saw-mill more than paid its way; his farms made a small profit, in spite of a cousin who worked one on halves, but who had a spendthrift wife; the ash-factory which his own initiative had started made no money, but the loss was only small; and he had even made profit out of his lime-kilns, although Sebastian Dolores, Carmen's father, had at one time mismanaged them—but of that anon. Jean Jacques himself managed the business of money-lending and horse-dealing; and he also was agent for fire insurance and a dealer in lightning rods.

In the thirteen years since he married he had been able to keep a good many irons in the fire, and also keep them more or less hot. Many people in his and neighbouring parishes were indebted to him, and it was worth their while to stand well with him. If he insisted on debts being paid, he was never exacting or cruel. If he lent money, he never demanded more than eight per cent.; and he never pressed his debtors unduly. His cheerfulness seldom deserted him, and he was notably kind to the poor. Not seldom in the winter time a poor man, here and there in the parish, would find dumped down outside his door in the early morning a half-cord of wood or a bag of flour.

It could not be said that Jean Jacques did not enjoy his own generosity. His vanity, however, did not come from an increasing admiration of his own personal appearance, a weakness which often belongs to middle age; but from the study of his so-called philosophy, which in time became an obsession with him. In vain the occasional college professors, who spent summer months at St. Saviour's, sought to interest him in science and history, for his philosophy had large areas of boredom; but science marched over too jagged a road for his tender intellectual feet; the wild places where it led dismayed him. History also meant numberless dates and facts. Perhaps he could have managed the dates, for he was quick at figures, but the facts were like bees in their hive,—he could scarcely tell one from another by looking at them.

So it was that Jean Jacques kept turning his eyes, as he thought, to the everlasting meaning of things, to "the laws of Life and the decrees of Destiny." He was one of those who had found, as he thought, what he could do, and was sensible enough to do it. Let the poor fellows, who gave themselves to science, trouble their twisted minds with trigonometry and the formula of some grotesque chemical combination; let the dull people rub their noses in the ink of Greek and Latin, which was no use for everyday consumption; let the heads of historians ache with the warring facts of the lives of nations; it all made for sleep. But philosophy—ah, there was a field where a man could always use knowledge got from books or sorted out of his own experiences!

It happened, therefore, that Jean Jacques, who not too vaguely realized that there was reputation to be got from being thought a philosopher, always carried about with him his little compendium from the quay at Quebec, which he had brought ashore inside his redflannel shirt, with the antique silver watch, when the Antoine went down.

Thus also it was that when a lawyer in court at Vilray, four miles from St. Saviour's, asked him one day, when he stepped into the witness-box, what he was, meaning what was his occupation, his reply was, "Moi-je suis M'sieu' Jean Jacques, philosophe—(Me—I am M'sieu' Jean Jacques, philosopher)."

A little later outside the court-house, the Judge who had tried the case—M. Carcasson—said to the Clerk of the Court:

"A curious, interesting little man, that Monsieur Jean Jacques. What's his history?"

"A character, a character, monsieur le juge," was the reply of M. Amand Fille. "His family has been here since Frontenac's time. He is a figure in the district, with a hand in everything. He does enough foolish things to ruin any man, yet swims along—swims along. He has many kinds of business—mills, stores, farms, lime-kilns, and all that, and keeps them all going; and as if he hadn't enough to do, and wasn't risking enough, he's now organizing a cheese-factory on the co-operative principle, as in Upper Canada among the English."

"He has a touch of originality, that's sure," was the reply of the Judge.

The Clerk of the Court nodded and sighed. "Monseigneur Giron of Laval, the greatest scholar in Quebec, he said to me once that M'sieu' Jean Jacques missed being a genius by an inch. But, monsieur le juge, not to have that inch is worse than to be an ignoramus."

Judge Carcasson nodded. "Ah, surely! Your Jean Jacques lacks a balance-wheel. He has brains, but not enough. He has vision, but it is not steady; he has argument, but it breaks down just where it should be most cohesive. He interested me. I took note of every turn of his mind as he gave evidence. He will go on for a time, pulling his strings, doing this and doing that, and then, all at once, when he has got a train of complications, his brain will not be big enough to see the way out. Tell me, has he a balance-wheel in his home—a sensible wife, perhaps?"

The Clerk of the Court shook his head mournfully and seemed to hesitate. Then he said, "Comme ci, comme ca—but no, I will speak the truth about it. She is a Spaniard—the Spanische she is called by the neighbours. I will tell you all about that, and you will wonder that he has carried on as well as he has, with his vanity and his philosophy."

"He'll have need of his philosophy before he's done, or I don't know human nature; he'll get a bad fall one of these days," responded the Judge. "'Moi-je suis M'sieu' Jean Jacques, philosophe'—that is what he said. Bumptious little man, and yet—and yet there's something in him. There's a sense of things which everyone doesn't have—a glimmer of life beyond his own orbit, a catching at the biggest elements of being, a hovering on the confines of deep understanding, as it were. Somehow I feel almost sorry for him, though he annoyed me while he was in the witness-box, in spite of myself. He was as the English say, so 'damn sure.'"

"So damn sure always," agreed the Clerk of the Court, with a sense of pleasure that his great man, this wonderful aged little judge, should have shown himself so human as to use such a phrase.

"But, no doubt, the sureness has been a good servant in his business," returned the Judge. "Confidence in a weak world gets unearned profit often. But tell me about his wife—the Spanische. Tell me the how and why, and everything. I'd like to trace our little money-man wise to his source."

Again M. Fille was sensibly agitated. "She is handsome, and she has great, good gifts when she likes to use them," he answered. "She can do as much in an hour as most women can do in two; but then she will not keep at it. Her life is but fits and starts. Yet she has a good head for business, yes, very good. She can see through things. Still, there it is—she will not hold fast from day to day."

"Yes, yes, but where did she come from? What was the field where she grew?"

"To be sure, monsieur. It was like this," responded the other.

Thereupon M. Fille proceeded to tell the history, musical with legend, of Jean Jacques' Grand Tour, of the wreck of the Antoine, of the marriage of the "seigneur," the home-coming, and the life that followed, so far as rumour, observation, and a mind with a gift for narrative, which was not to be incomplete for lack of imagination, could make it. It was only when he offered his own reflections on Carmen Dolores, now Carmen Barbille, and on women generally, that Judge Carcasson pulled him up.

"So, so, I see. She has temperament and so on, but she's unsteady, and regarded by her neighbours not quite as one that belongs. Bah, the conceit of every race! They are all the same. The English are the worst—as though the good God was English. But the child—so beautiful, you say, and yet more like the father than the mother. He is not handsome, that Jean Jacques, but I can understand that the little one should be like him and yet beautiful too. I should like to see the child."

Suddenly the Clerk of the Court stopped and touched the arm of his distinguished friend and patron. "That is very easy, monsieur," he said eagerly, "for there she is in the red wagon yonder, waiting for her father. She adores him, and that makes trouble sometimes. Then the mother gets fits, and makes things hard at the Manor Cartier. It is not all a bed of roses for our Jean Jacques. But there it is. He is very busy all the time. Something doing always, never still, except when you will find him by the road-side, or in a tavern with all the people round him, talking, jesting, and he himself going into a trance with his book of philosophy. It is very strange that everlasting going, going, going, and yet that love of his book. I sometimes think it is all pretence, and that he is all vanity—or almost so. Heaven forgive me for my want of charity!"

The little round judge cocked his head astutely. "But you say he is kind to the poor, that he does not treat men hardly who are in debt to him, and that he will take his coat off his back to give to a tramp—is it so?"

"As so, as so, monsieur."

"Then he is not all vanity, and because of that he will feel the blow when it comes—alas, so much he will feel it!"

"What blow, monsieur le juge?—but ah, look, monsieur!" He pointed eagerly. "There she is, going to the red wagon—Madame Jean Jacques. Is she not a figure of a woman? See the walk of her—is it not distinguished? She is half a hand-breadth taller than Jean Jacques. And her face, most sure it is a face to see. If Jean Jacques was not so busy with his farms and his mills and his kilns and his usury, he would see what a woman he has got. It is his good fortune that she has such sense in business. When Jean Jacques listens to her, he goes right. She herself did not want her father to manage the lime-kilns—the old Sebastian Dolores. She was for him staying at Mirimachi, where he kept the books of the lumber firm. But no, Jean Jacques said that he could make her happy by having her father near her, and he would not believe she meant what she said. He does not understand her; that is the trouble. He knows as much of women or men as I know of—"

"Of the law—hein?" laughed the great man.

"Monsieur—ah, that is your little joke! I laugh, yes, but I laugh," responded the Clerk of the Court a little uncertainly. "Now once when she told him that the lime-kilns—"

The Judge, who had retraced his steps down the street of the town—it was little more than a large village, but because it had a court-house and a marketplace it was called a town—that he might have a good look at Madame Jean Jacques and her child before he passed them, suddenly said:

"How is it you know so much about it all, Maitre Fille—as to what she says and of the inner secrets of the household? Ah, ha, my little Lothario, I have caught you—a bachelor too, with time on his hands, and the right side of seventy as well! The evidence you have given of a close knowledge of the household of our Jean Jacques does not have its basis in hearsay, but in acute personal observation. Tut-tut! Fie-fie! my little gay Clerk of the Court. Fie! Fie!"

M. Fille was greatly disconcerted. He had never been a Lothario. In forty years he had never had an episode with one of "the other sex," but it was not because he was impervious to the softer emotions. An intolerable shyness had ever possessed him when in the presence of women, and even small girl children had frightened him, till he had made friends with little Zoe Barbille, the daughter of Jean Jacques. Yet even with Zoe, who was so simple and companionable and the very soul of childish confidence, he used to blush and falter till she made him talk. Then he became composed, and his tongue was like a running stream, and on that stream any craft could sail. On it he became at ease with madame the Spanische, and he even went so far as to look her full in the eyes on more than one occasion.

"Answer me—ah, you cannot answer!" teasingly added the Judge, who loved his Clerk of the Court, and had great amusement out of his discomfiture.

"You are convicted. At an age when a man should be settling down, you are gallivanting with the wife of a philosopher."

"Monsieur—monsieur le juge!" protested M. Fille with slowly heightening colour. "I am innocent, yes, altogether. There is nothing, believe me. It is the child, the little Zoe—but a maid of charm and kindness. She brings me cakes and the toffy made by her own hands; and if I go to the Manor Cartier, as I often do, it is to be polite and neighbourly. If Madame says things to me, and if I see what I see, and hear what I hear, it is no crime; it is no misdemeanour; it is within the law—the perfect law."

Suddenly the Judge linked his arm within that of the other, for he also was little, and he was fat and round and ruddy, and even smaller than M. Fille, who was thin, angular and pale.

"Ah, my little Confucius," he said gently, "have you seen and heard me so seldom that you do not know me yet, or what I really think? Of course it is within the law—the perfect law—to visit at m'sieu' the philosopher's house and talk at length also to m'sieu' the philosopher's wife; while to make the position regular by friendship with the philosopher's child is a wisdom which I can only ascribe to"—his voice was charged with humour and malicious badinage "to an extended acquaintance with the devices of human nature, as seen in those episodes of the courts with which you have been long familiar."

"Oh, monsieur, dear monsieur!" protested the Clerk of the Court, "you always make me your butt."

"My friend," said the Judge, squeezing his arm, "if I could have you no other way, I would make you my butler!"

Then they both laughed at the inexpensive joke, and the Clerk of the Court was in high spirits, for on either side of the street were people with whom he lived every day, and they could see the doyen of the Bench, the great Judge Carcasson, who had refused to be knighted, arm in arm with him. Aye, and better than all, and more than all, here was Zoe Barbille drawing her mother's attention to him almost in the embrace of the magnificent jurist.

The Judge, with his small, round, quizzical eyes which missed nothing, saw too; and his attention was strangely arrested by the faces of both the mother and the child. His first glance at the woman's face made him flash an inward light on the memory of Jean Jacques' face in the witness-box, and a look of reflective irony came into his own. The face of Carmen Dolores, wife of the philosophic miller and money-master, did not belong to the world where she was placed—not because she was so unlike the habitant women, or even the wives of the big farmers, or the sister of the Cure, or the ladies of the military and commercial exiles who lived in that portion of the province; but because of an alien something in her look—a lonely, distant sense of isolation, a something which might hide a companionship and sympathy of a rare kind, or might be but the mask of a furtive, soulless nature. In the child's face was nothing of this. It was open as the day, bright with the cheerfulness of her father's countenance, alive with a humour which that countenance did not possess. The contour was like that of Jean Jacques, but with a fineness and delicacy to its fulness absent from his own; and her eyes were a deep and lustrous brown, under a forehead which had a boldness of gentle dignity possessed by neither father nor mother. Her hair was thick, brown and very full, like that of her father, and in all respects, save one, she had an advantage over both her parents. Her mouth had a sweetness which might not unfairly be called weakness, though that was balanced by a chin of commendable strength.

But the Judge's eyes found at once this vulnerable point in her character as he had found that of her mother. Delightful the child was, and alert and companionable, with no remarkable gifts, but with a rare charm and sympathy. Her face was the mirror of her mind, and it had no ulterior thought. Her mother's face, the Judge had noted, was the foreground of a landscape which had lonely shadows. It was a face of some distinction and suited to surroundings more notable, though the rural life Carmen had led since the Antoine went down and her fortunes came up, had coarsened her beauty a very little.

"There's something stirring in the coverts," said the Judge to himself as he was introduced to the mother and child. By a hasty gesture Zoe gave a command to M. Fille to help her down. With a hand on his shoulder she dropped to the ground. Her object was at once apparent. She made a pretty old-fashioned curtsey to the Judge, then held out her hand, as though to reassert her democratic equality.

As the Judge looked at Madame Barbille, he was involuntarily, but none the less industriously, noting her characteristics; and the sum of his reflections, after a few moments' talk, was that dangers he had seen ahead of Jean Jacques, would not be averted by his wife, indeed might easily have their origin in her.

"I wonder it has gone on as long as it has," he said to himself; though it seemed unreasonable that his few moments with her, and the story told him by the Clerk of the Court, should enable him to come to any definite conclusion. But at eighty-odd Judge Carcasson was a Solon and a Solomon in one. He had seen life from all angles, and he was not prepared to give any virtue or the possession of any virtue too much rope; while nothing in life surprised him.

"How would you like to be a judge?" he asked of Zoe, suddenly taking her hand in his. A kinship had been at once established between them, so little has age, position, and intellect to do with the natural gravitations of human nature.

She did not answer direct, and that pleased him. "If I were a judge I should have no jails," she said. "What would you do with the bad people?" he asked.

"I would put them alone on a desert island, or out at sea in a little boat, or out on the prairies without a horse, so that they'd have to work for their lives."

"Oh, I see! If M. Fille here set fire to a house, you would drop him on the prairie far away from everything and everybody and let him 'root hog or die'?"

"Don't you think it would kill him or cure him?" she asked whimsically.

The Judge laughed, his eyes twinkling. "That's what they did when the world was young, dear ma'm'selle. There was no time to build jails. Alone on the prairie—a separate prairie for every criminal—that would take a lot of space; but the idea is all right. It mightn't provide the proper degree of punishment, however. But that is being too particular. Alone on the prairie for punishment—well, I should like to see it tried."

He remembered that saying of his long after, while yet he was alive, and a tale came to him from the prairies which made his eyes turn more intently towards a land that is far off, where the miserable miscalculations and mistakes of this world are readjusted. Now he was only conscious of a primitive imagination looking out of a young girl's face, and making a bridge between her understanding and his own.

"What else would you do if you were a judge?" he asked presently.

"I would make my father be a miller," she replied. "But he is a miller, I hear."

"But he is so many other things—so many. If he was only a miller we should have more of him. He is at home only a little. If I get up early enough in the morning, or if I am let stay up at night late enough, I see him; but that is not enough—is it, mother?" she added with a sudden sense that she had gone too far, that she ought not to say this perhaps.

The woman's face had darkened for an instant, and irritation showed in her eyes, but by an effort of the will she controlled herself.

"Your father knows best what he can do and can't do," she said evenly.

"But you would not let a man judge for himself, would you, ma'm'selle?" asked the old inquisitor. "You would judge for the man what was best for him to do?"

"I would judge for my father," she replied. "He is too good a man to judge for himself."

"Well, there's a lot of sense in that, ma'm'selle philosophe," answered Judge Carcasson. "You would make the good idle, and make the bad work. The good you would put in a mill to watch the stones grind, and the bad you would put on a prairie alone to make the grist for the grinding. Ma'm'selle, we must be friends—is it not so?"

"Haven't we always been friends?" the young girl asked with the look of a visionary suddenly springing up in her eyes.

Here was temperament indeed. She pleased Judge Carcasson greatly. "But yes, always, and always, and always," he replied. Inwardly he said to himself, "I did not see that at first. It is her father in her.

"Zoe!" said her mother reprovingly.

CHAPTER V. THE CLERK OF THE COURT ENDS HIS STORY

A moment afterwards the Judge, as he walked down the street still arm in arm with the Clerk of the Court, said: "That child must have good luck, or she will not have her share of happiness. She has depths that are not deep enough." Presently he added, "Tell me, my Clerk, the man—Jean Jacques— he is so much away—has there never been any talk about—about."

"About—monsieur le juge?" asked M. Fille rather stiffly. "For instance— about what?"

"For instance, about a man—not Jean Jacques."

The lips of the Clerk of the Court tightened. "Never at any time—till now, monsieur le juge."

"Ah—till now!"

The Clerk of the Court blushed. What he was about to say was difficult, but he alone of all the world guessed at the tragedy which was hovering over Jean Jacques' home. By chance he had seen something on an afternoon of three days before, and he had fled from it as a child would fly from a demon. He was a purist at law, but he was a purist in life also, and not because the flush of youth had gone and his feet were on the path which leads into the autumn of a man's days. The thing he had seen had been terribly on his mind, and he had felt that his own judgment was not sufficient for the situation, that he ought to tell someone.

The Cure was the only person who had come to his mind when he became troubled to the point of actual mental agony. But the new curb, M. Savry, was not like the Old Cure, and, besides, was it not stepping between the woman and her confessional? Yet he felt that something ought to be done. It never occurred to him to speak to Jean Jacques. That would have seemed so brutal to the woman. It came to him to speak to Carmen, but he knew that he dared not do so. He could not say to a woman that which must shame her before him, she who had kept her head so arrogantly high—not so much to him, however, as to the rest of the world. He had not the courage; and yet he had fear lest some awful thing would at any moment now befall the Manor Cartier. If it did, he would feel himself to blame had he done nothing to stay the peril. So far he was the only person who could do so, for he was the only person who knew!

The Judge could feel his friend's arm tremble with emotion, and he said: "Come, now, my Plato, what is it? A man has come to disturb the peace of Jean Jacques, our philosophe, eh?"

"That is it, monsieur—a man of a kind."

"Oh, of course, my bambino, of course, a man 'of a kind,' or there would be no peace disturbed. You want to tell me, I see. Proceed then; there is no reason why you should not. I am secret. I have seen much. I have no prejudices. As you will, however; but I can see it would relieve your mind to tell me. In truth I felt there was something when I saw you look at her first, when you spoke to her, when she talked with me. She is a fine figure of a woman, and Jean Jacques, as you say, is much away from home. In fact he neglects her—is it not so?"

"He means it not, but it is so. His life is full of—"

"Yes, yes, of stores and ash-factories and debtors and lightning-rods and lime-kilns, and mortgaged farms, and the price of wheat—but certainly, I understand it all, my Fille. She is too much alone, and if she has travelled by the compass all these thirteen years without losing the track, it is something to the credit of human nature."

"Ah, monsieur, a vow before the good God—!" The Judge interrupted sharply. "Tut, tut—these vows! Do you not know that a vow may be a thing that ruins past redemption? A vow is sacred. Well, a poor mortal in one moment of weakness breaks it. Then there is a sense of awful shame of being lost, of never being able to put right the breaking of the vow, though the rest can be put right by sorrow and repentance! I would have no vows. They haunt like ghosts when they are broken, they torture like fire then. Don't talk to me of vows. It is not vows that keep the world right, but the prayer of a man's soul from day to day."

The Judge's words sounded almost blasphemous to M. Fille. A vow not keep the world right! Then why the vows of the Church at baptism, at confirmation, at marriage? Why the vows of the priests, of the nuns, of those who had given themselves to eternal service? Monsieur had spoken terrible things. And yet he had said at the last: "It is not vows that keep the world right, but the prayer of a man's soul from day to day." That was not heretical, or atheistic, or blasphemous. It sounded logical and true and good.

He was about to say that, to some people, vows were the only way of keeping them to their duty—and especially women—but the Judge added gently: "I would not for the world hurt your sensibilities, my little Clerk, and we are not nearly so far apart as you think at the minute. Thank God, I keep the faith that is behind all faith—the speech of a man's soul with God.... But there, if you can, let us hear what man it is who disturbs the home of the philosopher. It is not my Fille, that's sure."

He could not resist teasing, this judge who had a mind of the most rare uprightness; and he was not always sorry when his teasing hurt; for, to his mind, men should be lashed into strength, when they drooped over the tasks of life; and what so sharp a lash as ridicule or satire!

"Proceed, my friend," he urged brusquely, not waiting for the gasp of pained surprise of the little Clerk to end. He was glad to see the figure beside him presently straighten itself, as though to be braced for a task of difficulty. Indignation and resentment were good things to stiffen a man's back.

"It was three days ago," said M. Fille. "I saw it with my own eyes. I had come to the Manor Cartier by the road, down the hill—Mont Violet—behind the house. I could see into the windows of the house. There was no reason why I should not see—there never has been a reason," he added, as though to justify himself.

"Of course, of course, my friend. One's eyes are open, and one sees what one sees, without looking for it. Proceed."

"As I looked down I saw Madame with a man's arms round her, and his lips to hers. It was not Jean Jacques."

"Of course, of course. Proceed. What did you do?"

"I stopped. I fell back—"

"Of course. Behind a tree?"

"Behind some elderberry bushes."

"Of course. Elderberry bushes—that's better than a tree. I am very fond of elderberry wine when it is new. Proceed."

The Clerk of the Court shrank. What did it matter whether or no the Judge liked elderberry wine, when the world was falling down for Jean Jacques and his Zoe—and his wife. But with a sigh he continued: "There is nothing more. I stayed there for awhile, and then crept up the hill again, and came back to my home and locked myself in."

"What had you done that you should lock yourself in?"

"Ah, monsieur, how can I explain such things? Perhaps I was ashamed that I had seen things I should not have seen. I do not blush that I wept for the child, who is—but you saw her, monsieur le juge."

"Yes, yes, the little Zoe, and the little philosopher. Proceed."

"What more is there to tell!"

"A trifle perhaps, as you will think," remarked the Judge ironically, but as one who, finding a crime, must needs find the criminal too. "I must ask you to inform the Court who was the too polite friend of Madame."

"Monsieur, pardon me. I forgot. It is essential, of course. You must know that there is a flume, a great wooden channel—"

"Yes, yes. I comprehend. Once I had a case of a flume. It was fifteen feet deep and it let in the water of the river to the mill-wheels. A flume regulates, concentrates, and controls the water power. I comprehend perfectly. Well?"

"So. This flume for Jean Jacques' mill was also fifteen feet deep or more. It was out of repair, and Jean Jacques called in a master-carpenter from Laplatte, Masson by name—George Masson—to put the flume right."

"How long ago was that?"

"A month ago. But Masson was not here all the time. It was his workmen who did the repairs, but he came over to see—to superintend. At first he came twice in the week. Then he came every day."

"Ah, then he came every day! How do you know that?"

"It was my custom to walk to the mill every day—to watch the work on the flume. It was only four miles away across the fields and through the woods, making a walk of much charm—especially in the autumn, when the colours of the foliage are so fine, and the air has a touch of pensiveness, so that one is induced to reflection."

There was the slightest tinge of impatience in the Judge's response. "Yes, yes, I understand. You walked to study life and to reflect and to enjoy your intimacy with nature, but also to see our friend Zoe and her home. And I do not wonder. She has a charm which makes me sad—for her."

"So I have felt, so I have felt for her, monsieur. When she is gayest, and when, as it might seem, I am quite happy, talking to her, or picnicking, or idling on the river, or helping her with her lessons, I have sadness, I know not why."

The Judge pressed his friend's arm firmly. His voice grew more insistent. "Now, Maitre Fille, I think I understand the story, but there are lacunee which you must fill. You say the thing happened three days ago—now, when will the work be finished?"

"The work will be finished to-morrow, monsieur. Only one workman is left, and he will be quit of his task to-night."

"So the thing—the comedy or tragedy will come to an end to-morrow?" remarked the Judge seriously. "How did you find out that the workmen go tomorrow, maitre?"

"Jean Jacques—he told me yesterday."

"Then it all ends to-morrow," responded the Judge.

The puzzled subordinate stood almost still, and looked at the Judge in wonder. Why should it all end to-morrow simply because the work was finished at the flume? At last he spoke.

"It is only twelve miles to Laplatte where George Masson lives, and he has, besides, another contract near here, but three miles from the Manor Cartier. Also besides, how can we know what she will do—Jean Jacques' wife. How can we tell but that she will perhaps go and leave the beloved Zoe alone!"

"And leave our little philosopher—miller also alone?" remarked the Judge quizzically, yet with solemnity. M. Fille was agitated; he made a protesting gesture. "Jean Jacques can find comfort, but the child—ah, no, it is too terrible! Someone should speak. I tried to do it—to Madame Carmen, to Jean Jacques; but it was no use. How could I betray her to him, how could I tell her that I knew her shame!"

The Judge turned brusquely and caught his friend by the shoulders, fastening him with the eyes which had made many a witness forget to lie.

"If you were an avocat in practice I would ruin your reputation, Fille," he said. "A fool would tell Jean Jacques, or speak to the woman, and spoil all; for women go mad when they are in danger, and they do the impossible things. But did it not occur to you that the one person to have in a quiet room with the doors shut, with the light of the sun in his face, with the book of the law open on your desk and the damages to be got by an injured husband, in a Catholic province with a Catholic Judge, written down on a piece of paper, to hand over at the right moment—did it not strike you that that person was your George Masson?"

M. Fille's head dropped before the disdainful eyes of M. Carcasson. He who prided himself in keeping the court right on points of procedure, who was looked upon almost with the respect given the position of the Judge himself, that he should fail in thinking of the obvious thing was humiliating, and alas! so disconcerting.

"I am a fool, an imbecile," he responded, in great dejection.

"This much must be said, my imbecile, that every man some time or other makes just such a fool of his intelligence," was the soft reply.

A thin hand made a gesture of dissent. "Not you, monsieur. Never!"

"If it is any comfort to you, know then, my Solon, that I have done so publicly in my time, while you have only done it privately. But let us see. That Masson must be struck of a heap. What sort of a man is he to look at? Apart from his morals, what class of creature is he?"

"He is a man of strength, of force in his way, monsieur. He made himself from an apprentice without a cent, and he has now thirty men at work."

"Then he does not drink or gamble?"

"Neither, monsieur."

"Has he a family?"

"No, monsieur."

"How old is he?"

"Forty or thereabouts, monsieur."

The Judge cogitated for a moment, then said: "Ah, that's bad—unmarried and forty, and no vices except this. It gives him few escape-valves. Is he good-looking? What is his appearance?"

"Nor short, nor tall, and square shoulders. His face like the yellow brown of a peach, hair that curls close to his head, blue eyes that see everything, and a big hand that knows what it is doing."

The Judge nodded. "Ah, you have watched him, maitre.... When? Since then?"

"No, no, monsieur, not since. If I had watched him since, I should perhaps have thought of the right thing to do. But I did not. I used to study him while the work was going on, when he first came, but I have known him some time from a distance. If a man makes himself what he is, you look at him, of course."

"Truly. His temper—his disposition, what is it?" M. Fille was very much alive now. He replied briskly. "Like the snap of a whip. He flies into anger and flies out. He has a laugh that makes men say, 'How he enjoys himself!' and his mind is very quick and sure."

The Judge nodded with satisfaction. "Well done! Well done! I have got him in my eye. He will not be so easy to handle; but, if he has brains, he will see that you have the right end of the stick; and he will kiss and ride away. It will not be easy, but the game is in your hands, my Fille. In a quiet room, with the book of the law open, and figures of damages given by a Catholic court and Judge—I think that will do it; and then the course of true philosophy will not long be interrupted in the house of Jean Jacques Barbille."

"Monsieur—monsieur le juge, you mean that I shall do this, shall see George Masson and warn him—me?"

"Who else? You are a friend of the family. You are a public officer, to whom the good name of your parish is dear. As all are aware, no doubt, you are the trusted ancient comrade of the daughter of the woman—I speak legally—Carmen Barbille nee Dolores, a name of charm to the ear. Who but you then to do it?"

"There is yourself, monsieur."

"Dismiss me from your mind. I go to Quebec to-night, as you know, and there is not time; but even if there were, I should not be the best person to do this. I am known to few; you are known to all. I have no locus standi. You have. No, no, it would not be for me."

Suddenly, in his desperation, the Clerk of the Court sought release for himself from this solemn and frightening duty.

"Monsieur," he said eagerly, "there is another. I had forgotten. It is Madame Carmen's father, Sebastian Dolores."

"Ah, a father! Yes, I had forgotten to ask about him; so we are one in our imbecility, my little Aristotle. This Sebastian Dolores, where is he?"

"In the next parish, Beauharnais, keeping books for a lumber-firm. Ah, monsieur, that is the way to deal with the matter—through Sebastian Dolores, her father!"

"What sort is he?"

The other shook his head and did not answer. "Ah, not of the best? Drinks?"

M. Fille nodded.

"Has a weak character?"

Again M. Fille nodded.

"Has no good reputation hereabouts?"

The nod was repeated. "He has never been steady He goes here and there, but always he comes back to get Jean Jacques' help. He and his daughter are not close friends, and yet he likes to be near her. She can endure him at least. He can command her interest. He is a stranger in a strange land, and he drifts back to where she is always. But that is all."

"Then he is out of the question, and he would be always out of the question except as a last resort; for sooner or later he would tell his daughter, and challenge our George Masson too; and that is what you do not wish, eh?"

"Precisely so," remarked M. Fille, dropping back again into gloom. "To be quite honest, monsieur, even though it gives me a task which I abhor, I do not think that M. Dolores could do what is needed without mistakes which could not be mended. At least I can—" He stopped.

The Judge interposed at once, well pleased with the way things were going for this "case." "Assuredly. You can as can no other, my Solon. The secret of success in such things is a good heart, a right mind, a clear intelligence and some astuteness, and you have it all. It is your task and yours only."

The little man's self-respect seemed restored. He preened himself somewhat and bowed to the Judge. "I take your commands, monsieur, to obey them as heaven gives me power so to do. Shall it be tomorrow?"

The Judge reflected a moment, then said: "Tonight would be better, but—"

"I can do it better to-morrow morning," interposed M. Fille, "for George Masson has a meeting here at Vilray with the avocat Prideaux at ten o'clock to sign a contract, and I can ask him to step into my office on a little affair of business. He will not guess, and I shall be armed"—the Judge frowned— "with the book of the law on such misdemeanours, and the figures of the damages,"—the Judge smiled—"and I think perhaps I can frighten him as he has never been frightened before."

A courage and confidence had now taken possession of the Clerk in strange contrast to his timidity and childlike manner of a few minutes before. He was now as he appeared in court, clothed with an austere authority which gave him a vicarious strength and dignity. The Judge had done his work well, and he was of those folk in the world who are not content to do even the smallest thing ill.

Arm in arm they passed into the garden which fronted the vine-covered house, where Maitre Fille lived alone with his sister, a tiny edition of himself, who whispered and smiled her way through life.

She smiled and whispered now in welcome to the Judge; and as she did so, the three saw Jean Jacques, laughing, and cracking his whip, drive past with his daughter beside him, chirruping to the horses; while, moody and abstracted, his wife sat silent on the backseat of the red wagon.

CHAPTER VI. JEAN JACQUES HAD HAD A GREAT DAY

Jean Jacques was in great good humour as he drove away to the Manor Cartier. The day, which was not yet aged, had been satisfactory from every point of view. He had impressed the Court, he had got a chance to pose in the witness-box; he had been able to repeat in evidence the numerous businesses in which he was engaged; had referred to his acquaintance with the Lieutenant-Governor and a Cardinal; to his Grand Tour (this had been hard to do in the cross-examination to which he was subjected, but he had done it); and had been able to say at the very start in reply as to what was his occupation—"Moi je suis M'sieu' Jean Jacques, philosophe."

Also he had, during the day, collected a debt long since wiped off his books; he had traded a poor horse for a good cow; he had bought all the wheat of a Vilray farmer below market-price, because the poor fellow needed ready money; he had issued an insurance policy; his wife and daughter had conversed in the public streets with the great judge who was the doyen of the provincial Bench; and his daughter had been kissed by the same judge in the presence of at least a dozen people. He was, in fact, very proud of his Carmen and his Carmencita, as he called the two who sat in the red wagon sharing his glory—so proud that he did not extol them to others; and he was quite sure they were both very proud of him. The world saw what his prizes of life were, and there was no need to praise or brag. Dignity and pride were both sustained by silence and a wave of the hand, which in fact said to the world, "Look you, my masters, they belong to Jean Jacques. Take heed."

There his domestic scheme practically ended. He was so busy that he took his joys by snatches, in moments of suspension of actual life, as it were. His real life was in the eddy of his many interests, in the field of his superficial culture, in the eyes of the world. The worst of him was on the surface. He showed what other men hid, that was all. Their vanity was concealed, he wore it in his cap. They put on a manner as they put on their clothes, and wore it out in the world, or took it off in their own homes-behind the door of life; but he was the same vain, frank, cocksure fellow in his home as in the street. There was no difference at all. He was vain, but he had no conceit; and therefore he did not deceive, and was not tyrannous or dictatorial; in truth, if you but estimated him at his own value, he was the least insistent man alive. Many a debtor knew this; and, by asking Jean Jacques' advice, making an appeal to his logic, as it were—and it was always worth listening to, even when wrong or sadly obvious, because of the glow with which he declared things this or that—found his situation immediately eased. Many a hard-up countryman, casting about for a five-dollar bill, could get it of Jean Jacques by telling him what agreeable thing some important person had said about him; or by writing to a great newspaper in Montreal a letter, saying that the next candidate for the provincial legislature should be M. Jean Jacques Barbille, of St. Saviour's. This never failed to draw a substantial "bill" from the wad which Jean Jacques always carried in his pocket-loose, not tied up in a leather roll, as so many lesser men freighted the burdens of their wealth.

He had changed since the day he left Bordeaux on the Antoine; since he had first caught the flash of interest in Carmen Dolores' eyes—an interest roused from his likeness to a conspirator who had been shot for his country's good. He was no stouter in body, for he was of the kind that wear away the flesh by much doing and thinking; but there were occasional streaks of grey in his bushy hair, and his eye roamed less than it did once. In the days when he first brought Carmen home, his eye was like a bead of brown light on a swivel. It flickered and flamed; it saw here, saw there; it twinkled, and it pierced into life's mysteries; and all the while it was a good eye. Its whites never showed, as it were. As an animal, his eye showed a nature free from vice. In some respects he was easy to live with, for he never found fault with what was given him to eat, or the way the house was managed; and he never interfered with the "kitchen people," or refused a dollar or ten dollars to Carmen for finery. In fact, he was in a sense too lavish, for he used at one time to bring her home presents of silks and clothes and toilet things and stockings and hats, which were not in accord with her taste, and only vexed her. Indeed, she resented wearing them, and could hardly bring herself to thank him for them. At last, however, she induced him to let her buy what she wanted with the presents of money which he might give her.

On the whole Carmen fared pretty well, for he would sometimes give her a handful of bills from his pocket, bidding her take ten dollars, and she would coolly take twenty, while he shrugged his shoulders and declared she would be his ruin. He had never repented of marrying her, in spite of the fact that she did not always keep house as his mother and grandmother had kept it; that she was gravely remiss in going to mass; and that she quarrelled with more than one of her neighbours, who had an idea that Spain was an inferior country because it was south of France, just as the habitants regarded the United States as a low and inferior country because it was south of Quebec. You went north towards heaven and south towards hell, in their view; but when they went so far as to patronize or slander Carmen, she drove her verbal stilettos home without a button; so that on one occasion there would have been a law-suit for libel if the Old Cure had not intervened. To Jean Jacques' credit, be it said, he took his wife's part on this occasion, though in his heart he knew that she was in the wrong.

He certainly was not always in the right himself. If he had been told that he neglected his wife he would have been justly indignant. Also, it never occurred to him that a woman did not always want to talk philosophy or discuss the price of wheat or the cost of flour-barrels; and that for a man to be stupidly and foolishly fond was dearer to a woman than anything else. How should he know—yet he ought to have done so, if he really was a philosopher—that a woman would want the cleverest man in the world to be a boy and play the fool sometimes; that she would rather, if she was a healthy woman, go to a circus than to a revelation of the mysteries of the mind from an altar of culture, if her own beloved man was with her.

Carmen had been left too much alone, as M. Fille had said to Judge Carcasson. Her spirits had moments of great dullness, when she was ready to fling herself into the river—or the arms of the schoolmaster or the farrier. When she first came to St. Saviour's, the necessity of adapting herself to the new conditions, of keeping faith with herself, which she had planned on the Antoine, and making a good wife to the man who was to solve all her problems for her, prevailed. She did not at first miss so much the life of excitement, of danger, of intrigue, of romance, of colour and variety, which she had left behind in Spain. When her child was born, she became passionately fond of it; her maternal spirit smothered it. It gave the needed excitement in the routine of life at St. Saviour's.

Yet the interest was not permanent. There came a time when she resented the fact that Jean Jacques made more of the child than he did of herself. That was a bad day for all concerned, for dissimulation presently became necessary, and the home of Jean Jacques was a home of mystery which no philosophy could interpret. There had never been but the one child. She was not less handsome than when Jean Jacques married her and brought her home, though the bloom of maiden youthfulness was no longer there; and she certainly was a cut far above the habitant women or even the others of a higher social class, in a circle which had an area equal to a principality in Europe.

The old cure, M. Langon, had had much influence over her, for few could resist the amazing personal influence which his rare pure soul secured over the worst. It was a sad day to her when he went to his long home; and inwardly she felt a greater loss than she had ever felt, save that once when her Carvillho Gonzales went the way of the traitor. Memories of her past life far behind in Madrid did not grow fainter; indeed, they grew more distinct as the years went on. They seemed to vivify, as her discontent and restlessness grew.

Once, when there had come to St. Saviour's a middle-aged baron from Paris who had heard the fishing was good at St. Saviour's, and talked to her of Madrid and Barcelona, of Cordova and Toledo, as one who had seen and known and (he declared) loved them; who painted for her in splashing impressionist pictures the life that still eddied in the plazas and dreamed in the patios, she had been almost carried off her feet with longing; and she nearly gave that longing an expression which would have brought a tragedy, while still her Zoe was only eight years old. But M. Langon, the wise priest whose eyes saw and whose heart understood, had intervened in time; and she never knew that the sudden disappearance of the Baron, who still owed fifty dollars to Jean Jacques, was due to the practical wisdom of a great soul which had worked out its own destiny in a little back garden of the world.

When this good priest was alive she felt she had a friend who was as large of heart as he was just, and who would not scorn the fool according to his folly, or chastise the erring after his deserts. In his greatness of soul Pere Langon had shut his eyes to things that pained him more than they shocked him, for he had seen life in its most various and demoralized forms, and indeed had had his own temptations when he lived in Belgium and France, before he had finally decided to become a priest. He had protected Carmen with a quiet persistency since her first day in the parish, and had had a saving influence over her. Pere Langon reproved those who criticized her and even slandered her, for it was evident to all that she would rather have men talk to her than women; and any summer visitor who came to fish, gave her an attention never given even to the youngest and brightest in the district; and the eyes of the habitant lass can be very bright at twenty. Yet whatever Carmen's coquetry and her sport with fire had been, her own emotions had never been really involved till now.

The new cure, M. Savry, would have said they were involved now because she never came to confession, and indeed, since the Old Cure died, she had seldom gone to mass. Yet when, with accumulated reproof on his tongue, M. Savry did come to the Manor Cartier, he felt the inherent supremacy of beauty, not the less commanding because it had not the refinement of the duchess or the margravine.

Once M. Savry ventured to do what the Old Cure would never have done—he spoke to Jean Jacques concerning Carmen's neglect of mass and confession, and he received a rebuff which was almost au seigneur; for in Jean Jacques' eyes he was now the figure in St. Saviour's; and this was an occasion when he could assert his position as premier of the secular world outside the walls of the parish church. He did it in good style for a man who had had no particular training in the social arts.

This is how he did it and what he said:

"There have been times when I myself have thought it would be a good thing to have a rest from the duties of a Catholic, m'sieu' le cure," he remarked to M. Savry, when the latter had ended his criticism. He said it with an air of conflict, and with full intent to make his supremacy complete.

"No Catholic should speak like that," returned the shocked priest.

"No priest should speak to me as you have done," rejoined Jean Jacques. "What do you know of the reasons for the abstention of madame? The soul must enjoy rest as well as the body, and madame has a—mind which can judge for itself. I have a body that is always going, and it gets too little rest, and that keeps my soul in a flutter too. It must be getting to mass and getting to confession, and saying aves and doing penance, it is such a busy little soul of mine; but we are not all alike, and madame's body goes in a more stately way. I am like a comet, she is like the sun steady, steady, round and round, with plenty of sleep and the comfortable darkness. Sometimes madame goes hard; so does the sun in summer-shines, shines, shines like a furnace. Madame's body goes like that—at the dairy, in the garden, with the loom, among the fowls, growing her strawberries, keeping the women at the beating of the flax; and then again it is all still and idle like the sun on a cloudy day; and it rests. So it is with the human soul—I am a philosopher—I think the soul goes hard the same as the body, churning, churning away in the heat of the sun; and then it gets quiet and goes to sleep in the cloudy day, when the body is sick of its bouncing, and it has a rest—the soul has a rest, which is good for it, m'sieu'. I have worked it all out so. Besides, the soul of madame is her own. I have not made any claim upon it, and I will not expect you to do more, m'sieu' le cure."

"It is my duty to speak," protested the good priest. "Her soul is God's, and I am God's vicar—"

Jean Jacques waved a hand. "T'sh, you are not the Pope. You are not even an abbe. You were only a deacon a few years ago. You did not know how to hold a baby for the christening when you came to St. Saviour's first. For the mass, you have some right to speak; it is your duty perhaps; but the confession, that is another thing; that is the will of every soul to do or not to do. What do you know of a woman's soul-well, perhaps, you know what they have told you; but madame's soul—"

"Madame has never been to confession to me," interjected M. Savry indignantly. Jean Jacques chuckled. He had his New Cure now for sure.

"Confession is for those who have sinned. Is it that you say one must go to confession, and in order to go to confession it is needful to sin?"

M. Savry shivered with pious indignation. He had a sudden desire to rend this philosophic Catholic—to put him under the thumb-screw for the glory of the Lord, and to justify the Church; but the little Catholic miller-magnate gave freely to St. Saviour's; he was popular; he had a position; he was good to the poor; and every Christmas-time he sent a half-dozen bags of flour to the presbytery!

All Pere Savry ventured to say in reply was: "Upon your head be it, M. Jean Jacques. I have done my duty. I shall hope to see madame at mass next Sunday."

Jean Jacques had chuckled over that episode, for he had conquered; he had shown M. Savry that he was master in his own household and outside it. That much his philosophy had done for him. No other man in the parish would have dared to speak to the Cure like that. He had never scolded Carmen when she had not gone to church. Besides, there was Carmen's little daughter always at his side at mass; and Carmen always insisted on Zoe going with him, and even seemed anxious for them to be off at the first sound of the bells of St. Saviour's. Their souls were busy, hers wanted rest; that was clear. He was glad he had worked it out so cleverly to the Cure— and to his own mind. His philosophy surely had vindicated itself.

But Jean Jacques was far from thinking of these things as he drove back from Vilray and from his episode in Court to the Manor Cartier. He was indeed just praising himself, his wife, his child, and everything that belonged to him. He was planning, planning, as he talked, the new things to do—the cheese-factory, the purchase of a steam-plough and a steam-thresher which he could hire out to his neighbours. Only once during the drive did he turn round to Carmen, and then it was to ask her if she had seen her father of late.

"Not for ten months," was her reply. "Why do you ask?"

"Wouldn't he like to be nearer you and Zoe? It's twelve miles to Beauharnais," he replied.

"Are you thinking of offering him another place at the Manor?" she asked sharply.

"Well, there is the new cheese-factory—not to manage, but to keep the books! He's doing them all right for the lumber-firm. I hear that he—"

"I don't want it. No good comes from relatives working together. Look at the Latouche farm where your cousin makes his mess. My father is well enough where he is."

"But you'd like to see him oftener—I was only thinking of that," said Jean Jacques in a mollifying voice. It was the kind of thing in which he showed at once the weakness and the kindness of his nature. He was in fact not a philosopher, but a sentimentalist.

"If mother doesn't think it's sensible, why do it, father?" asked Zoe anxiously, looking up into her father's face.

She had seen the look in her mother's eyes, and also she had no love for her grandfather. Her instinct had at one time wavered regarding him; but she had seen an incident with a vanished female cook, and though she had not understood, a prejudice had been created in her mind. She was always contrasting him with M. Fille, who, to her mind, was what a grandfather ought to be.

"I won't have him beholden to you," said Carmen, almost passionately.

"He is of my family," said Jean Jacques firmly and chivalrously. "There is no question of being beholden."

"Let well enough alone," was the gloomy reply. With a sigh, Jean Jacques turned back to the study of the road before him, to gossip with Zoe, and to keep on planning subconsciously the new things he must do.

Carmen sighed too, or rather she gave a gasp of agitation and annoyance. Her father? She had lost whatever illusion once existed regarding him. For years he had clung to her—to her pocket. He was given to drinking in past years, and he still had his sprees. Like the rest of the world, she had not in earlier years seen the furtiveness in his handsome face; but at last, as his natural viciousness became stereotyped, and bad habits matured and emphasized, she saw beneath his mask of low-class comeliness. When at last she had found it necessary to dismiss the best cook she ever had, because of him, they saw little of each other. This was coincident with his failure at the ash-factory, where he mismanaged and even robbed Jean Jacques right and left; and she had firmly insisted on Jean Jacques evicting him, on the ground that it was not Sebastian Dolores' bent to manage a business.

This little episode, as they drove home from Vilray, had an unreasonable effect upon her.

It was like the touch of a finger which launches a boat balancing in the ways onto the deep. It tossed her on a sea of agitation. She was swept away on a flood of morbid reflection.

Her husband and her daughter, laughing and talking in the front seat of the red wagon, seemed quite oblivious of her, and if ever there was a time when their influence was needed it was now. George Masson was coming over late this afternoon to inspect the work he had been doing; and she was trembling with an agitation which, however, did not show upon the surface. She had not seen him for two days—since the day after the Clerk of the Court had discovered her in the arms of a man who was not her husband; but he was coming this evening, and he was coming to-morrow for the last time; for the repair work on the flume of the dam would all be finished then.

But would the work he had been doing all be finished then? As she thought of that incident of three days ago and of its repetition on the following day, she remembered what he had said to her as she snatched herself almost violently from his arms, in a sudden access of remorse. He had said that it had to be, that there was no escape now; and at his words she had felt every pulse in her body throbbing, every vein expanding with a hot life which thrilled and tortured her. Life had been so meagre and so dull, and the man who had worshipped her on the Antoine now worshipped himself only, and also Zoe, the child, maybe; or so she thought; while the man who had once possessed her whole mind and whole heart, and never her body, back there in Spain, he, Carvillho Gonzales, would have loved her to the end, in scenes where life had colour and passion and danger and delightful movement.

She was one of those happy mortals who believe that the dead and gone lover was perfect, and that in losing him she was losing all that life had in store; but the bare, hard truth was that her Gonzales could have been true neither to her nor to any woman in the world for longer than one lingering year, perhaps one lunar month. It did not console her—she did not think of it-that the little man on the seat of the red wagon, chirruping with their daughter, had been, would always be, true to her. Of what good was fidelity if he that was faithful desired no longer as he once did?

A keen observer would have seen in the glowing, unrestful look, in the hot cheek, in the interlacing fingers, that a contest was going on in the woman's soul, as she drove homeward with all that was her own in the world. The laughter of her husband and child grated painfully on her ears. Why should they be mirthful while her life was being swept by a storm of doubt, temptation, and dark passion? Why was it?

Yet she smiled at Jean Jacques when he lifted her down from the red wagon at the door of the Manor Cartier, even though he lifted his daughter down first.

Did she smile at Jean Jacques because, as they came toward the Manor, she saw George Masson in the distance by the flume, and in that moment decided to keep her promise and meet him at a secluded point on the river-bank at sunset after supper?

CHAPTER VII. JEAN JACQUES AWAKES FROM SLEEP

The pensiveness of a summer evening on the Beau Cheval was like a veil hung over all the world. While yet the sun was shining, there was the tremor of life in the sadness; but when the last glint of amethyst and gold died away behind Mont Violet, and the melancholy swish of the river against the osiered banks rose out of the windless dusk, all the region around Manor Cartier, with its cypresses, its firs, its beeches, and its elms, became gently triste. Even the weather-vane on the Manor—the gold Cock of Beaugard, as it was called—did not move; and the stamping of a horse in the stable was like the thunderous knock of a traveller from Beyond. The white mill and the grey manor stood out with ghostly vividness in the light of the rising moon. Yet there were times innumerable when they looked like cool retreats for those who wanted rest; when, in the summer solstice, they offered the pleasant peace of the happy fireside. How often had Jean Jacques stood off from it all of a summer night and said to himself: "Look at that, my Jean Jacques. It is all yours, Manor and mills and farms and factory—all."

"Growing, growing, fattening, while I drone in my feather bed," he had as often said, with the delighted observation of the philosopher. "And me but a young man yet—but a mere boy," he would add. "I have piled it up—I have piled it up, and it keeps on growing, first one thing and then another."

Could such a man be unhappy? Finding within himself his satisfaction, his fountain of appeasement, why should not his days be days of pleasantness and peace? So it appeared to him during that summer, just passed, when he had surveyed the World and his world within the World, and it seemed to his innocent mind that he himself had made it all. There he was, not far beyond forty, and eligible to become a member of Parliament, or even a count of the Holy Roman Empire! He had thought of both these honours, but there was so much to occupy him—he never had a moment to himself, except at night; and then there was planning and accounting to do, his foremen to see, or some knotty thing to disentangle. But when the big clock in the Manor struck ten, and he took out his great antique silver watch, to see if the two marched to the second, he would go to the door, look out into the night, say, "All's well, thank the good God," and would go to bed, very often forgetting to kiss Carmen, and even forgetting his darling little Zoe.

After all, a mind has to be very big and to have very many tentacles to hold so many things all at once, and also to remember to do the right thing at the right moment every time. He would even forget to ask Carmen to play on the guitar, which in the first days of their married life was the recreation of every evening. Seldom with the later years had he asked her to sing, because he was so busy; and somehow his ear had not that keenness of sound once belonging to it. There was a time when he himself was wont to sing, when he taught his little Zoe the tunes of the Chansons Canadiennes; but even that had dropped away, except at rare intervals, when he would sing Le Petit Roger Bontemps, with Petite Fleur de Bois, and a dozen others; but most he would sing—indeed there was never a sing-song in the Manor Cartier but he would burst forth with A la Claire Fontaine and its haunting refrain:

> "Il y a longtemps que je t'aime,
>
> Jamais je ne t'oublierai."

But this very summer, when he had sung it on the birthday of the little Zoe, his voice had seemed out of tune. At first he had thought that Carmen was playing his accompaniment badly on the guitar, but she had sharply protested against that, and had appealed to M. Fille, who was present at the pretty festivity. He had told the truth, as a Clerk of the Court should. He said that Jean Jacques' voice was not as he had so often heard it; but he would also frankly admit that he did not think madame played the song as he had heard her play it aforetime, and that covered indeed twelve years or more—in fact, since the birth of the renowned Zoe.

M. Fille had wondered much that night of June at the listless manner and listless playing of Carmen Barbille. For a woman of such spirit and fire it would seem as though she must be in ill-health to play like that. Yet when he looked at her he saw only the comeliness of a woman whom the life of the haut habitant had not destroyed or, indeed, dimmed. Her skin was smooth, she had no wrinkles, and her neck was a pillar of softly moulded white flesh, around which a man might well string unset jewels, if he had them; for the tint and purity of her skin would be a better setting than platinum or fine gold. But the Clerk of the Court was really unsophisticated, or he would have seen that Carmen played the guitar badly because she was not interested in Jean Jacques' singing. He would have known that she had come to that stage in her married life when the tenure is pitifully insecure. He would have seen that the crisis was near. If he had had any real observation he would have noticed that Carmen's eyes at once kindled, and that the guitar became a different thing, when M. Colombin, the young schoolmaster, one of the guests, caught up the refrain of A la Claire Fontaine, and in a soft tenor voice sang it with Jean Jacques to the end, and then sang it again with Zoe. Then Carmen's dark eyes deepened with the gathering light in them, her body seemed to vibrate and thrill with emotion; and when M. Colombin and Zoe ceased, with her eyes fixed on the distance, and as though unconscious of them all, she began to sing a song of Cadiz which she had not sung since boarding the Antoine at Bordeaux. Her mind had, suddenly flown back out of her dark discontent to the days when all life was before her, and, with her Gonzales, she had moved in an atmosphere of romance, adventure and passion.

In a second she was transformed from the wife of the brown money-master to the girl she was when she came to St. Saviour's from the plaza, where her Carvillho Gonzales was shot, with love behind her and memory blazoned in the red of martyrdom. She sang now as she had not sung for some years. Her guitar seemed to leap into life, her face shone with the hot passion of memory, her voice rang with the pain of a disappointed life:

"Granada, Granada, thy gardens are gay,

And bright are thy stars, the high stars above;

But as flowers that fade and are gray,

But as dusk at the end of the day,

Are ye to the light in the eyes of my love

In the eyes, in the soul, of my love.

"Granada, Granada, oh, when shall I see

My love in thy gardens, there waiting for me?

"Beloved, beloved, have pity, and make

Not the sun shut its eyes, its hot, envious eyes,

And the world in the darkness of night

Be debtor to thee for its light.

Turn thy face, turn thy face from the skies

To the love, to the pain in my eyes.

"Granada, Granada, oh, when shall I see

My love in thy gardens, there waiting for me!"

From that night forward she had been restless and petulant and like one watching and waiting. It seemed to her that she must fly from the life which was choking her. It was all so petty and so small. People went about sneaking into other people's homes like detectives; they turned yellow and grew scrofulous from too much salt pork, green tea, native tobacco, and the heat of feather beds. The making of a rag carpet was an event, the birth of a baby every year till the woman was forty-five was a commonplace; but the exit of a youth to a seminary to become a priest, or the entrance to the novitiate of a young girl, were matters as important as a battle to Napoleon the Great.

How had she gone through it all so long, she asked herself? The presence of Jean Jacques had become almost unbearable when, the day done, he retired to the feather bed which she loathed, though he would have looked upon discarding it like the abdication of his social position. A feather bed was a sign of social position; it was as much the dais to his honour as is the woolsack to the Lord Chancellor in the House of Lords.

She was waiting for something. There was a restless, vagrant spirit alive in her now. She had been so long inactive, tied by the leg, with wings clipped; now her mind roamed into pleasant places of the imagination where life had freedom, where she could renew the impulses of youth. A true philosopher-a man of the world-would have known for what she was waiting with that vague, disordered expectancy and yearning; but there was no man of the world to watch and guide her this fateful summer, when things began to go irretrievably wrong.

Then George Masson came. He was a man of the world in his way; he saw and knew better than the philosopher of the Manor Cartier. He grasped the situation with the mind of an artist in his own sphere, and with the knowledge got by experience. Thus there had been the thing which the Clerk of the Court saw from Mont Violet behind the Manor; and so it was that as Jean Jacques helped Carmen down from the red wagon on their return from Vilray, she gave him a smile which was meant to deceive; for though given to him it was really given to another man in her mind's eye. At sunset she gave it again to George Masson on the river-bank, only warmer and brighter still, with eyes that were burning, with hands that trembled, and with an agitated bosom more delicately ample than it was on the day the Antoine was wrecked.

Neither of these two adventurers into a wild world of feeling noticed that a man was sitting on a little knoll under a tree, not far away from their meeting-place, busy with pencil and paper.

It was Jean Jacques, who had also come to the river-bank to work out a business problem which must be settled on the morrow. He had stolen out immediately after supper from neighbours who wished to see him, and had come here by a roundabout way, because he wished to be alone.

George Masson and Carmen were together for a few moments only, but Jean Jacques heard his wife say, "Yes, to-morrow—for sure," and then he saw her kiss the master-carpenter—kiss him twice, thrice. After which they vanished, she in one direction, and the invader and marauder in another.

If either of these two had seen the face of the man with a pencil and paper under the spreading beechtree, they would not have been so impatient for tomorrow, and Carmen would not have said "for sure."

Jean Jacques was awake at last, man as well as philosopher.

CHAPTER VIII. THE GATE IN THE WALL

Jean Jacques was not without originality of a kind, and not without initiative; but there were also the elements of the very old Adam in him, and the strain of the obvious. If he had been a real genius, rather than a mere lively variation of the commonplace—a chicken that could never burst its shell, a bird which could not quite break into song—he might have made his biographer guess hard and futilely, as to what he would do after having seen his wife's arms around the neck of another man than himself—a man little more than a manual labourer, while he, Jean Jacques Barbille, had come of the people of the Old Regime. As it was, this magnate of St. Saviour's, who yesterday posed so sympathetically and effectively in the Court at Vilray as a figure of note, did the quite obvious thing: he determined to kill the master-carpenter from Laplatte.

There was no genius in that. When, from under the spreading beech-tree, Jean Jacques saw his wife footing it back to her house with a light, wayward step; when he watched the master-carpenter vault over a stone fence five feet high with a smile of triumph mingled with doubt on his face, he was too stunned at first to move or speak. If a sledge-hammer strikes you on the skull, though your skull is of such a hardness that it does not break, still the shock numbs activity for awhile, at any rate. The sledge-hammer had descended on Jean Jacques' head, and also had struck him between the eyes; and it is in the credit balance of his ledger of life, that he refrained from useless outcry at the moment. Such a stroke kills some men, either at once, or by lengthened torture; others it sends mad, so that they make a clamour which draws the attention of the astonished and not sympathetic world; but it only paralysed Jean Jacques. For a time he sat fascinated by the ferocity of the event, his eyes following the hurrying wife and the jaunty, swaggering master-carpenter with a strange, animal-like dismay and apprehension. They remained fixed with a kind of blank horror and distraction on the landscape for some time after both had disappeared.

At last, however, he seemed to recover his senses, and to come back from the place where he had been struck by the hammer of treachery. He seemed to realize again that he was still a part of the common world, not a human being swung through the universe on his heart-strings by a Gorgon.

The paper and pencil in his hand brought him back from the far Gehenna where he had been, to the world again—how stony and stormy a world it was, with the air gone as heavy as lead, with his feet so loaded down with chains that he could not stir! He had had great joy of this his world; he had found it a place where every day were problems to be solved by an astute mind, problems which gave way before the master-thinker. There was of course unhappiness in his world. There was death, there was accident occasionally—had his own people not gone down under the scythe of time? But in going they had left behind in real estate and other things good compensation for their loss. There was occasional suffering and poverty and trouble in his little kingdom; but a cord of wood here, a barrel of flour there, a side of beef elsewhere, a little debt remitted, a bag of dried apples, or an Indian blanket—these he gave, and had great pleasure in giving; and so the world was not a place where men should hang their heads, but a place where the busy man got more than the worth of his money.

It had never occurred to him that he was ever translating the world into terms of himself, that he went on his way saying in effect, "I am coming. I am Jean Jacques Barbille. You have heard of me. You know me. Wave a hand to me, duck your head to me, crack the whip or nod when I pass. I am M'sieu' Jean Jacques, philosopher."

And all the while he had only been vaguely, not really, conscious of his wife and child. He did not know that he had only made of his wife an incident in his life, in spite of the fact that he thought he loved her; that he had been proud of her splendid personality; and that, with passionate chivalry, he had resented any criticism of her.

He thought still, as he did on the Antoine, that Carmen's figure had the lines of the Venus of Milo, that her head would have been a model either for a Madonna, or for Joan of Arc, or the famous Isabella of Aragon. Having visited the Louvre and the Luxembourg all in one day, he felt he was entitled to make such comparisons, and that in making them he was on sure ground. He had loved to kiss Carmen in the neck, it was so full and soft and round; and when she went about the garden with her dress shortened, and he saw her ankles, even after he had been married thirteen years, and she was thirty-four, he still admired, he still thought that the world was a good place when it produced such a woman. And even when she had lashed him with her tongue, as she did sometimes, he still laughed—after the smart was over—because he liked spirit. He would never have a horse that had not some blood, and he had never driven a sluggard in his life more than once. But wife and child and world, and all that therein was, existed largely because they were necessary to Jean Jacques.

That is the way it had been; and it was as though the firmament had been rolled up before his eyes, exposing the everlasting mysteries, when he saw his wife in the arms of the master-carpenter. It was like some frightening dream.

The paper and pencil waked him to reality. He looked towards his house, he looked the way George Masson had gone, and he knew that what he had seen was real life and not a dream. The paper fell from his hand. He did not pick it up. Its fall represented the tumbling walls of life, was the earthquake which shook his world into chaos. He ground the sheet into the gravel with his heel. There would be no cheese-factory built at St. Saviour's for many a year to come. The man of initiative, the man of the hundred irons would not have the hundred and one, or keep the hundred hot any more; because he would be so busy with the iron which had entered into his soul.

When the paper had been made one with the earth, a problem buried for ever, Jean Jacques pulled himself up to his full height, as though facing a great thing which he must do.

"Well, of course!" he said firmly.

That was what his honour, Judge Carcasson, had said a few hours before, when the little Clerk of the Court had remarked an obvious thing about the case of Jean Jacques.

And Jean Jacques said only the obvious thing when he made up his mind to do the obvious thing—to kill George Masson, the master-carpenter.

This was evidence that he was no genius. Anybody could think of killing a man who had injured him, as the master-carpenter had done Jean Jacques. It is the solution of the problem of the Patagonian. It is old as Rameses.

Yet in his own way Jean Jacques did what he felt he had to do. The thing he was going to do was hopelessly obvious, but the doing of it was Jean Jacques' own; and it was not obvious; and that perhaps was genius after all. There are certain inevitable things to do, and for all men to do; and they have been doing them from the beginning of time; but the way it is done—is not that genius? There is no new story in the world; all the things that happen have happened for untold centuries; but the man who tells the story in a new way, that is genius, so the great men say. If, then, Jean Jacques did the thing he had to do with a turn of his own, he would justify to some degree the opinion he had formed of himself.

As he walked back to his desecrated home he set himself to think. How should it be done? There was the rifle with which he had killed deer in the woods beyond the Saguenay and bear beyond the Chicoutimi. That was simple—and it was obvious; and it could be done at once. He could soon overtake the man who had spoiled the world for him.

Yet he was a Norman, and the Norman thinks before he acts. He is the soul of caution; he wants to get the best he can out of his bargain. He will throw nothing away that is to his advantage. There should be other ways than the gun with which to take a man's life—ways which might give a Norman a chance to sacrifice only one life; to secure punishment where it was due, but also escape from punishment for doing the obvious thing.

Poison? That was too stupid even to think of once. A pitch-fork and a dung-heap? That had its merits; but again there was the risk of more than one life.

All the way to his house, Jean Jacques, with something of the rage of passion and the glaze of horror gone from his eyes, and his face not now so ghastly, still brooded over how, after he had had his say, he was to put George Masson out of the world. But it did not come at once. All makers of life-stories find their difficulty at times. Tirelessly they grope along a wall, day in, day out, and then suddenly a great gate swings open, as though to the touch of a spring, and the whole way is clear to the goal.

Jean Jacques went on thinking in a strange, new, intense abstraction. His restless eyes were steadier than they had ever been; his wife noticed that as he entered the house after the Revelation. She noticed also his paleness and his abstraction. For an instant she was frightened; but no, Jean Jacques could not know anything. Yet—yet he had come from the direction of the river!

"What is it, Jean Jacques?" she asked. "Aren't you well?"

He put his hand to his head, but did not look her in the eyes. His gesture helped him to avoid that. "I have a head—la, such a head! I have been thinking, thinking-it is my hobby. I have been planning the cheese-factory, and all at once it comes on-the ache in my head. I will go to bed. Yes, I will go at once." Suddenly he turned at the door leading to the bedroom. "The little Zoe—is she well?"

"Of course. Why should she not be well? She has gone to the top of the hill. Of course, she's well, Jean Jacques."

"Good-good!" he remarked. Somehow it seemed strange to him that Zoe should be well. Was there not a terrible sickness in his house, and had not that woman, his wife, her mother, brought the infection? Was he himself not stricken by it?

Carmen was calm enough again. "Go to bed, Jean Jacques," she said, "and I'll bring you a sleeping posset. I know those headaches. You had one when the ash-factory was burned."

He nodded without looking at her, and closed the door behind him.

When she came to the bedroom a half-hour later, his face was turned to the wall. She spoke, but he did not answer. She thought he was asleep. He was not asleep. He was only thinking how to do the thing which was not obvious, which was also safe for himself. That should be his triumph, if he could but achieve it.

When she came to bed he did not stir, and he did not answer her when she spoke.

"The poor Jean Jacques!" he heard her say, and if there had not been on him the same courage that possessed him the night when the Antoine was wrecked, he would have sobbed.

He did not stir. He kept thinking; and all the time her words, "The poor Jean Jacques!" kept weaving themselves through his vague designs. Why had she said that—she who had deceived, betrayed him? Had he then seen what he had seen?

She did not sleep for a long time, and when she did it was uneasily. But the bed was an immense one, and she was not near him. There was no sleep for him—not even for an hour. Once, in exhaustion, he almost rolled over into the poppies of unconsciousness; but he came back with a start and a groan to sentient life again, and kept feeling, feeling along the wall of purpose for a masterly way to kill.

At dawn it came, suddenly spreading out before him like a picture. He saw himself standing at the head of the flume out there by the Mill Cartier with his hand on the lever. Below him in the empty flume was the master-carpenter giving a last inspection to the repairs. Beyond the master-carpenter—far beyond—was the great mill-wheel! Behind himself, Jean Jacques, was the river held back by the dam; and if the lever was opened,— the river would sweep through the raised gates down the flume to the millwheel—with the man. And then the wheel would turn and turn, and the man would be in the wheel.

It was not obvious; it was original; and it looked safe for Jean Jacques. How easily could such an "accident" occur!

CHAPTER IX. "MOI-JE SUIS PHILOSOPHE"

The air was like a mellow wine, and the light on the landscape was full of wistfulness. It was a thing so exquisite that a man of sentiment like Jean Jacques in his younger days would have wept to see. And the feeling was as palpable as the seeing; as in the early spring the new life which is being born in the year, produces a febrile kind of sorrow in the mind. But the glow of Indian summer, that compromise, that after-thought of real summer, which brings her back for another good-bye ere she vanishes for ever—its sadness is of a different kind. Its longing has a sharper edge; there stir in it the pangs of discontent; and the mind and body yearn for solace. It is a dangerous time, even more dangerous than spring for those who have passed the days of youth.

It had proved dangerous to Carmen Barbille. The melancholy of the gorgeously tinted trees, the flights of the birds to the south, the smell of the fallow field, the wind with the touch of the coming rains—these had given to a growing discontent with her monotonous life the desire born of self-pity. In spite of all she could do she was turning to the life she had left behind in Cadiz long ago.

It seemed to her that Jean Jacques had ceased to care for the charms which once he had so proudly proclaimed. There was in her the strain of the religion of Epicurus. She desired always that her visible corporeal self should be admired and desired, that men should say, "What a splendid creature!" It was in her veins, an undefined philosophy of life; and she had ever measured the love of Jean Jacques by his caresses. She had no other vital standard. This she could measure, she could grasp it and say, "Here I have a hold; it is so much harvested." But if some one had written her a poem a thousand verses long, she would have said, "Yes, all very fine, but let me see what it means; let me feel that it is so."

She had an inherent love of luxury and pleasure, which was far more active in her now than when she married Jean Jacques. For a Spanish woman she had matured late; and that was because, in her youth, she had been active and athletic, unlike most Spanish girls; and the microbes of a sensuous life, or what might have become a sensual life, had not good chance to breed.

It all came, however, in the dullness of the winter days and nights, in the time of deep snows, when they could go abroad but very little. Then her body and her mind seemed to long for the indolent sun-spaces of Spain. The artificial heat of the big stoves in the rooms with the low ceilings only irritated her, and she felt herself growing more ample from lassitude of the flesh. This particular autumn it seemed to her that she could not get through another winter without something going wrong, without a crisis of some sort. She felt the need of excitement, of change. She had the desire for pleasures undefined.

Then George Masson came, and the undefined took form almost at once. It was no case of the hunter pursuing his prey with all the craft and subtlety of his trade. She had answered his look with spontaneity, due to the fact that she had been surprised into the candour of her feelings by the appearance of one who had the boldness of a brigand, the health of a Hercules, and the intelligence of a primitive Jesuit. He had not hesitated; he had yielded himself to the sumptuous attraction, and the fire in his eyes was only the window of the furnace within him. He had gone headlong to the conquest, and by sheer force of temperament and weight of passion he had swept her off her feet.

He had now come to the last day of his duty at the Mill Cartier, when all he had to do was to inspect the work done, give assurance and guarantee that it was all right, and receive his cheque from Jean Jacques. He had come early, because he had been unable to sleep well, and also he had much to do before keeping his tryst with Carmen Barbille in the afternoon.

As he passed the Manor Cartier this fateful morning, he saw her at the window, and he waved his hat at her with a cheery salutation which she did not hear. He knew that she did not hear or see. "My beauty!" he said aloud. "My splendid girl, my charmer of Cadiz! My wonder of the Alhambra, my Moorish maid! My bird of freedom—hand of Charlemagne, your lips are sweet, yes, sweet as one-and-twenty!"

His lips grew redder at the thought of the kisses he had taken, his cheek flushed with the thought of those he meant to take; and he laughed greedily as he lowered himself into the flume by a ladder, just under the lever that opened the gates, to begin his inspection.

It was not a perfunctory inspection, for he was a good craftsman, and he had pride in what his workmen did.

"Ah!"

It was a sound of dumbfounded amazement, a hoarse cry of horror which was not in tune with the beauty of the morning.

"Ah!"

It came from his throat like the groan of a trapped and wounded lion. George Masson had almost finished his inspection, when he heard a noise behind him. He turned and looked back. There stood Jean Jacques with his hand on the lever. The noise he had heard was the fourteen-foot ladder being dropped, after Jean Jacques had drawn it up softly out of the flume.

"Ah! Nom de Dieu!" George Masson exclaimed again in helpless fury and with horror in his eyes.

By instinct he understood that Carmen's husband knew all. He realized what Jean Jacques meant to do. He knew that the lever locking the mill-wheel had been opened, and that Jean Jacques had his hand on the lever which raised the gate of the flume.

By instinct—for there was no time for thought—he did the only thing which could help him, he made a swift gesture to Jean Jacques, a gesture that bade him wait. Time was his only friend in this—one minute, two minutes, three minutes, anything. For if the gates were opened, he would be swept into the millwheel, and there would be the end—the everlasting end.

"Wait!" he called out after his gesture. "One second!"

He ran forward till he was about thirty feet from Jean Jacques standing there above him, with the set face and the dark malicious, half-insane eyes. Even in his fear and ghastly anxiety, the subconscious mind of George Masson was saying, "He looks like the Baron of Beaugard—like the Baron of Beaugard that killed the man who abused his wife."

It was so. Great-great-grand-nephew of the Baron of Beaugard as he was, Jean Jacques looked like the portrait of him which hung in the Manor Cartier. "Wait—but wait one minute!" exclaimed George Masson; and now, all at once, he had grown cool and determined, and his brain was at work again with an activity and a clearness it had never known. He had gained one minute of time, he might be able to gain more. In any case, no one could save him except himself. There was Jean Jacques with his hand on the lever—one turn and the thing was done for ever. If a rescuer was even within one foot of Jean Jacques, the deed could still be done. It was so much easier opening than shutting the gates of the flume!

"Why should I wait, devil and rogue?" The words came from Jean Jacques' lips with a snarl. "I am going to kill you. It will do you no good to whine—cochon!"

To call a man a pig is the worst insult which could be offered by one man to another in the parish of St. Saviour's. To be called a pig as you are going to die, is an offensive business indeed.

"I know you are going to kill me—that you can kill me, and I can do nothing," was the master-carpenter's reply. "There it is—a turn of the lever, and I am done. Bien sur, I know how easy! I do not want to die, but I will not squeal even if I am a pig. One can only die once. And once is enough.... No, don't—not yet! Give me a minute till I tell you something; then you can open the gates. You will have a long time to live—yes, yes, you are the kind that live long. Well, a minute or two is not much to ask. If you want to murder, you will open the gates at once; but if it is punishment, if you are an executioner, you will give me time to pray."

Jean Jacques did not soften. His voice was harsh and grim. "Well, get on with your praying, but don't talk. You are going to die," he added, his hands gripping the lever tighter.

The master-carpenter had had the true inspiration in his hour of danger. He had touched his appeal with logic, he had offered an argument. Jean Jacques was a logician, a philosopher! That point made about the difference between a murder and an execution was a good one. Beside it was an acknowledgment, by inference, from his victim, that he was getting what he deserved.

"Pray quick and have it over, pig of an adulterer!" added Jean Jacques.

The master-carpenter raised a protesting hand. "There you are mistaken; but it is no matter. At the end of to-day I would have been an adulterer, if you hadn't found out. I don't complain of the word. But see, as a philosopher"—Jean Jacques jerked a haughty assent—"as a philosopher you will want to know how and why it is. Carmen will never tell you—a woman never tells the truth about such things, because she does not know how. She does not know the truth ever, exactly, about anything. It is because she is a woman. But I would like to tell you the exact truth; and I can, because I am a man. For what she did you are as much to blame as she ... no, no—not yet!"

Jean Jacques' hand had spasmodically tightened on the lever as though he would wrench the gates open, and a snarl came from his lips.

"Figure de Christ, but it is true, as true as death! Listen, M'sieu' Jean Jacques. You are going to kill me, but listen so that you will know how to speak to her afterwards, understanding what I said as I died."

"Get on—quick!" growled Jean Jacques with white wrinkled lips and the sun in his agonized eyes. George Masson continued his pleading. "You were always a man of mind"—Jean Jacques' fierce agitation visibly subsided, and a surly sort of vanity crept into his face—"and you married a girl who cared more for what you did than what you thought—that is sure, for I know women. I am not married, and I have had much to do with many of them. I will tell you the truth. I left the West because of a woman—of two women. I had a good business, but I could not keep out of trouble with women. They made it too easy for me."

"Peacock-pig!" exclaimed Jean Jacques with an ugly sneer.

"Let a man when he is dying tell all the truth, to ease his mind," said the master-carpenter with a machiavellian pretence and cunning. "It was vanity, it was, as you say; it was the peacock in me made me be the friend of many women and not the husband of one. I came down here to Quebec from the Far West to get away from consequences. It was expensive. I had to sacrifice. Well, here I am in trouble again—my last trouble, and with the wife of a man that I respect and admire, not enough to keep my hands off his wife, but still that I admire. It is my weakness that I could not be, as a man, honourable to Jean Jacques Barbille. And so I pay the price; so I have to go without time to make my will. Bless heaven above, I have no wife—"

"If you had a wife you would not be dying now. You would not then meddle with the home of Jean Jacques Barbille," sneered Jean Jacques. The note was savage yet.

"Ah, for sure, for sure! It is so. And if I lived I would marry at once."

Desperate as his condition was, the master-carpenter could almost have laughed at the idea of marriage preventing him from following the bent of his nature. He was the born lover. If he had been as high as the Czar, or as low as the ditcher, he would have been the same; but it would be madness to admit that to Jean Jacques now.

"But, as you say, let me get on. My time has come—"

Jean Jacques jerked his head angrily. "Enough of this. You keep on saying 'Wait a little,' but your time has come. Now take it so, and don't repeat."

"A man must get used to the idea of dying, or he will die hard," replied the master-carpenter, for he saw that Jean Jacques' hands were not so tightly clenched on the lever now; and time was everything. He had already been near five minutes, and every minute was a step to a chance of escape—somehow.

"I said you were to blame," he continued. "Listen, Jean Jacques Barbille. You, a man of mind, married a girl who cared more for a touch of your hand than a bucketful of your knowledge, which every man in the province knows is great. At first you were almost always thinking of her and what a fine woman she was, and because everyone admired her, you played the peacock, too. I am not the only peacock. You are a good man—no one ever said anything against your character. But always, always, you think most of yourself. It is everywhere you go as if you say, 'Look out. I am coming. I am Jean Jacques Barbille.

"'Make way for Jean Jacques. I am from the Manor Cartier. You have heard of me.'... That is the way you say things in your mind. But all the time the people say, 'That is Jean Jacques Barbille, but you should see his wife. She is a wonder. She is at home at the Manor with the cows and the geese. Jean Jacques travels alone through the parish to Quebec, to Three Rivers, to Tadousac, to the great exhibition at Montreal, but madame, she stays at home. M'sieu' Jean Jacques is nothing beside her'—that is what the people say. They admire you for your brains, but they would have fallen down before your wife, if you had given her half a chance."

"Ah, that's bosh—what do you know!" exclaimed Jean Jacques fiercely, but he was fascinated too by the argument of the man whose life he was going to take.

"I know the truth, my money-man. Do you think she'd have looked at me if you'd been to her what she thought I might be? No, bien sur! Did you take her where she could see the world? No. Did you bring her presents? No. Did you say, 'Come along, we will make a little journey to see the world?' No. Do you think that a woman can sit and darn your socks, and tidy your room, and bake you pancakes in the morning while you roast your toes, and be satisfied with just that, and not long for something outside?"

Jean Jacques was silent. He did not move. He was being hypnotized by a mind of subtle strength, by the logic of which he was so great a lover.

The master-carpenter pressed his logic home. "No, she must sit in your shadow always. She must wait till you come. And when you come, it was 'Here am I, your Jean Jacques. Fall down and worship me. I am your husband.' Did you ever say, 'Heavens, there you are, the woman of all the world, the rising and the setting sun, the star that shines, the garden where all the flowers of love grow'? Did you ever do that? But no, there was only one person in the world—there was only you, Jean Jacques. You were the only pig in the sty."

It was a bold stroke, but if Jean Jacques could stand that, he could stand anything. There was a savage start on the part of Jean Jacques, and the lever almost moved.

"Stop one second!" cried the master-carpenter, sharply now, for in spite of the sudden savagery on Jean Jacques' part, he felt he had an advantage, and now he would play his biggest card.

"You can kill me. It is there in your hand. No one can stop you. But will that give you anything? What is my life? If you take it away, will you be happier? It is happiness you want. Your wife—she will love you, if you give her a chance. If you kill me, I will have my revenge in death, for it is the end of all things for you. You lose your wife for ever. You need not do so. She would have gone with me, not because of me, but because I was a man who she thought would treat her like a friend, like a comrade; who would love her— sacre, what husband could help make love to such a woman, unless he was in love with himself instead of her!"

Jean Jacques rocked to and fro over the lever in his agitation, yet he made no motion to move it. He was under a spell.

Straight home drove the master-carpenter's reasoning now. "Kill me, and you lose her for ever. Kill me, and she will hate you. You think she will not find out? Then see: as I die I will shriek out so loud that she can hear me, and she will understand. She will go mad, and give you over to the law. And then—and then! Did you ever think what will become of your child, of your Zoe, if you go to the gallows? That would be your legacy and your blessing to her—the death of a murderer; and she would be left alone with the woman that would hate you in death! Voila—do you not see?"

Jean Jacques saw. The terrific logic of the thing smote him. His wife hating him, himself on the scaffold, his little Zoe disgraced and dishonoured all her life; and himself out of it all, unable to help her, and bringing irremediable trouble on her! As a chemical clears a muddy liquid, leaving it pure and atomless, so there seemed to pass over Jean Jacques' face a thought like a revelation.

He took his hand from the lever. For a moment he stood like one awakened out of a sleep. He put his hands to his eyes, then shook his head as though to free it of some hateful burden. An instant later he stooped, lifted up the ladder beside him, and let it down to the floor of the flume.

"There, go—for ever," he said.

Then he turned away with bowed head. He staggered as he stepped down from the bridge of the flume, where the lever was. He swayed from side to side. Then he raised his head and looked towards his house. His child lived there—his Zoe.

"Moi je suis philosophe!" he said brokenly.

After a moment or two, as he stumbled on, he said it again—"Me, I am a philosopher!"

CHAPTER X. "QUIEN SABE"—WHO KNOWS!

This much must be said for George Masson, that after the terrible incident at the flume he would have gone straight to the Manor Cartier to warn Carmen, if it had been possible, though perhaps she already knew. But there was Jean Jacques on his way back to the Manor, and nothing remained but to proceed to Laplatte, and give the woman up for ever. He had no wish to pull up stakes again and begin life afresh, though he was only forty, and he had plenty of initiative left. But if he had to go, he would want to go alone, as he had done before. Yes, he would have liked to tell Carmen that Jean Jacques knew everything; but it was impossible. She would have to face the full shock from Jean Jacques' own battery. But then again perhaps she knew already. He hoped she did.

At the very moment that Masson was thinking this, while he went to the main road where he had left his horse and buggy tied up, Carmen came to know.

Carmen had not seen her husband that morning until now. She had waked late, and when she was dressed and went into the dining-room to look for him, with an apprehension which was the reflection of the bad dreams of the night, she found that he had had his breakfast earlier than usual and had gone to the mill. She also learned that he had eaten very little, and that he had sent a man into Vilray for something or other. Try as she would to stifle her anxiety, it obtruded itself, and she could eat no breakfast. She kept her eyes on the door and the window, watching for Jean Jacques.

Yet she reproved herself for her stupid concern, for Jean Jacques would have spoken last night, if he had discovered anything. He was not the man to hold his tongue when he had a chance of talking. He would be sure to make the most of any opportunity for display of intellectual emotion, and he would have burst his buttons if he had known. That was the way she put it in a vernacular which was not Andalusian. Such men love a grievance, because it gives them an opportunity to talk—with a good case and to some point, not into the air at imaginary things, as she had so often seen Jean Jacques do. She knew her Jean Jacques. That is, she thought she knew her Jean Jacques after living with him for over thirteen years; but hers was a very common mistake. It is not time which gives revelation, or which turns a character inside out, and exposes a new and amazing, maybe revolting side to it. She had never really seen Jean Jacques, and he had never really seen himself, as he was, but only as circumstances made him seem to be. What he had showed of his nature all these forty odd years was only the ferment of a more or less shallow life, in spite of its many interests: but here now at last was life, with the crust broken over a deep well of experience and tragedy. She knew as little what he would do in such a case as he himself knew beforehand. As the incident of the flume just now showed, he knew little indeed, for he had done exactly the opposite of what he meant to do. It was possible that Carmen would also do exactly the opposite of what she meant to do in her own crisis.

Her test was to come. Would she, after all, go off with the master-carpenter, leaving behind her the pretty, clever, volatile Zoe ... Zoe—ah, where was Zoe? Carmen became anxious about Zoe, she knew not why. Was it the revival of the maternal instinct?

She was told that Zoe had gone off on her pony to take a basket of good things to a poor old woman down the river three miles away. She would be gone all morning. By so much, fate was favouring her; for the child's presence would but heighten the emotion of her exit from that place where her youth had been wasted. Already the few things she had meant to take away were secreted in a safe place some distance from the house, beside the path she meant to take when she left Jean Jacques for ever. George Masson wanted her, they were to meet to-day, and she was going—going somewhere out of this intolerable dullness and discontent.

When she pushed her coffee-cup aside and rose from the table without eating, she went straight to her looking-glass and surveyed herself with a searching eye. Certainly she was young enough (she said to herself) to draw the eyes of those who cared for youth and beauty. There was not a grey hair in the dark brown of her head, there was not a wrinkle—yes, there were two at the corners of her mouth, which told the story of her restlessness, of her hunger for the excitement of which she had been deprived all these years. To go back to Cadiz?—oh, anywhere, anywhere, so that her blood could beat faster; so that she could feel the stir of life which had made her spirit flourish even in the dangers of the far-off day when Gonzales was by her side.

She looked at her guitar. She was sorry she could not take that away with her. But Jean Jacques would, no doubt, send it after her with his curse. She would love to play it once again with the old thrill; with the thrill she had felt on the night of Zoe's birthday a little while ago, when she was back again with her lover and the birds in the gardens of Granada. She would sing to someone who cared to hear her, and to someone who would make her care to sing, which was far more important. She would sing to the master-carpenter. Though he had not asked her to go with him—only to meet in a secret place in the hills—she meant to do so, just as she once meant to marry Jean Jacques, and had done so. It was true she would probably not have married Jean Jacques, if it had not been for the wreck of the Antoine; but the wreck had occurred, and she had married him, and that was done and over so far as she was concerned. She had determined to go away with the master-carpenter, and though he might feel the same hesitation as that which Jean Jacques had shown—she had read her Norman aright aboard the Antoine—yet, still, George Masson should take her away. A catastrophe had thrown Jean Jacques into her arms; it would not be a catastrophe which would throw the master-carpenter into her arms. It would be that they wanted each other.

The mirror gave her a look of dominance—was it her regular features and her classic head? Does beauty in itself express authority, just because it has the transcendent thing in it? Does the perfect form convey something of the same thing that physical force—an army in arms, a battleship—conveys? In any case it was there, that inherent masterfulness, though not in its highest form. She was not an aristocrat, she was no daughter of kings, no duchess of Castile, no dona of Segovia; and her beauty belonged to more primary manifestations; but it was above the lower forms, even if it did not reach to the highest. "A handsome even splendid woman of her class" would have been the judgment of the connoisseur.

As she looked in the glass at her clear skin, at the wonderful throat showing so soft and palpable and tower-like under the black velvet ribbon brightened by a paste ornament; as she saw the smooth breadth of brow, the fulness of the lips, the limpid lustre of the large eyes, the well-curved ear, so small and so like ivory, it came home to her, as it had never done before, that she was wasted in this obscure parish of St. Saviour's.

There was not a more restless soul or body in all the hemisphere than the soul and body of Carmen Barbille, as she went from this to that on the morning when Jean Jacques had refrained from killing the soul-disturber, the master-carpenter, who had with such skill destroyed the walls and foundations of his home. Carmen was pointlessly busy as she watched for the return of Jean Jacques.

At last she saw him coming from the flume of the mill! She saw that he stumbled as he walked, and that, every now and then, he lifted his head with an effort and threw it back, and threw his shoulders back also, as though to assert his physical manhood. He wore no hat, his hands were making involuntary gestures of helplessness. But presently he seemed to assert authority over his fumbling body and to come erect. His hands clenched at his sides, his head came up stiffly and stayed, and with quickened footsteps he marched rigidly forward towards the Manor.

Then she guessed at the truth, and as soon as she saw his face she was sure beyond peradventure that he knew.

His figure darkened the doorway. Her first thought was to turn and flee, not because she was frightened of what he would do, but because she did not wish to hear what he would say. She shrank from the uprolling of the curtain of the last thirteen years, from the grim exposure of the nakedness of their life together. Her indolent nature in repose wanted the dust of existence swept into a corner out of sight; yet when she was roused, and there were no corners into which the dust could be swept, she could be as bold as any better woman.

She hesitated till it was too late to go, and then as he entered the house from the staring sunlight and the peace of the morning, she straightened herself, and a sulky, stubborn look came into her eyes. He might try to kill her, but she had seen death in many forms far away in Spain, and she would not be afraid till there was cause. Imagination would not take away her courage. She picked up a half-knitted stocking which lay upon the table, and standing there, while he came into the middle of the room, she began to ply the needles.

He stood still. Her face was bent over her knitting. She did not look at him.

"Well, why don't you look at me?" he asked in a voice husky with passion.

She raised her head and looked straight into his dark, distracted eyes.

"Good morning," she said calmly.

A kind of snarling laugh came to his lips. "I said good morning to my wife yesterday, but I will not say it to-day. What is the use of saying good morning, when the morning is not good!"

"That's logical, anyhow," she said, her needles going faster now. She was getting control of them—and of herself.

"Why isn't the morning good? Speak. Why isn't it good, Carmen?"

"Quien sabe—who knows!" she replied with exasperating coolness.

"I know—I know all; and it is enough for a lifetime," he challenged.

"What do you know—what is the 'all'?" Her voice had lost timbre. It was suddenly weak, but from suspense and excitement rather than from fear.

"I saw you last night with him, by the river. I saw what you did. I heard you say, 'Yes, to-morrow, for sure.' I saw what you did."

Her eyes were busy with the knitting now. She did not know what to say. Then, he had known all since the night before! He knew it when he pretended that his head ached—knew it as he lay by her side all night. He knew it, and said nothing! But what had he done—what had he done? She waited for she knew not what. George Masson was to come and inspect the flume early that morning. Had he come? She had not seen him. But the river was flowing through the flume: she could hear the mill-wheel turning—she could hear the mill-wheel turning!

As she did not speak, with a curious husky shrillness to his voice he said: "There he was down in the flume, there was I at the lever above, there was the mill-wheel unlocked. There it was. I gripped the lever, and—"

Her great eyes stared with horror. The knitting-needles stopped; a pallor swept across her face. She felt as she did when she heard the court-martial sentence Carvillho Gonzales to death.

The mill-wheel sounded louder and louder in her ears.

"You let in the river!" she cried. "You drove him into the wheel—you killed him!"

"What else was there to do?" he demanded. "It had to be done, and it was the safest way. It would be an accident. Such a thing might easily happen."

"You have murdered him!" she gasped with a wild look.

"To call it murder!" he sneered. "Surely my wife would not call it murder."

"Fiend—not to have the courage to fight him!" she flung back at him. "To crawl like a snake and let loose a river on a man! In any other country, he'd have been given a chance."

This was his act in a new light. He had had only one idea in his mind when he planned the act, and that was punishment. What rights had a man who had stolen what was nearer and dearer than a man's own flesh, and for which he would have given his own flesh fifty times? Was it that Carmen would now have him believe he ought to have fought the man, who had spoiled his life and ruined a woman's whole existence.

"What chance had I when he robbed me in the dark of what is worth fifty times my own life to me?" he asked savagely.

"Murderer—murderer!" she cried hoarsely. "You shall pay for this."

"You will tell—you will give me up?"

Her eyes were on the mill and the river... "Where—where is he? Has he gone down the river? Did you kill him and let him go—like that!"

She made a flinging gesture, as one would toss a stone.

He stared at her. He had never seen her face like that—so strained and haggard. George Masson was right when he said that she would give him up; that his life would be in danger, and that his child's life would be spoiled.

"Murderer!" she repeated. "And when you go to the gallows, your child's life—you did not think of that, eh? To have your revenge on the man who was no more to blame than I, thinking only of yourself, you killed him; but you did not think of your child."

Ah, yes, surely George Masson was right! That was what he had said about his child, Zoe. What a good thing it was he had not killed the ravager of his home!

But suddenly his logic came to his aid. In terrible misery as he was, he was almost pleased that he could reason. "And you would give me over to the law? You would send me to the gallows—and spoil your child's life?" he retorted.

She threw the knitting down and flung her hands up. "I have no husband. I have no child. Take your life. Take it. I will go and find his body," she said, and she moved swiftly towards the door. "He has gone down the river—I will find him!"

"He has gone up the river," he exclaimed. "Up the river, I say!"

She stopped short and looked at him blankly. Then his meaning became clear to her.

"You did not kill him?" she asked scarce above a whisper.

"I let him go," he replied.

"You did not fight him—why?" There was scorn in her tone.

"And if I had killed him that way?" he asked with terrible logic, as he thought.

"There was little chance of that," she replied scornfully, and steadied herself against a chair; for, now that the suspense was over, she felt as though she had been passed between stones which ground the strength out of her.

A flush of fierce resentment crossed over his face. "It is not everything to be big," he rejoined. "The greatest men in the world have been small like me, but they have brought the giant things to their feet."

She waved a hand disdainfully. "What are you going to do now?" she asked.

He drew himself up. He seemed to rearrange the motions of his mind with a little of the old vanity, which was at once grotesque and piteous. "I am going to forgive you and to try to put things right," he said. "I have had my faults. You were not to blame altogether. I have left you too much alone. I did not understand everything all through. I had never studied women. If I had I should have done the right thing always. I must begin to study women." The drawn look was going a little from his face, the ghastly pain was fading from his eyes; his heart was speaking for her, while his vain intellect hunted the solution of his problem.

She could scarcely believe her ears. No Spaniard would ever have acted as this man was doing. She had come from a land of No Forgiveness. Carvillho Gonzales would have killed her, if she had been untrue to him; and she would have expected it and understood it.

But Jean Jacques was going to forgive her—going to study women, and so understand her and understand women, as he understood philosophy! This was too fantastic for human reason. She stared at him, unable to say a word, and the distracted look in her face did not lessen. Forgiveness did not solve her problem.

"I am going to take you to Montreal—and then out to Winnipeg, when I've got the cheese-factory going," he said with a wise look in his face, and with tenderness even coming into his eyes. "I know what mistakes I've made"—had not George Masson the despoiler told him of them?—"and I know what a scoundrel that fellow is, and what tricks of the tongue he has. Also he is as sleek to look at as a bull, and so he got a hold on you. I grasp things now. Soon we will start away together again as we did at Gaspe."

He came close to her. "Carmen!" he said, and made as though he would embrace her.

"Wait—wait a little. Give me time to think," she said with dry lips, her heart beating hard. Then she added with a flattery which she knew would tell, "I cannot think quick as you do. I am slow. I must have time. I want to work it all out. Wait till to-night," she urged. "Then we can—"

"Good, we will make it all up to-night," he said, and he patted her shoulder as one would that of a child. It had the slight flavour of the superior and the paternal.

She almost shrank from his touch. If he had kissed her she would have felt that she must push him away; and yet she also knew how good a man he was.

CHAPTER XI. THE CLERK OF THE COURT KEEPS A PROMISE

"Well, what is it, M'sieu' Fille? What do you want with me? I've got a lot to do before sundown, and it isn't far off. Out with it."

George Masson was in no good humour; from the look on the face of the little Clerk of the Court he had no idea that he would disclose any good news. It was probably some stupid business about "money not being paid into the Court," which had been left over from cases tried and lost; and he had had a number of cases that summer. His head was not so clear to-day as usual, but he had had little difficulties with M'sieu' Fille before, and he was sure that there was something wrong now.

"Do you want to make me a present?" he added with humorous impatience, for though he was not in a good temper, he liked the Clerk of the Court, who was such a figure at Vilray.

The opening for his purpose did not escape M. Fille. He had been at a loss to begin, but here was a natural opportunity for him.

"Well, good advice is not always a present, but I should like mine to be taken as such, monsieur," he said a little oracularly.

"Oh, advice—to give me advice—that's why you've brought me in here, when I've so much to do I can't breathe! Time is money with me, old 'un."

"Mine is advice which may be money in your pocket, monsieur," remarked the Clerk of the Court with meaning. "Money saved is money earned."

"How do you mean to save me money—by getting the Judge to give decisions in my favour? That would be money in my pocket for sure. The Court has been running against my interests this year. When I think I was never so right in my life—bang goes the judgment of the Court against me, and into my pocket goes my hand. I don't only need to save money, I need to make it; so if you can help me in that way I'm your man, M'sieu' la Fillette?"

The little man bristled at the misuse of his name, and he flushed slightly also; but there was always something engaging in the pleasure-loving master-carpenter. He had such an eloquent and warm temperament, the atmosphere of his personality was so genial, that his impertinence was insulated. Certainly the master-carpenter was not unpopular, and people could not easily resist the grip of his physical influence, while mentally he was far indeed from being deficient. He looked as little like a villain as a man could, and yet—and yet—a nature like that of George Masson (even the little Clerk could see that) was not capable of being true beyond the minute in which he took his oath of fidelity. While the fit of willingness was on him he would be true; yet in reality there was no truth at all—only self-indulgence unmarked by duty or honour.

"Give me a judgment for defamation of character. Give me a thousand dollars or so for that, m'sieu', and you'll do a good turn to a deserving fellow-citizen and admirer—one little thousand, that's all, m'sieu'. Then I'll dance at your wedding and weep at your tomb—so there!"

How easy he made the way for the little Clerk of the Court! "Defamation of character"—could there possibly be a better opening for what he had promised Judge Carcasson he would say!

"Ah, Monsieur Masson," very officially and decorously replied M. Fille, "but is it defamation of character? If the thing is true, then what is the judgment? It goes against you—so there!" There was irony in the last words.

"If what thing is true?" sharply asked the mastercarpenter, catching at the fringe of the idea in M. Fille's mind. "What thing?"

"Ah, but it is true, for I saw it! Yes, alas! I saw it with my own eyes. By accident of course; but there it was—absolute, uncompromising, deadly and complete."

It was a happy moment for the little Clerk of the Court when he could, in such an impromptu way, coin a phrase, or a set of adjectives, which would bear inspection of purists of the language. He loved to talk, though he did not talk a great deal, but he made innumerable conversations in his mind, and that gave him facility when he did speak. He had made conversations with George Masson in his mind since yesterday, when he gave his promise to Judge Carcasson; but none of them was like the real conversation now taking place. It was all the impression of the moment, while the phrases in his mind had been wonderfully logical things which, from an intellectual standpoint, would have delighted the man whose cause he was now engaged in defending.

"You saw what, M'sieu' la Fillette? Out with it, and don't use such big adjectives. I'm only a carpenter. 'Absolute, uncompromising, deadly, complete'—that's a mouthful of grammar, my lords! Come, my sprig of jurisprudence, tell us what you saw." There was an apparent nervousness in Masson's manner now. Indeed he showed more agitation than when, a few hours before, Jean Jacques had stood with his hand on the lever of the gates of the flume, and the life of the master-carpenter at his feet, to be kicked into eternity.

"Four days ago at five o'clock in the afternoon"—in a voice formal and exact, the little Clerk of the Court seemed to be reading from a paper, since he kept his eyes fixed on the blotter before him, as he did in Court—"I was coming down the hill behind the Manor Cartier, when my attention—by accident—

was drawn to a scene below me in the Manor. I stopped short, of course, and—"

"Diable! You stopped short 'of course' before what you saw! Spit it out—what did you see?" George Masson had had a trying day, and there was danger of losing control of himself. There was a whiteness growing round the eyes, and eating up the warmth of the cheek; his admirably smooth brow was contracted into heavy wrinkles, and a foot shifted uneasily on the floor with a scraping sole. This drew the attention of M. Fille, who raised his head reprovingly—he could not get rid of the feeling that he was in court, and that a case was being tried; and the severity of a Judge is naught compared with the severity of a Clerk of the Court, particularly if he is small and unmarried, and has no one to beat him into manageable humanity.

M. Fille's voice was almost querulous.

"If you will but be patient, monsieur! I saw a man with a woman in his arms, and I fear that I must mention the name of the man. It is not necessary to give the name of the woman, but I have it written here"—he tapped the paper—"and there is no mistake in the identity. The man's name is George Masson, master-carpenter, of the town of Laplatte in the province of Quebec."

George Masson was as one hit between the eyes. He made a motion as though to ward off a blow. "Name of Peter, old cock!" he exclaimed abruptly. "You saw enough certainly, if you saw that, and you needn't mention the lady's name, as you say. The evidence is not merely circumstantial. You saw it with your own eyes, and you are an official of the Court, and have the ear of the Judge, and you look like a saint to a jury. Well for sure, I can't prove defamation of character, as you say. But what then—what do you want?"

"What I want I hope you may be able to grant without demur, monsieur. I want you to give your pledge on the Book"—he laid his hand on a Testament lying on the table—"that you will hold no further communication with the lady."

"Where do you come in here? What's your standing in the business?" Masson jerked out his words now. The Clerk of the Court made a reproving gesture. "Knowing what I did, what I had seen, it was clear that I must approach one or other of the parties concerned. Out of regard for the lady I could not approach her husband, and so betray her; out of regard for the husband I could not approach himself and destroy his peace; out of regard for all concerned I could not approach the lady's father, for then—"

Masson interrupted with an oath.

"That old reprobate of Cadiz—well no, bagosh!

"And so you whisked me into your office with the talk of urgent business and—"

"Is not the business urgent, monsieur?"

"Not at all," was the sharp reply of the culprit.

"Monsieur, you shock me. Do you consider that your conduct is not criminal? I have here"—he placed his hand on a book—"the Statutes of Victoria, and it lays down with wholesome severity the law concerning the theft of the affection of a wife, with the accompanying penalty, going as high as twenty thousand dollars."

George Masson gasped. Here was a new turn of affairs. But he set his teeth.

"Twenty thousand dollars—think of that!" he sneered angrily.

"That is what I said, monsieur. I said I could save you money, and money saved is money earned. I am your benefactor, if you will but permit me to be so, monsieur. I would save you from the law, and from the damages which the law gives. Can you not guess what would be given in a court of the Catholic province of Quebec, against the violation of a good man's home? Do you not see that the business is urgent?"

"Not at all," curtly replied the master-carpenter. M. Fille bridled up, and his spare figure seemed to gain courage and dignity.

"If you think I will hold my peace unless you give your sacred pledge, you are mistaken, monsieur. I am no meddler, but I have had much kindness at the hands of Monsieur and Madame Barbille, and I will do what I can to protect them and their daughter—that good and sweet daughter, from the machinations, corruptions and malfeasance—"

"Three damn good words for the Court, bagosh!" exclaimed Masson with a jeer.

"No, with a man devoid of honour, I shall not hesitate, for the Manor Cartier has been the home of domestic peace, and madame, who came to us a stranger, deserves well of the people of that ancient abode of chivalry-the chivalry of France."

"When we are wound up, what a humming we can make!" laughed George Masson sourly. "Have you quite finished, m'sieu'?"

"The matter is urgent, you will admit, monsieur?" again demanded M. Fille with austerity.

"Not at all."

The master-carpenter was defiant and insolent, yet there was a devilish kind of humour in his tone as in his attitude.

"You will not heed the warning I give?" The little Clerk pointed to the open page of the Victorian statutes before him.

"Not at all."

"Then I shall, with profound regret—"

Suddenly George Masson thrust his face forward near that of M. Fille, who did not draw back.

"You will inform the Court that the prisoner refuses to incriminate himself, eh?" he interjected.

"No, monsieur, I will inform Monsieur Barbille of what I saw. I will do this without delay. It is the one thing left me to do."

In quite a grand kind of way he stood up and bowed, as though to dismiss his visitor.

As George Masson did not move, the other went to the door and opened it. "It is the only thing left to do," he repeated, as he made a gentle gesture of dismissal.

"Not at all, my legal bombardier. Not at all, I say. All you know Jean Jacques knows, and a good deal more—what he has seen with his own eyes, and understood with his own mind, without legal help. So, you see, you've kept me here talking when there's no need and while my business waits. It is urgent, M'sieu' la Fillette—your business is stale. It belongs to last session of the Court." He laughed at his joke. "M'sieu' Jean Jacques and I understand each other." He laughed grimly now. "We know each other like a book, and the Clerk of the Court couldn't get in an adjective that would make the sense of it all clearer."

Slowly M. Fille shut the door, and very slowly he came back. Almost blindly, as it might seem, and with a moan, he dropped into his chair. His eyes fixed themselves on George Masson.

"Ah—that!" he said helplessly. "That! The little Zoe—dear God, the little Zoe, and the poor madame!" His voice was aching with pain and repugnance.

"If you were not such an icicle naturally, I'd be thinking your interest in the child was paternal," said the master-carpenter roughly, for the virtuous horror of the other's face annoyed him. He had had a vexing day.

The Clerk of the Court was on his feet in a second. "Monsieur, you dare!" he exclaimed. "You dare to multiply your crimes in that shameless way. Begone! There are those who can make you respect decency. I am not without my friends, and we all stand by each other in our love of home—of sacred home, monsieur."

There was something right in the master-carpenter at the bottom, with all his villainy. It was not alone that he knew there were fifty men in the Parish of St. Saviour's who would man-handle him for such a suggestion, and for what he had done at the Manor Cartier, if they were roused; but he also had a sudden remorse for insulting the man who, after all, had tried to do him a service. His amende was instant.

"I take it back with humble apology—all I can hold in both hands, m'sieu'," he said at once. "I would not insult you so, much less Madame Barbille. If she'd been like what I've hinted at, I wouldn't have gone her way, for the promiscuous is not for me. I'll tell you the whole truth of what happened to-day this morning. Last night I met her at the river, and—Then briefly he told all that had happened to the moment when Jean Jacques had left him at the flume with the words, 'Moi, je suis philosophe!' And at the last he said:

"I give you my word—my oath on this"—he laid his hand on the Testament on the table—"that beyond what you saw, and what Jean Jacques saw, there has been nothing." He held up a hand as though taking an oath.

"Name of God, is it not enough what there has been?" whispered the little Clerk.

"Oh, as you think, and as you say! It is quite enough for me after to-day. I'm a teetotaller, but I'm not so fond of water as to want to take my eternal bath in it." He shuddered slightly. "Bien sur, I've had my fill of the Manor Cartier for one day, my Clerk of the Court."

"Bien sur, it was enough to set you thinking, monsieur," was the dry comment of M. Fille, who was now recovering his composure.

At that moment there came a knock at the door, and another followed quickly; then there entered without waiting for a reply—Carmen Barbille.

CHAPTER XII. THE MASTER-CARPENTER HAS A PROBLEM

The Clerk of the Court came to his feet with a startled "Merci!" and the master-carpenter fell back with a smothered exclamation. Both men stared confusedly at the woman as she shut the door slowly and, as it might seem, carefully, before she faced them.

"Here I am, George," she said, her face alive with vital adventure.

His face was instantly swept by a storm of feeling for her, his nature responded to the sound of her voice and the passion of her face.

"Carmen—ah!" he said, and took a step forward, then stopped. The hoarse feeling in his voice made her eyes flash gratitude and triumph, and she waited for him to take her in his arms; but she suddenly remembered M. Fille. She turned to him.

"I am sorry to intrude, m'sieu'," she said. "I beg your pardon. They told me at the office of avocat Prideaux that M'sieu' Masson was here. So I came; but be sure I would not interrupt you if there was not cause."

M. Fille came forward and took her hand respectfully. "Madame, it is the first time you have honoured me here. I am very glad to receive you. Monsieur and Mademoiselle Zoe, they are with you? They will also come in perhaps?"

M. Fille was courteous and kind, yet he felt that a duty was devolving on him, imposed by his superior officer, Judge Carcasson, and by his own conscience, and with courage he faced the field of trouble which his simple question opened up. George Masson had but now said there had been nothing more than he himself had seen from the hill behind the Manor; and he had further said, in effect, that all was ended between Carmen Barbille and himself; yet here they were together, when they ought to be a hundred miles apart for many a day. Besides, there was the look in the woman's face, and that intense look also in the face of the master-carpenter! The Clerk of the Court, from sheer habit of his profession, watched human faces as other people watch the weather, or the rise or fall in the price of wheat and potatoes. He was an archaic little official, and apparently quite unsophisticated; yet there was hidden behind his ascetic face a quiet astuteness which would have been a valuable asset to a worldly-minded and ambitious man. Besides, affection sharpens the wits. Through it the hovering, protecting sense becomes instinctive, and prescience takes on uncanny certainty. He had a real and deep affection for Jean Jacques and his Carmen, and a deeper one still for the child Zoe; and the danger to the home at the Manor Cartier now became again as sharp as the knife of the guillotine. His eyes ran from the woman to the man, and back again, and then with great courage he repeated his question:

"Monsieur and mademoiselle, they are well—they are with you, I hope, madame?"

She looked at him in the eyes without flinching, and on the instant she was aware that he knew all, and that there had been talk with George Masson. She knew the little man to be as good as ever can be, but she resented the fact that he knew. It was clear George Masson had told him—else how could he know; unless, perhaps, all the world knew!

"You know well enough that I have come alone, my friend," she answered. "It is no place for Zoe; and it is no place for my husband and him together," she made a motion of the head towards the mastercarpenter. "Santa Maria, you know it very well indeed!"

The Clerk of the Court bowed, but made no reply. What was there to say to a remark like that! It was clear that the problem must be worked out alone between these two people, though he was not quite sure what the problem was. The man had said the thing was over; but the woman had come, and the look of both showed that it was not all over.

What would the man do? What was it the woman wished to do? The master-carpenter had said that Jean Jacques had spared him, and meant to forgive his wife. No doubt he had done so, for Jean Jacques was a man of sentiment and chivalry, and there was no proof that there had been anything more than a few mad caresses between the two misdemeanants; yet here was the woman with the man for whom she had imperilled her future and that of her husband and child!

As though Carmen understood what was going on in his mind, she said: "Since you know everything, you can understand that I want a few words with M'sieu' George here alone."

"Madame, I beg of you," the Clerk of the Court answered instantly, his voice trembling a little—"I beg that you will not be alone with him. As I believe, your husband is willing to let bygones be bygones, and to begin to-morrow as though there was no to-day. In such case you should not see Monsieur Masson here alone. It is bad enough to see him here in the office of the Clerk of the Court, but to see him alone—what would Monsieur Jean Jacques say? Also, outside there in the street, if our neighbours should come to know of the trouble, what would they say? I wish not to be tiresome, but as a friend, a true friend of your whole family, madame—yes, in spite of all, your whole family—I hope you will realize that I must remain here. I owe it to a past made happy by kindness which is to me like life itself. Monsieur Masson, is it not so?" he added, turning to the master-carpenter. More flushed and agitated than when he had faced Jean Jacques in the flume, the master-carpenter said: "If she wants a few words-of farewell—alone with me, she must have it, M'sieu' Fille. The other room—eh? Outside there"—he jerked a finger towards the street—"they won't know that you are not with us; and as for Jean Jacques, isn't it possible for a Clerk of the Court to stretch the truth a little? Isn't the Clerk of the Court a man as well as a mummy? I'd do as much for you, little lawyer, any time. A word to say farewell, you understand!" He looked M. Fille squarely in the eye.

"If I had to answer M. Jean Jacques on such a matter—and so much at stake—"

Masson interrupted. "Well, if you like we'll bind your eyes and put wads in your ears, and you can stay, so that you'll have been in the room all the time, and yet have heard and seen nothing at all. How is that, m'sieu'? It's all right, isn't it?"

M. Fille stood petrified for a moment at the audacity of the proposition. For him, the Clerk of the Court, to be blinded and made ridiculous with wads in his ears-impossible!

"Grace of Heaven, I would prefer to lie!" he answered quickly. "I will go into the next room, but I beg that you be brief, monsieur and madame. You owe it to yourselves and to the situation to be brief, and, if I may say so, you owe it to me. I am not a practised Ananias."

"As well be hung for a sheep as a lamb, m'sieu'," returned Masson.

"I must beg that you will make your farewells of a minute and no more," replied the Clerk of the Court firmly. He took out his watch. "It is six o'clock. I will come again at three minutes past six. That is long enough for any farewell—even on the gallows."

Not daring to look at the face of the woman, he softly disappeared into the other room, and shut the door without a sound.

"Too good for this world," remarked the master-carpenter when the door closed tight. He said it after the disappearing figure and not to Carmen. "I don't suppose he ever kissed a real grown-up woman in his life. It would have shattered his frail little carcass if, if"—he turned to his companion—"if you had kissed him, Carmen. He's made of tissue-paper,—not tissue—and apple-jelly. Yes, but a stiff little backbone, too, or he'd not have faced me down."

Masson talked as though he were trying to gain time. "He said three minutes," she returned with a look of death in her face. As George Masson had talked with the Clerk of the Court, she had come to see, in so far as agitation would permit, that he was not the same as when he left her by the river the evening before.

"There's no time to waste," she continued. "You spoke of farewells—twice you spoke, and three times he spoke of farewells between us. Farewells—farewells—George—!"

With sudden emotion she held out her arms, and her face flushed with passion and longing.

The tempest which shook her shook him also, and he swayed from side to side like an animal uncertain if the moment had come to try its strength with its foe; and in truth the man was fighting with himself. His moments with Jean Jacques at the flume had expanded him in a curious kind of way. His own arguments while he was fighting for his life had, in a way, convinced himself. She was a rare creature, and she was alluring—more alluring than she had ever been; for a tragic sense had made her thinner, had refined the boldness of her beauty, had given a wonderful lustre to her eyes; and suffering has its own attraction to the degenerate. But he, George Masson, had had a great shock, and he had come out of the jaws of death by the skin of his teeth. It had been the nearest thing he had ever known; for though once he had had a pistol pointed at him, there was the chance that it might miss at half-a-dozen yards, while there was no chance of the lever of the flume going wrong; and water and a mill-wheel were as absolute as the rope of the gallows.

In a sense he had saved himself by his cleverness, but if Jean Jacques had not been just the man he was, he could not have saved himself. It did not occur to him that Jean Jacques had acted weakly. He would not have done what Jean Jacques had done, had Jean Jacques spoiled his home. He would have sprung the lever; but he was not so mean as to despise Jean Jacques because he had foregone his revenge. This master-carpenter had certain gifts, or he could not have caused so much trouble in the world. There is a kind of subtlety necessary to allure or delude even the humblest of women, if she is not naturally bad; and Masson had had experiences with the humblest, and also with those a little higher up. This much had to be said for him, that he did not think Jean Jacques contemptible because he had been merciful, or degraded because he had chosen to forgive his wife.

The sight of the woman, as she stood with arms outstretched, had made his pulses pound in his veins, but the heat was suddenly chilled by the wave of tragedy which had passed over him. When he had climbed out of the flume, and opened the lever for the river to rush through, he had felt as though ice—cold liquid flowed in his veins, not blood; and all day he had been like that. He had moved much as one in a dream, and he had felt for the first time in his life that he was not ready to bluff creation. He had always faced things down, as long as it could be done; and when it could not, he had retreated, with the comment that no man was wise who took gruel when he needn't. He was now face to face with his greatest problem. One thing was clear—they must either part for ever, or go together, and part no more. There could be no half measures. She was a remarkable woman in her way, with a will of her own, and a kind of madness in her; and there could be no backing and filling. They only had three minutes to talk together alone, and two of them were up.

Her arms were held out to him, but he stood still, and before the fire of her eyes his own eyes dropped. "No, not yet!" he exclaimed. "It's been a day— heaven and hell, what a day it's been! He had me like that!" He opened and shut his hand with fierce, spasmodic strength. "And he let me go—oh, let me go like a fox out of a trap! I've had enough for one day—blood of St. Peter, enough, enough!"

The flame of desire in her eyes suddenly turned to fury. "It is farewell, then, that you wish," she said hoarsely. "It is no more and farewell then? You said it to him"—she pointed to the other room—"you said it to Jean Jacques, and you say it to me—to me that's given you all I have. Ah, what a beast you are, George Masson!"

"No, Carmen, you have not given me all. If you had, there would be no farewell. I would stand by you to the end of life, if I had taken all." He lied, but that does not matter here.

"All—all!" she cried. "What is all? Is it but the one thing that the world says must part husband and wife? Caramba! Is that all? I have given everything—I have had your arms around me—"

"Yes, the Clerk of the Court saw that," he interrupted. "He saw from the hill behind the Manor on Tuesday last."

There was a tap at the door of the other room; it slowly opened, and the figure of the Clerk appeared. "Two minutes—just two minutes more, old trump!" said the master-carpenter, stretching out a hand. "One minute will be enough," said Carmen, who was suffering the greatest humiliation which can come to a woman.

The Clerk looked at them both, and he was content. He saw that one minute would certainly be enough. "Very well, monsieur and madame," he said, and closed the door again.

Carmen turned fiercely on the man. "M. Fille saw, did he, from Mont Violet? Well, when I came here I did not care who saw. I only thought of you—that you wanted me, and that I wanted you. What the world thought was nothing, if you were as when we parted last night.... I could not face Jean Jacques' forgiveness. To stay there, feeling that I must be always grateful, that I must be humble, that I must pretend, that I must kiss Jean Jacques, and lie in his arms, and go to mass and to confession, and—"

"There is the child, there is Zoe—"

"Oh, it is you that preaches now—you that tempted me, that said I was wasted at the Manor; that the parish did not understand me; that Jean Jacques did not know a jewel of price when he saw it—little did you think of Zoe then!"

He made a protesting gesture. "Maybe so, Carmen, but I think now before it is too late."

"The child loves her father as she never loved me," she declared. "She is twelve years old. She will soon be old enough to keep house for him, and then to marry—ah, before there is time to think she will marry!"

"It would be better then for you to wait till she marries before—before—"

"Before I go away with you!" She gave a shrill, agonized laugh. "So that is the end of it all! What did you think of my child when you forced your way into my life, when you made me think of you—ah, quel bete—what a coward and beast you are!"

"No, I am not all coward, though I may be a beast," he answered. "I didn't think of your child when I began to talk to you as I did. I was out for all I could get. I was the hunter. And you were the finest woman that I'd ever met and talked with; you—"

"Oh, stop lying!" she cried with a face suddenly grown white and cold.

"It isn't lying. You're the sort of woman to drive men mad. I went mad, and I didn't think of your child. But this morning in the flume I saved my life by thinking of her, and I saved your life, too, maybe, by thinking of her; and I owe her something. I'm going to try to pay back by letting her keep her mother. I never felt towards a woman as I've felt towards you; and that's why I want to make things not so bad for you as they might be."

In her bitter eagerness she took a step nearer to him. "As things might be, if you were the man you were yesterday, willing to throw up everything for me?"

"Like that—if you put it so," he answered.

She walked slowly up to him, looking as though she would plunge a knife into his heart. "I wish Jean Jacques had opened the gates," she said. "It would have saved the hangman trouble."

Then suddenly, and with a cry, she raised her hand and struck him full in the face with her fist. At that instant came a tap at the door of the other room, and the Clerk of the Court appeared. He saw the blow, and drew back with an exclamation.

Carmen turned to him. "Farewell has been said, M'sieu' Fille," she remarked in a voice sombre with rage and despair, and she went to the door leading to the street.

Masson had winced at the blow, but he remained silent. He knew not what to say or do.

M. Fille hastily followed Carmen to the door. "You are going home, dear madame? Permit me to accompany you," he said gently. "I have to do business with Jean Jacques."

A hand upon his chest, she pushed him back. "Where I go I'm going alone," she said. Opening the door she went out, but turning back again she gave George Masson a look that he never forgot. Then the door closed.

"Grace of God, she is not going home!" brokenly murmured the Clerk of the Court.

With a groan the master-carpenter started forward towards the door, but M. Fille stepped between, laid a hand on his arm, and stopped him.

CHAPTER XIII. THE MAN FROM OUTSIDE

"Oh, who will walk the wood with me,

I fear to walk alone;

So young am I, as you may see;

No dangers have I known.

So young, so small—ah, yes, m'sieu',

I'll walk the wood with you!"

In the last note of the song applause came instantaneously, almost impatiently, as it might seem. With cries of "Encore! Encore!" it lasted some time, while the happy singer looked around with frank pleasure on the little group encircling her in the Manor Cartier.

"Did you like it so much?" she asked in a general way, and not looking at any particular person. A particular person, however, replied, and she had addressed the question to him, although not looking at him. He was the Man from Outside, and he sat near the bright wood-fire; for though it was almost June the night was cool and he was delicate.

"Ah, but splendid, but splendid—it got into every corner of every one of us," the Man from Outside responded, speaking his fluent French with a slight English accent, which had a pleasant piquancy—at least to the ears of the pretty singer, Mdlle. Zoe Barbille. He was a man of about thirty-three, clean-shaven, dark-haired, with an expression of cleverness; yet with an irresponsible something about him which M. Fille had reflected upon with concern. For this slim, eager, talkative, half-invalid visitor to St. Saviour's had of late shown a marked liking for the presence and person of Zoe Barbille; and Zoe was as dear to M. Fille as though she were his own daughter. He it was who, in sarcasm, had spoken of this young stranger as "The Man from Outside."

Ever since Zoe's mother had vanished—alone—seven years before from the Manor Cartier, or rather from his office at Vilray, M. Fille had been as much like a maiden aunt or a very elder brother to the Spanische's daughter as a man could be. Of M. Fille's influence over his daughter and her love of his companionship, Jean Jacques had no jealousy whatever. Very often indeed, when he felt incompetent to do for his child all that he wished—philosophers are often stupid in human affairs—he thought it was a blessing Zoe had a friend like M. Fille. Since the terrible day when he found that his wife had gone from him—not with the master-carpenter who only made his exit from Laplatte some years afterwards—he had had no desire to have a woman at the Manor to fill her place, even as housekeeper. He had never swerved from that. He had had a hard row to hoe, but he had hoed it with a will not affected by domestic accidents or inconveniences. The one woman from outside whom he permitted to go and come at will—and she did not come often, because she and M. Fille agreed it would be best not to do so—was the sister of the Cure. To be sure there was Seraphe Corniche, the old cook, but she was buried in her kitchen, and Jean Jacques treated her like a man.

When Zoe was confirmed, and had come back from Montreal, having spent two years in a convent there—the only time she had been away from her father in seven years—having had her education chiefly from a Catholic "brother," the situation developed in a new way. Zoe at once became as conspicuous in the country-side as her father had been over so many years. She was fresh, volatile, without affectation or pride, and had a temperament responsive to every phase of life's simple interests. She took the attention of the young men a little bit as her due, but yet without conceit. The gallants had come about her like bees, for there was Jean Jacques' many businesses and his reputation for wealth; and there was her own charm, concerning which there could be far less doubt than about Jean Jacques' magnificent solvency.

Zoe had gone heart-whole and with no especial preference for any young man, until the particular person came, the Man from Outside.

His name was Gerard Fynes, and his business was mumming. He was a young lawyer turned actor, and he had lived in Montreal before he went on the stage. He was English—that was a misfortune; he was an actor—that was a greater misfortune, for it suggested vagabondage of morals as well as of profession; and he was a Protestant, which was the greatest misfortune of all. But he was only at St. Saviour's for his convalescence after a so-called attack of congestion of the lungs; and as he still had a slight cough and looked none too robust, and as, more than all, he was simple in his ways, enjoying the life of the parish with greater zest than the residents, he found popularity. Undoubtedly he had a taking way with him. He was lodging with Louis Charron, a small farmer and kinsman of Jean Jacques, who sold whisky—"white whisky"—without a license. It was a Charron family habit to sell liquor illegally, and Louis pursued the career with all an amateur's enthusiasm. He had a sovereign balm for "colds," composed of camomile flowers, boneset, liquorice, pennyroyal and gentian root, which he sold to all comers; and it was not unnatural that a visitor with weak lungs should lodge with him.

Louis and his wife had only good things to say about Gerard Fynes; for the young man lived their life as though he was born to it. He ate the slap-jacks, the buttermilk-pop, the pork and beans, the Indian corn on the cob, the pea-soup, and the bread baked in the roadside oven, with a relish which was not all pretence; for indeed he was as primitive as he was subtle. He himself could not have told how much of him was true and how much was make-believe. But he was certainly lovable, and he was not bad by nature. Since coming to St. Saviour's he had been constant to one attraction, and he had not risked his chances with Zoe by response to the shy invitations of dark eyes, young and not so young, which met his own here and there in the parish.

Only M. Fille and Jean Jacques himself had feelings of real antagonism to him. Jean Jacques, though not naturally suspicious, had, however, seen an understanding look pass between his Zoe and this stranger—this Protestant English stranger from the outer world, to which Jean Jacques went less frequently since his fruitless search for his vanished Carmen. The Clerk of the Court saw that Jean Jacques had observed the intimate glances of the two young people, and their eyes met in understanding. It was just before Zoe had sung so charmingly, 'Oh, Who Will Walk the Wood With Me'.

At first after Carmen's going Jean Jacques had found it hard to endure singing in his house. Zoe's trilling was torture to him, though he had never forbidden her to sing, and she had sung on to her heart's content. By a subtle instinct, however, and because of the unspoken sorrow in her own heart, she never sang the songs like 'La Manola'. Never after the day Carmen went did Zoe speak of her mother to anyone at all. It was worse than death; it was annihilation, so far as speech was concerned. The world at large only knew that Carmen Barbille had run away, and that even Sebastian Dolores her father did not know where she was. The old man had not heard from her, and he seldom visited at the Manor Cartier or saw his grand-daughter. His own career of late years had been marked by long sojourns in Quebec, Montreal and even New York; yet he always came back to St. Saviour's when he was penniless, and was there started afresh by Jean Jacques. Some said that Carmen had gone back to Spain, but others discredited that, for, if she had done so, certainly old Sebastian Dolores would have gone also. Others continued to insist that she had gone off with a man; but there was George Masson at Laplatte living alone, and never going twenty miles away from home, and he was the only person under suspicion. Others again averred that since her flight Carmen had become a loose woman in Montreal; but the New Cure came down on that with a blow which no one was tempted to invite again.

M. Savry's method of punishing was of a kind to make men shrink. If Carmen Barbille had become a loose woman in Montreal, how did any member of his flock know that it was the case? What company had he kept in Montreal that he could say that? Did he see the woman—or did he hear about her? And if he heard, what sort of company was he keeping when he went to Montreal without his wife to hear such things? That was final, and the slanderer was under a cloud for a time, by reason of the anger of his own wife. It was about this time that the good priest preached from the text, "Judge not that ye be not judged," and said that there were only ten commandments on the tables of stone; but that the ten included all the commandments which the Church made for every man, and which every man, knowing his own weakness, must also make for himself.

His flock understood, though they did refrain, every one, from looking towards the place where Jean Jacques sat with Ma'm'selle—she was always called that, as though she was a great lady; or else she was called "the little Ma'm'selle Zoe," even when she had grown almost as tall as her mother had been.

Though no one looked towards the place where Jean Jacques and his daughter sat when this sermon was preached, and although Zoe seemed not to apprehend personal reference in the priest's words, when she reached home, after talking to her father about casual things all the way, she flew to her room, and, locking the door, flung herself on her bed and cried till her body felt as though it had been beaten by rods. Then she suddenly got up and, from a drawer, took out two things—an old photograph of her mother at the time of her marriage, and Carmen's guitar, which she had made her own on the day after the flight, and had kept hidden ever since. She lay on the bed with her cheek pressed to the guitar, and her eyes hungrily feeding on the face of a woman whose beauty belonged to spheres other than where she had spent the thirteen years of her married life.

Zoe had understood more even at the time of the crisis than they thought she did, child though she was; and as the years had gone on she had grasped the meaning of it all more clearly perhaps than anyone at all except her adored friends Judge Carcasson, at whose home she had visited in Montreal, and M. Fille.

The thing last rumoured about her mother in the parish was that she had become an actress. To this Zoe made no protest in her mind. It was better than many other possibilities, and she fixed her mind on it, so saving herself from other agonizing speculations. In a fixed imagination lay safety. In her soul she knew that, no matter what happened, her mother would never return to the Manor Cartier.

The years had not deepened confidence between father and daughter. A shadow hung between them. They laughed and talked together, were even boisterous in their fun sometimes, and yet in the eyes of both was the forbidden thing—the deserted city into which they could not enter. He could not speak to the child of the shame of her mother; she could not speak of that in him which had contributed to that mother's shame—the neglect which existed to some degree in her own life with him. This was chiefly so because his enterprises had grown to such a number and height, that he seemed ever to be counting them, ever struggling to the height, while none of his ventures ever reached that state of success when it "ran itself", although as years passed men called him rich, and he spent and loaned money so freely that they called him the Money Master, or the Money Man Wise, in deference to his philosophy.

Zoe was not beautiful, but there was a wondrous charm in her deep brown eyes and in the expression of her pretty, if irregular, features. Sometimes her face seemed as small as that of a young child, and alive with eerie fancies; and always behind her laughter was something which got into her eyes, giving them a haunting melancholy. She had no signs of hysteria, though now and then there came heart-breaking little outbursts of emotion which had this proof that they were not hysteria—they were never seen by others. They were sacred to her own solitude. While in Montreal she had tasted for the first time the joys of the theatre, and had then secretly read numbers of plays, which she bought from an old bookseller, who was wise enough to choose them for her. She became possessed of a love for the stage even before Gerard Fynes came upon the scene. The beginning of it all was the rumour that her mother was now an actress; yet the root-cause was far down in a temperament responsive to all artistic things.

The coming of the Man from Outside acted on the confined elements of her nature like the shutter of a camera. It let in a world of light upon unexplored places, it set free elements of being which had not before been active. She had been instantly drawn to Gerard Fynes. He had the distance from her own life which provoked interest, and in that distance was the mother whom perhaps it was her duty to forget, yet for whom she had a longing which grew greater as the years went on.

Gerard Fynes could talk well, and his vivid pictures of his short play-acting career absorbed her; and all the time she was vigilant for some name, for the description of some actress which would seem to be a clue to the lost spirit of her life. This clue never came, but before she gave up hope of it, the man had got nearer to her than any man had ever done.

After meeting him she awoke to the fact that there was a difference between men, that it was not the same thing to be young as to be old; that the reason why she could kiss the old Judge and the little Clerk of the Court, and not kiss, say, the young manager of the great lumber firm who came every year for a fortnight's fishing at St. Saviour's, was one which had an understandable cause and was not a mere matter of individual taste. She had been good friends with this young manager, who was only thirty years of age, and was married, but when he had wanted to kiss her on saying good-bye one recent summer, she had said, "Oh, no, oh, no, that would spoil it all!" Yet when he had asked her why, and what she meant, she could not tell him. She did not know; but by the end of the first week after Gerard Fynes had been brought to the Manor Cartier by Louis Charron, she knew.

She had then been suddenly awakened from mere girlhood. Judge Carcasson saw the difference in her on a half-hour's visit as he passed westward, and he had said to M. Fille, "Who is the man, my keeper of the treasure?" The reply had been of such a sort that the Judge was startled:

"Tut, tut," he had exclaimed, "an actor—an actor once a lawyer! That's serious. She's at an age—and with a temperament like hers she'll believe anything, if once her affections are roused. She has a flair for the romantic, for the thing that's out of reach—the bird on the highest branch, the bird in the sky beyond ours, the song that was lost before time was, the light that never was on sea or land. Why, damn it, damn it all, my Solon, here's the beginning of a case in Court unless we can lay the fellow by the heels! How long is he here for?"

When M. Fille had told him that he would stay for another month for certain, and no doubt much longer, if there seemed a prospect of winning the heiress of the Manor Cartier, the Judge gave a groan.

"We must get him away, somehow," he said. "Where does he stay?"

"At the house of Louis Charron," was the reply. "Louis Charron—isn't he the fellow that sells whisky without a license?"

"It is so, monsieur."

The Judge moved his head from side to side like a bear in a cage. "It is that, is it, my Fille? By the thumb of the devil, isn't it time then that Louis Charron was arrested for breaking the law? Also how do we know but that the interloping fellow Fynes is an agent for a whisky firm perhaps? Couldn't he, then, on suspicion, be arrested with—"

The Clerk of the Court shook his head mournfully. His Judge was surely becoming childish in his old age. He looked again closely at the great man, and saw a glimmer of moisture in the grey eyes. It was clear that Judge Carcasson felt deeply the dangers of the crisis, and that the futile outburst had merely been the agitated protest of the helpless.

"The man is what he says he is—an actor; and it would be folly to arrest him. If our Zoe is really fond of him, it would only make a martyr of him."

As he made this reply M. Fille looked furtively at the other—out of the corner of his eye, as it were. The reply of the Judge was impatient, almost peevish and rough. "Did you think I was in earnest, my punchinello? Surely I don't look so young as all that. I am over sixty-five, and am therefore mentally developed!"

M. Fille was exactly sixty-five years of age, and the blow was a shrewd one. He drew himself up with rigid dignity.

"You must feel sorry sometimes for those who suffered when your mind was undeveloped, monsieur," he answered. "You were a judge at forty-nine, and you defended poor prisoners for twenty years before that."

The Judge was conquered, and he was never the man to pretend he was not beaten when he was. He admired skill too much for that. He squeezed M. Fille's arm and said:

"I've been quick with my tongue myself, but I feel sure now, that it's through long and close association with my Clerk of the Court."

"Ah, monsieur, you are so difficult to understand!" was the reply. "I have known you all these years, and yet—"

"And yet you did not know how much of the woman there was in me!... But yes, it is that. It is that which I fear with our Zoe. Women break out—they break out, and then there is the devil to pay. Look at her mother. She broke out. It was not inevitable. It was the curse of opportunity, the wrong thing popping up to drive her mad at the wrong moment. Had the wrong thing come at the right time for her, when she was quite sane, she would be yonder now with our philosopher. Perhaps she would not be contented if she were there, but she would be there; and as time goes on, to be where we were in all things which concern the affections, that is the great matter."

"Ah, yes, ah, yes," was the bright-eyed reply of that Clerk, "there is no doubt of that! My sister and I there, we are fifty years together, never with the wrong thing at the wrong time, always the thing as it was, always to be where we were."

The Judge shook his head. "There is an eternity of difference, Fille, between the sister and brother and the husband and wife. The sacredness of isolation is the thing which holds the brother and sister together. The familiarity of—but never mind what it is that so often forces husband and wife apart. It is there, and it breaks out in rebellion as it did with the wife of Jean Jacques Barbille. As she was a strong woman in her way, it spoiled her life, and his too when it broke out."

M. Fille's face lighted with memory and feeling. "Ah, a woman of powerful emotions, monsieur, that is so! I think I never told you, but at the last, in my office, when she went, she struck George Masson in the face. It was a blow that—but there it was; I have never liked to think of it. When I do, I shudder. She was a woman who might have been in other circumstances—but there!"

The Judge suddenly stopped in his walk and faced round on his friend. "Did you ever know, my Solon," he said, "that it was not Jean Jacques who saved Carmen at the wreck of the Antoine, but it was she who saved him; and yet she never breathed of it in all the years. One who was saved from the Antoine told me of it. Jean Jacques was going down. Carmen gave him her piece of wreckage to hang on to, and swam ashore without help. He never gave her the credit. There was something big in the woman, but it did not come out right."

M. Fille threw up his hands. "Grace de Dieu, is it so that she saved Jean Jacques? Then he would not be here if it had not been for her?"

"That is the obvious deduction, Maitre Fille," replied the Judge.

The Clerk of the Court seemed moved. "He did not treat her ill. I know that he would take her back to-morrow if he could. He has never forgotten. I saw him weeping one day—it was where she used to sing to the flax-beaters by the Beau Cheval. I put my hand on his shoulder, and said, 'I know, I comprehend; but be a philosopher, Jean Jacques.'"

"What did he say?" asked the Judge.

"He drew himself up. 'In my mind, in my soul, I am philosopher always,' he said, 'but my eyes are the windows of my heart, m'sieu'. They look out and see the sorrow of one I loved. It is for her sorrow that I weep, not for my own. I have my child, I have money; the world says to me, "How goes it, my friend?" I have a home—a home; but where is she, and what does the world say to her?'"

The Judge shook his head sadly. "I used to think I knew life, but I come to the belief in the end that I know nothing. Who could have guessed that he would have spoken like that!"

"He forgave her, monsieur."

The Judge nodded mournfully. "Yes, yes, but I used to think it is such men who forgive one day and kill the next. You never can tell where they will explode, philosophy or no philosophy."

The Judge was right. After all the years that had passed since his wife had left him, Jean Jacques did explode. It was the night of his birthday party at which was present the Man from Outside. It was in the hour when he first saw what the Clerk of the Court had seen some time before—the understanding between Zoe and Gerard Fynes. It had never occurred to him that there was any danger. Zoe had been so indifferent to the young men of St. Saviour's and beyond, had always been so much his friend and the friend of those much older than himself, like Judge Carcasson and M. Fille, that he had not yet thought of her electing to go and leave him alone.

To leave him alone! To be left alone—it had never become a possibility to his mind. It did not break upon him with its full force all at once. He first got the glimmer of it, then the glimmer grew to a glow, and the glow to a great red light, in which his brain became drunk, and all his philosophy was burned up like wood-shavings in a fiery furnace.

"Did you like it so much?" Zoe had asked when her song was finished, and the Man from Outside had replied, "Ah, but splendid, splendid! It got into every corner of every one of us."

"Into the senses—why not into the heart? Songs are meant for the heart," said Zoe.

"Yes, yes, certainly," was the young man's reply, "but it depends upon the song whether it touches the heart more than the senses. Won't you sing that perfect thing, 'La Claire Fontaine'?" he added, with eyes as bright as passion and the hectic fires of his lung-trouble could make them.

She nodded and was about to sing, for she loved the song, and it had been ringing in her head all day; but at that point M. Fille rose, and with his glass raised high—for at that moment Seraphe Corniche and another carried round native wine and cider to the company—he said:

"To Monsieur Jean Jacques Barbille, and his fifty years, good health—bonne sante! This is his birthday. To a hundred years for Jean Jacques!"

Instantly everyone was up with glass raised, and Zoe ran and threw her arms round her father's neck. "Kiss me before you drink," she said.

With a touch almost solemn in its tenderness Jean Jacques drew her head to his shoulder and kissed her hair, then her forehead. "My blessed one—my angel," he whispered; but there was a look in his eyes which only M. Fille had seen there before. It was the look which had been in his eyes at the flax-beaters' place by the river.

"Sing—father, you must sing," said Zoe, and motioned to the fiddler. "Sing It's Fifty Years," she cried eagerly. They all repeated her request, and he could but obey.

Jean Jacques' voice was rather rough, but he had some fine resonant notes in it, and presently, with eyes fastened on the distance, and with free gesture and much expression, he sang the first verse of the haunting ballad of the man who had reached his fifty years:

"Wherefore these flowers?

This fete for me?

Ah, no, it is not fifty years,

Since in my eyes the light you see

First shone upon life's joys and tears!

How fast the heedless days have flown

Too late to wail the misspent hours,

To mourn the vanished friends I've known,

To kneel beside love's ruined bowers.

Ah, have I then seen fifty years,

With all their joys and hopes and fears!"

Through all the verses he ranged, his voice improving with each phrase, growing more resonant, till at last it rang out with a ragged richness which went home to the hearts of all. He was possessed. All at once he was conscious that the beginning of the end of things was come for him; and that now, at fifty, in no sphere had he absolutely "arrived," neither in home nor fortune, nor—but yes, there was one sphere of success; there was his fatherhood. There was his daughter, his wonderful Zoe. He drew his eyes from the distance, and saw that her ardent look was not towards him, but towards one whom she had known but a few weeks.

Suddenly he stopped in the middle of a verse, and broke forward with his arms outstretched, laughing. He felt that he must laugh, or he would cry; and that would be a humiliating thing to do.

"Come, come, my friends, my children, enough of that!" he cried. "We'll have no more maundering. Fifty years—what are fifty years! Think of Methuselah! It's summer in the world still, and it's only spring at St. Saviour's. It's the time of the first flowers. Let's dance—no, no, never mind the Cure to-night! He will not mind. I'll settle it with him. We'll dance the gay quadrille."

He caught the hands of the two youngest girls present, and nodded at the fiddler, who at once began to tune his violin afresh. One of the joyous young girls, however, began to plead with him.

"Ah, no, let us dance, but at the last—not yet, M'sieu' Jean Jacques! There is Zoe's song, we must have that, and then we must have charades. Here is M'sieu' Fynes—he can make splendid charades for us. Then the dance at the last—ah, yes, yes, M'sieu' Jean Jacques! Let it be like that. We all planned it, and though it is your birthday, it's us are making the fete."

"As you will then, as you will, little ones," Jean Jacques acquiesced with a half-sigh; but he did not look at his daughter. Somehow, suddenly, a strange constraint possessed him where Zoe was concerned. "Then let us have Zoe's song; let us have 'La Claire Fontaine'," cried the black-eyed young madcap who held Jean Jacques' arms.

But Zoe interrupted. "No, no," she protested, "the singing spell is broken. We will have the song after the charades—after the charades."

"Good, good—after the charades!" they all cried, for there would be charades like none which had ever been played before, with a real actor to help them, to carry them through as they did on the stage. To them the stage was compounded of mystery, gaiety and the forbidden.

So, for the next half-hour they were all at the disposal of the Man from Outside, who worked as though it was a real stage, and they were real players, and there were great audiences to see them. It was all quite wonderful, and it involved certain posings, attitudes, mimicry and pantomime, for they were really ingenious charades.

So it happened that Zoe's fingers often came in touch with those of the stage-manager, that his hands touched her shoulders, that his cheek brushed against her dark hair once, and that she had sensations never experienced before. Why was it that she thrilled when she came near to him, that her whole body throbbed and her heart fluttered when their shoulders or arms touched? Her childlike nature, with all its warmth and vibration of life, had never till now felt the stir of sex in its vital sense. All men had in one way been the same to her; but now she realized that there was a world-wide difference between her Judge Carcasson, her little Clerk of the Court, and this young man whose eyes drank hers. She had often been excited, even wildly agitated, had been like a sprite let loose in quiet ways; but that was mere spirit. Here was body and senses too; here was her whole being alive to a music, which had an aching sweetness and a harmony coaxing every sense into delight.

"To-morrow evening, by the flume, where the beechtrees are—come—at six. I want to speak with you. Will you come?"

Thus whispered the maker of this music of the senses, who directed the charades, but who was also directing the course of another life than his own.

"Yes, if I can," was Zoe's whispered reply, and the words shook as she said them; for she felt that their meeting in the beech-trees by the flume would be of consequence beyond imagination.

Judge Carcasson had always said that Zoe had judgment beyond her years; M. Fille had remarked often that she had both prudence and shrewdness as well as a sympathetic spirit; but M. Fille's little whispering sister, who could never be tempted away from her home to any house, to whom the market and the church were like pilgrimages to distant wilds, had said to her brother:

"Wait, Armand—wait till Zoe is waked, and then prudence and wisdom will be but accident. If all goes well, you will see prudence and wisdom; but if it does not, you will see—ah, but just Zoe!"

The now alert Jean Jacques had seen the whispering of the two, though he did not know what had been said. It was, however, something secret, and if it was secret, then it was—yes, it was love; and love between his daughter and that waif of the world—the world of the stage—in which men and women were only grown-up children, and bad grown-up children at that—it was not to be endured. One thing was sure, the man should come to the Manor Cartier no more. He would see to that to-morrow. There would be no faltering or paltering on his part. His home had been shaken to its foundations once, and he was determined that it should not fall about his ears a second time. An Englishman, an actor, a Protestant, and a renegade lawyer! It was not to be endured.

The charade now being played was the best of the evening. One of the madcap friends of Zoe was to be a singing-girl. She was supposed to carry a tambourine. When her turn to enter came, with a look of mischief and a gay dancing step, she ran into the room. In her hands was a guitar, not a tambourine. When Zoe saw the guitar she gave a cry.

"Where did you get that?" she asked in a low, shocked, indignant voice.

"In your room—your bedroom," was the half-frightened answer. "I saw it on the dresser, and I took it."

"Come, come, let's get on with the charade," urged the Man from Outside.

On the instant's pause, in which Zoe looked at her lover almost involuntarily, and without fully understanding what he said, someone else started forward with a smothered exclamation—of anger, of horror, of dismay. It was Jean Jacques. He was suddenly transformed.

His eyes were darkened by hideous memory, his face alight with passion. He caught from the girl's hands the guitar—Carmen's forgotten guitar which he had not seen for seven years—how well he knew it! With both hands he broke it across his knee. The strings, as they snapped, gave a shrill, wailing cry, like a voice stopped suddenly by death. Stepping jerkily to the fireplace he thrust it into the flame.

"Ah, there!" he said savagely. "There—there!" When he turned round slowly again, his face—which he had never sought to control before he had his great Accident seven years ago—was under his command. A strange, ironic-almost sardonic-smile was on his lips.

"It's in the play," he said.

"No, it's not in the charade, Monsieur Barbille," said the Man from Outside fretfully.

"That is the way I read it, m'sieu'," retorted Jean Jacques, and he made a motion to the fiddler.

"The dance! The dance!" he exclaimed.

But yet he looked little like a man who wished to dance, save upon a grave.

CHAPTER XIV. "I DO NOT WANT TO GO"

It is a bad thing to call down a crisis in the night-time. A "scene" at midnight is a savage enemy of ultimate understanding, and that Devil, called Estrangement, laughs as he observes the objects of his attention in conflict when the midnight candle burns.

He should have been seized with a fit of remorse, however, at the sight he saw in the Manor Cartier at midnight of the day when Jean Jacques Barbille had reached his fiftieth year. There is nothing which, for pathos and for tragedy, can compare with a struggle between the young and the old.

The Devil of Estrangement when he sees it, may go away and indulge himself in sleep; for there will be no sleep for those who, one young and the other old, break their hearts on each other's anvils, when the lights are low and it is long till morning.

When Jean Jacques had broken the forgotten guitar which his daughter had retrieved from her mother's life at the Manor Cartier (all else he had had packed and stored away in the flour-mill out of sight) and thrown it in the fire, there had begun a revolt in the girl's heart, founded on a sense of injustice, but which itself became injustice also; and that is a dark thing to come between those who love—even as parent and child.

After her first exclamation of dismay and pain, Zoe had regained her composure, and during the rest of the evening she was full of feverish gaiety. Indeed her spirits and playful hospitality made the evening a success in spite of the skeleton at the feast. Jean Jacques had also roused himself, and, when the dance began, he joined in with spirit, though his face was worn and haggard even when lighted by his smile. But though the evening came to the conventional height of hilarity, there was a note running through it which made even the youngest look at each other, as though to say, "Now, what's going to happen next!"

Three people at any rate knew that something was going to happen. They were Zoe, the Man from Outside and M. Fille. Zoe had had more than one revelation that night, and she felt again as she did one day, seven years before, when, coming home from over the hills, she had stepped into a house where Horror brooded as palpably as though it sat beside the fire, or hung above the family table. She had felt something as soon as she had entered the door that far-off day, though the house seemed empty. It was an emptiness which was filled with a torturing presence or torturing presenes. It had stilled her young heart. What was it? She had learned the truth soon enough. Out of the sunset had come her father with a face twisted with misery, and as she ran to him, he had caught her by both shoulders, looked through her eyes to something far beyond, and hoarsely said: "She is gone—gone from us! She has run away from home! Curse her baptism—curse it, curse it!"

Zoe could never forget these last words she had ever heard her father speak of Carmen. They were words which would make any Catholic shudder to hear. It was a pity he had used them, for they made her think at last that her mother had been treated with injustice. This, in spite of the fact that in the days, now so far away, when her mother was with them she had ever been nearer to her father, and that, after first childhood, she and her mother were not so close as they had been, when she went to sleep to the humming of a chanson of Cadiz. Her own latent motherhood, however, kept stealing up out of the dim distances of childhood's ignorance and, with modesty and allusiveness, whispering knowledge in her ear. So it was that now she looked back pensively to the years she had spent within sight and sound of her handsome mother, and out of the hunger of her own spirit she had come to idealize her memory. It was good to have a loving father; but he was a man, and he was so busy just when she wanted—when she wanted she knew not what, but at least to go and lay her head on a heart that would understand what was her sorrow, her joy, or her longing.

And now here at last was come Crisis, which showed its thunderous head in the gay dance, and shook his war-locks in the fire, where her mother's guitar had shrieked in its last agony.

When all the guests had gone, when the bolts had been shot home, and old Seraphe Corniche had gone to bed, father and daughter came face to face.

There was a moment's pause, as the two looked at each other, and then Zoe came up to Jean Jacques to kiss him good-night. It was her way of facing the issue. Instinctively she knew that he would draw back, and that the struggle would begin. It might almost seem that she had invited it; for she had let the Man from Outside hold her hand for far longer than courtesy required, while her father looked on with fretful eyes—even with a murmuring which was not a benediction. Indeed, he had evaded shaking hands with his hated visitor by suddenly offering him a cigar, and then in the doorway itself handing a lighted match.

"His eminence, Cardinal Christophe, gave these cigars to me when he passed through St. Saviour's five years ago," Jean Jacques had remarked loftily, "and I always smoke one on my birthday. I am a good Catholic, and his eminence rested here for a whole day."

He had had a grim pleasure in avoiding the handshake, and in having the Protestant outsider smoke the Catholic cigar! In his anger it seemed to him that he had done something worthy almost of the Vatican, indeed of the great Cardinal Christophe himself. Even in his moments of crisis, in his hours of real tragedy, in the times when he was shaken to the centre, Jean Jacques fancied himself more than a little. It was as the master-carpenter had remarked seven years before, he was always involuntarily saying, "Here I come—look at me. I am Jean Jacques Barbille!"

When Zoe reached out a hand to touch his arm, and raised her face as though to kiss him good-night, Jean Jacques drew back.

"Not yet, Zoe," he said. "There are some things—What is all this between you and that man?... I have seen. You must not forget who you are—the daughter of Jean Jacques Barbille, of the Manor Cartier, whose name is known in the whole province, who was asked to stand for the legislature. You are Zoe Barbille—Mademoiselle Zoe Barbille. We do not put on airs. We are kind to our neighbours, but I am descended from the Baron of Beaugard. I have a place—yes, a place in society; and it is for you to respect it. You comprehend?"

Zoe flushed, but there was no hesitation whatever in her reply. "I am what I have always been, and it is not my fault that I am the daughter of M. Jean Jacques Barbille! I have never done anything which was not good enough for the Manor Cartier." She held her head firmly as she said it.

Now Jean Jacques flushed, and he did hesitate in his reply. He hated irony in anyone else, though he loved it in himself, when heaven gave him inspiration thereto. He was in a state of tension, and was ready to break out, to be a force let loose—that is the way he would have expressed it; and he was faced by a new spirit in his daughter which would surely spring the mine, unless he secured peace by strategy. He had sense enough to feel the danger.

He did not see, however, any course for diplomacy here, for she had given him his cue in her last words. As a pure logician he was bound to take it, though it might lead to drama of a kind painful to them both.

"It is not good enough for the Manor Cartier that you go falling in love with a nobody from nowhere," he responded.

"I am not falling in love," she rejoined.

"What did you mean, then, by looking at him as you did; by whispering together; by letting him hold your hand when he left, and him looking at you as though he'd eat you up—without sugar!"

"I said I was not falling in love," she persisted, quietly, but with characteristic boldness. "I am in love."

"You are in love with him—with that interloper! Heaven of heavens, do you speak the truth? Answer me, Zoe Barbille."

She bridled. "Certainly I will answer. Did you think I would let a man look at me as he did, that I would look at a man as I looked at him, that I would let him hold my hand as I did, if I did not love him? Have you ever seen me do it before?"

Her voice was even and quiet—as though she had made up her mind on a course, and meant to carry it through to the end.

"No, I never saw you look at a man like that, and everything is as you say, but—" his voice suddenly became uneven and higher—pitched and a little hoarse, "but he is English, he is an actor—only that; and he is a Protestant."

"Only that?" she asked, for the tone of his voice was such as one would use in speaking of a toad or vermin, and she could not bear it. "Is it a disgrace to be any one of those things?"

"The Barbilles have been here for two hundred years; they have been French Catholics since the time of"—he was not quite sure—"since the time of Louis XI.," he added at a venture, and then paused, overcome by his own rashness.

"Yes, that is a long time," she said, "but what difference does it make? We are just what we are now, and as if there never had been a Baron of Beaugard. What is there against Gerard except that he is an actor, that he is English, and that he is a Protestant? Is there anything?"

"Sacre, is it not enough? An actor, what is that—to pretend to be someone else and not to be yourself!"

"It would be better for a great many people to be someone else rather than themselves—for nothing; and he does it for money."

"For money! What money has he got? You don't know. None of us know. Besides, he's a Protestant, and he's English, and that ends it. There never has been an Englishman or a Protestant in the Barbille family, and it shan't begin at the Manor Cartier." Jean Jacques' voice was rising in proportion as he perceived her quiet determination. Here was something of the woman who had left him seven years ago—left this comfortable home of his to go to disgrace and exile, and God only knew what else! Here in this very room—yes, here where they now were, father and daughter, stood husband and wife that morning when he had his hand on the lever prepared to destroy the man who had invaded his home; who had cast a blight upon it, which remained after all the years; after he had done all a man could do to keep the home and the woman too. The woman had gone; the home remained with his daughter in it, and now again there was a fight for home and the woman. Memory reproduced the picture of the mother standing just where the daughter now stood, Carmen quiet and well in hand, and himself all shaken with weakness, and with all power gone out of him—even the power which rage and a murderous soul give.

But yet this was different. There was no such shame here as had fallen on him seven years ago. But there was a shame after its kind; and if it were not averted, there was the end of the home, of the prestige, the pride and the hope of "M'sieu' Jean Jacques, philosophe."

"What shall not begin here at the Manor Cartier?" she asked with burning cheek.

"The shame—it shall not begin here."

"What shame, father?"

"Of marriage with a Protestant and an actor."

"You will not let me marry him?" she persisted stubbornly.

Her words seemed to shake him all to pieces. It was as though he was going through the older tragedy all over again. It had possessed him ever since the sight of Carmen's guitar had driven him mad three hours ago. He swayed to and fro, even as he did when his hand left the lever and he let the master-carpenter go free. It was indeed a philosopher under torture, a spirit rocking on its anchor. Just now she had put into words herself what, even in his fear, he had hoped had no place in her mind—marriage with the man. He did not know this daughter of his very well. There was that in her which was far beyond his ken. Thousands of miles away in Spain it had origin, and the stream of tendency came down through long generations, by courses unknown to him.

"Marry him—you want to marry him!" he gasped. "You, my Zoe, want to marry that tramp of a Protestant!"

Her eyes blazed in anger. Tramp—the man with the air of a young Alexander, with a voice like the low notes of the guitar thrown to the flames! Tramp!

"If I love him I ought to marry him," she answered with a kind of calmness, however, though all her body was quivering. Suddenly she came close to her father, a great sympathy welled up in her eyes, and her voice shook.

"I do not want to leave you, father, and I never meant to do so. I never thought of it as possible; but now it is different. I want to stay with you; but I want to go with him too."

Presently as she seemed to weaken before him, he hardened. "You can't have both," he declared with as much sternness as was possible to him, and with a Norman wilfulness which was not strength. "You shall not marry an actor and a Protestant. You shall not marry a man like that—never—never—never. If you do, you will never have a penny of mine, and I will never—"

"Oh, hush—Mother of Heaven, hush!" she cried. "You shall not put a curse on me too."

"What curse?" he burst forth, passion shaking him. "You cursed my mother's baptism. It would be a curse to be told that you would see me no more, that I should be no more part of this home. There has been enough of that curse here.... Ah, why—why—" she added with a sudden rush of indignation, "why did you destroy the only thing I had of hers? It was all that was left—her guitar. I loved it so."

All at once, with a cry of pain, she turned and ran to the door—entering on the staircase which led to her room. In the doorway she turned.

"I can't help it. I can't help it, father. I love him—but I love you too," she cried. "I don't want to go—oh, I don't want to go! Why do you—?" her voice choked; she did not finish the sentence; or if she did, he could not hear.

Then she opened the door wide, and disappeared into the darkness of the unlighted stairway, murmuring, "Pity—have pity on me, holy Mother, Vierge Marie!" Then the door closed behind her almost with a bang.

After a moment of stupefied inaction Jean Jacques hurried over and threw open the door she had closed. "Zoe—little Zoe, come back and say good-night," he called. But she did not hear, for, with a burst of crying, she had hurried into her own room and shut and locked the door.

It was a pity, a measureless pity, as Mary the Mother must have seen, if she could see mortal life at all, that Zoe did not hear him. It might have altered the future. As it was, the Devil of Estrangement might well be content with his night's work.

CHAPTER XV. BON MARCHE

Vilray was having its market day, and everyone was either going to or coming from market, or buying and selling in the little square by the Court House. It was the time when the fruits were coming in, when vegetables were in full yield, when fish from the Beau Cheval were to be had in plenty—from mud-cats and suckers, pike and perch, to rock-bass, sturgeon and even maskinonge. Also it was the time of year when butter and eggs, chickens and ducks were so cheap that it was a humiliation not to buy. There were other things on sale also, not for eating and drinking, but for wear and household use—from pots and pans to rag-carpets and table-linen, from woollen yarn to pictures of the Virgin and little calvaries.

These were side by side with dried apples, bottled fruits, jars of maple syrup, and cordials of so generous and penetrating a nature that the currant and elderberry wine by which they were flanked were tipple for babes beside them. Indeed, when a man wanted to forget himself quickly he drank one of these cordials, in preference to the white whisky so commonly imbibed in the parishes. But the cordials being expensive, they were chiefly bought for festive occasions like a wedding, a funeral, a confirmation, or the going away of some young man or young woman to the monastery or the convent to forget the world. Meanwhile, if these spiritual argonauts drank it, they were likely to forget the world on the way to their voluntary prisons. It was very seldom that a man or woman bought the cordials for ordinary consumption, and when that was done, it would almost make a parish talk! Yet cordials of nice brown, of delicate green, of an enticing yellow colour, were here for sale at Vilray market on the morning after the painful scene at the Manor Cartier between Zoe and her father.

The market-place was full—fuller than it had been for many a day. A great many people were come in as much to "make fete" as to buy and sell. It was a saint's day, and the bell of St. Monica's had been ringing away cheerfully twice that morning. To it the bell of the Court House had made reply, for a big case was being tried in the court. It was a river-driving and lumber case for which many witnesses had been called; and there were all kinds of stray people in the place—red-shirted river-drivers, a black-coated Methodist minister from Chalfonte, clerks from lumber-firms, and foremen of lumber-yards; and among these was one who greatly loved such a day as this when he could be free from work, and celebrate himself!

Other people might celebrate saints dead and gone, and drink to 'La Patrie', and cry "Vive Napoleon!" or "Vive la Republique!" or "Vive la Reine!" though this last toast of the Empire was none too common—but he could only drink with real sincerity to the health of Sebastian Dolores, which was himself.

Sebastian Dolores was the pure anarchist, the most complete of monomaniacs.

"Here comes the father of the Spanische," remarked Mere Langlois, who presided over a heap of household necessities, chiefly dried fruits, preserves and pickles, as Sebastian Dolores appeared not far away.

"Good-for-nothing villain! I pity the poor priest that confesses him."

"Who is the Spanische?" asked a young woman from her own stall or stand very near, as she involuntarily arranged her hair and adjusted her waist-belt; for the rakish-looking reprobate, with the air of having been somewhere, was making towards them; and she was young enough to care how she looked when a man, who took notice, was near. Her own husband had been a horse-doctor, farmer, and sportsman of a kind, and she herself was now a farmer of a kind; and she had only resided in the parish during the three years since she had been married to, and buried, Palass Poucette.

Old Mere Langlois looked at her companion in merchanting irritably, then she remembered that Virginie Poucette was a stranger, in a way, and was therefore deserving of pity, and she said with compassionate patronage: "Newcomer you—I'd forgotten. Look you then, the Spanische was the wife of my third cousin, M'sieu' Jean Jacques, and—"

Virginie Poucette nodded, and the slight frown cleared from her low yet shapely forehead. "Yes, yes, of course I know. I've heard enough. What a fool she was, and M'sieu' Jean Jacques so rich and kind and good-looking! So this is her father—well, well, well!"

Palass Poucette's widow leaned forward, and looked intently at Sebastian Dolores, who had stopped near by, and facing a couple of barrels on which were exposed some bottles of cordial and home-made wine. He was addressing himself with cheerful words to the dame that owned the merchandise.

"I suppose you think it's a pity Jean Jacques can't get a divorce," said Mere Langlois, rather spitefully to Virginie, for she had her sex's aversion to widows who had had their share of mankind, and were afterwards free to have someone else's share as well. But suddenly repenting, for Virginie was a hard-working widow who had behaved very well for an outsider—having come from Chalfonte beyond the Beau Chevalshe added: "But if he was a Protestant and could get a divorce, and you did marry him, you'd make him have more sense than he's got; for you've a quiet sensible way, and you've worked hard since Palass Poucette died."

"Where doesn't he show sense, that M'sieu' Jean Jacques?" the younger woman asked.

"Where? Why, with his girl—with Ma'm'selle." "Everybody I ever heard speaks well of Ma'm'selle Zoe," returned the other warmly, for she had a very generous mind and a truthful, sentimental heart. Mere Langlois sniffed, and put her hands on her hips, for she had a daughter of her own; also she was a relation of Jean Jacques, and therefore resented in one way the difference in their social position, while yet she plumed herself on being kin.

"Then you'll learn something now you never knew before," she said. "She's been carrying on—there's no other word for it—with an actor fellow—"

"Yes, yes, I did hear about him—a Protestant and an Englishman."

"Well, then, why do you pretend you don't know—only to hear me talk, is it? Take my word, I'd teach cousin Zoe a lesson with all her education and her two years at the convent. Wasn't it enough that her mother should spoil everything for Jean Jacques, and make the Manor Cartier a place to point the finger at, without her bringing disgrace on the parish too! What happened last night—didn't I hear this morning before I had my breakfast! Didn't I—"

She then proceeded to describe the scene in which Jean Jacques had thrown the wrecked guitar of his vanished spouse into the fire. Before she had finished, however, something occurred which swept them into another act of the famous history of Jean Jacques Barbille and his house.

She had arrived at the point where Zoe had cried aloud in pain at her father's incendiary act, when there was a great stir at the Court House door which opened on the market-place, and vagrant cheers arose. These were presently followed by a more disciplined fusillade; which presently, in turn, was met by hisses and some raucous cries of resentment. These increased as a man appeared on the steps of the Court House, looked round for a moment in a dazed kind of way, then seeing some friends below who were swarming towards him, gave a ribald cry, and scrambled down the steps towards them.

He was the prisoner whose release had suddenly been secured by a piece of evidence which had come as a thunder-clap on judge and jury. Immediately after giving this remarkable evidence the witness—Sebastian Dolores—had left the court-room. He was now engaged in buying cordials in the market-place—in buying and drinking them; for he had pulled the cork out of a bottle filled with a rich yellow liquid, and had drained half the bottle at a gulp. Presently he offered the remainder to a passing carter, who made a gesture of contempt and passed on, for, to him, white whisky was the only drink worth while. Besides, he disliked Sebastian Dolores. Then, with a flourish, the Spaniard tendered the bottle to Madame Langlois and Palass Poucette's widow, at whose corner of merchandise he had now arrived.

Surely there never was a more benign villain and perjurer in the world than Sebastian Dolores! His evidence, given a half-hour before, with every sign of truthfulness, was false. The man—Rocque Valescure—for whom he gave it was no friend of his; but he owned a tavern called "The Red Eagle," a few miles from the works where the Spaniard was employed; also Rocque Valescure's wife set a good table, and Sebastian Dolores was a very liberal feeder; when he was not hungry he was always thirsty. The appeasement of hunger and thirst was now become a problem to him, for his employers at Beauharnais had given him a month's notice because of certain irregularities which had come to their knowledge. Like a wise man Sebastian Dolores had said nothing about this abroad, but had enlarged his credit in every direction, and had then planned this piece of friendly perjury for Rocque Valescure, who was now descending the steps of the Court House to the arms of his friends and amid the execrations of his foes. What the alleged crime was does not matter. It has no vital significance in the history of Jean Jacques Barbille, though it has its place as a swivel on which the future swung.

Sebastian Dolores had saved Rocque Valescure from at least three years in jail, and possibly a very heavy fine as well; and this service must have its due reward. Something for nothing was not the motto of Sebastian Dolores; and he confidently looked forward to having a home at "The Red Eagle" and a banker in its landlord. He was no longer certain that he could rely on help from Jean Jacques, to whom he already owed so much. That was why he wanted to make Rocque Valescure his debtor. It was not his way to perjure his soul for nothing. He had done so in Spain—yet not for nothing either. He had saved his head, which was now doing useful work for himself and for a needy fellow-creature. No one could doubt that he had helped a neighbour in great need, and had done it at some expense to his own nerve and brain. None but an expert could have lied as he had done in the witness-box. Also he had upheld his lies with a striking narrative of circumstantiality. He made things fit in "like mortised blocks" as the Clerk of the Court said to Judge Carcasson, when they discussed the infamy afterwards with clear conviction that it was perjury of a shameless kind; for one who would perjure himself to save a man from jail, would also swear a man into the gallows-rope. But Judge Carcasson had not been able to charge the jury in that sense, for there was no effective evidence to rebut the untruthful attestation of the Spaniard. It had to be taken for what it was worth, since the prosecuting attorney could not shake it; and yet to the Court itself it was manifestly false witness.

Sebastian Dolores was too wise to throw himself into the arms of his released tavern-keeper here immediately after the trial, or to allow Rocque Valescure a like indiscretion and luxury; for there was a strong law against perjury, and right well Sebastian Dolores knew that old Judge Carcasson would have little mercy on him, in spite of the fact that he was the grandfather of Zoe Barbille. The Judge would probably think that safe custody for his wayward character would be the kindest thing he could do for Zoe. Therefore it was that Sebastian Dolores paid no attention to the progress of the released landlord of "The Red Eagle," though, by a glance out of the corner of his eyes, he made sure that the footsteps of liberated guilt were marching at a tangent from where he was—even to the nearest tavern.

It was enough for Dolores that he should watch the result of his good deed from the isolated area where he now was, in the company of two virtuous representatives of domesticity. His time with liberated guilt would come! He chuckled to think how he had provided himself with a refuge against his hour of trouble. That very day he had left his employment, meaning to return no more, securing his full wages through having suddenly become resentful and troublesome, neglectful—and imperative. To avoid further unpleasantness the firm had paid him all his wages; and he had straightway come to Vilray to earn his bed and board by other means than through a pen, a ledger and a gift for figures. It would not be a permanent security against the future, but it would suffice for the moment. It was a rest-place on the road. If the worst came to the worst, there was his grand-daughter and his dear son-in-law whom he so seldom saw—blood was thicker than water, and he would see to it that it was not thinned by neglect.

Meanwhile he ogled Palass Poucette's widow with one eye, and talked softly with his tongue to Mere Langlois, as he importuned Madame to "Sip the good cordial in the name of charity to all and malice towards none."

"You're a bad man—you, and I want none of your cordials," was Mere Langlois's response. "Malice towards none, indeed! If you and the devil started business in the same street, you'd make him close up shop in a year. I've got your measure, for sure; I have you certain as an arm and a pair of stirrups."

"I go about doing good—only good," returned the old sinner with a leer at the young widow, whose fingers he managed to press unseen, as he swung the little bottle of cordial before the eyes of Mere Langlois. He was not wholly surprised when Palass Poucette's widow did not show abrupt displeasure at his bold familiarity.

A wild thought flashed into his mind. Might there not be another refuge here—here in Palass Poucette's widow! He was sixty-three, it was true, and she was only thirty-two; but for her to be an old man's darling who had no doubt been a young man's slave, that would surely have its weight with her. Also she owned the farm where she lived; and she was pleasant pasturage—

that was the phrase he used in his own mind, even as his eye swept from Mere Langlois to hers in swift, hungry inquiry.

He seemed in earnest when he spoke—but that was his way; it had done him service often. "I do good whenever it comes my way to do it," he continued. "I left my work this morning"—he lied of course—"and hired a buggy to bring me over here, all at my own cost, to save a fellow-man. There in the Court House he was sure of prison, with a wife and three small children weeping in 'The Red Eagle'; and there I come at great expense and trouble to tell the truth—before all to tell the truth—and save him and set him free. Yonder he is in the tavern, the work of my hands, a gift to the world from an honest man with a good heart and a sense of justice. But for me there would be a wife and three children in the bondage of shame, sorrow, poverty and misery"—his eyes again ravished the brown eyes of Palass Poucette's widow—"and here again I drink to my own health and to that of all good people—with charity to all and malice towards none!"

The little bottle of golden cordial was raised towards Mere Langlois. The fingers of one hand, however, were again seeking those of the comely young widow who was half behind him, when he felt them caught spasmodically away. Before he had time to turn round he heard a voice, saying: "I should have thought that 'With malice to all and charity towards none,' was your motto, Dolores."

He knew that voice well enough. He had always had a lurking fear that he would hear it say something devastating to him, from the great chair where its owner sat and dispensed what justice a jury would permit him to do. That devastating something would be agony to one who loved liberty and freedom—had not that ever been his watchword, liberty and freedom to do what he pleased in the world and with the world? Yes, he well knew Judge Carcasson's voice. He would have recognized it in the dark—or under the black cap. "M'sieu' le juge!" he said, even before he turned round and saw the faces of the tiny Judge and his Clerk of the Court. There was a kind of quivering about his mouth, and a startled look in his eyes as he faced the two. But there was the widow of Palass Poucette, and, if he was to pursue and frequent her, something must be done to keep him decently figured in her eye and mind.

"It cost me three dollars to come here and save a man from jail to-day, m'sieu' le juge," he added firmly. The Judge pressed the point of his cane against the stomach of the hypocrite and perjurer. "If the Devil and you meet, he will take off his hat to you, my escaped anarchist"—Dolores started almost violently now—"for you can teach him much, and Ananias was the merest aboriginal to you. But we'll get you—we'll get you, Dolores. You saved that guilty fellow by a careful and remarkable perjury to-day. In a long experience I have never seen a better performance—have you, monsieur?" he added to M. Fille.

"But once," was the pointed and deliberate reply. "Ah, when was that?" asked Judge Carcasson, interested.

"The year monsieur le juge was ill, and Judge Blaquiere took your place. It was in Vilray at the Court House here."

"Ah—ah, and who was the phenomenon—the perfect liar?" asked the Judge with the eagerness of the expert.

"His name was Sebastian Dolores," meditatively replied M. Fille. "It was even a finer performance than that of to-day."

The Judge gave a little grunt of surprise. "Twice, eh?" he asked. "Yet this was good enough to break any record," he added. He fastened the young widow's eyes. "Madame, you are young, and you have an eye of intelligence. Be sure of this: you can protect yourself against almost anyone except a liar—eh, madame?" he added to Mere Langlois. "I am sure your experience of life and your good sense—"

"My good sense would make me think purgatory was hell if I saw him"—she nodded savagely at Dolores as she said it, for she had seen that last effort of his to take the fingers of Palass Poucette's widow—"if I saw him there, m'sieu' le juge."

"We'll have you yet—we'll have you yet, Dolores," said the Judge, as the Spaniard prepared to move on. But, as Dolores went, he again caught the eyes of the young widow.

This made him suddenly bold. "'Thou shalt not bear false witness against thy neighbour,'—that is the commandment, is it not, m'sieu' le juge? You are doing against me what I didn't do in Court to-day. I saved a man from your malice."

The crook of the Judge's cane caught the Spaniard's arm, and held him gently.

"You're possessed of a devil, Dolores," he said, "and I hope I'll never have to administer justice in your case. I might be more man than judge. But you will come to no good end. You will certainly—"

He got no further, for the attention of all was suddenly arrested by a wagon driving furiously round the corner of the Court House. It was a red wagon. In it was Jean Jacques Barbille.

His face was white and set; his head was thrust forward, as though looking at something far ahead of him; the pony stallions he was driving were white with sweat, and he had an air of tragic helplessness and panic.

Suddenly a child ran across the roadway in front of the ponies, and the wild cry of the mother roused Jean Jacques out of his agonized trance. He sprang to his feet, wrenching the horses backward and aside with deftness and presence of mind. The margin of safety was not more than a foot, but the child was saved.

The philosopher of the Manor Cartier seemed to come out of a dream as men and women applauded, and cries arose of "Bravo, M'sieu' Jean Jacques!"

At any other time this would have made Jean Jacques nod and smile, or wave a hand, or exclaim in good fellowship. Now, however, his eyes were full of trouble, and the glassiness of the semi-trance leaving them, they shifted restlessly here and there. Suddenly they fastened on the little group of which Judge Carcasson was the centre. He had stopped his horses almost beside them.

"Ah!" he said, "ah!" as his eyes rested on the Judge. "Ah!" he again exclaimed, as the glance ran from the Judge to Sebastian Dolores. "Ah, mercy of God!" he added, in a voice which had both a low note and a high note-deep misery and shrill protest in one. Then he seemed to choke, and words would not come, but he kept looking, looking at Sebastian Dolores, as though fascinated and tortured by the sight of him.

"What is it, Jean Jacques?" asked the little Clerk of the Court gently, coming forward and laying a hand on the steaming flank of a spent and trembling pony.

As though he could not withdraw his gaze from Sebastian Dolores, Jean Jacques did not look at M. Fille; but he thrust out the long whip he carried towards the father of his vanished Carmen and his Zoe's grandfather, and with the deliberation of one to whom speaking was like the laceration of a nerve he said: "Zoe's run away—gone—gone!"

At that moment Louis Charron, his cousin, at whose house Gerard Fynes had lodged, came down the street galloping his horse. Seeing the red wagon, he made for it, and drew rein.

"It's no good, Jean Jacques," he called. "They're married and gone to Montreal—married right under our noses by the Protestant minister at Terrebasse Junction. I've got the telegram here from the stationmaster at Terrebasse.... Ah, the villain to steal away like that—only a child—from her own father! Here it is—the telegram. But believe me, an actor, a Protestant and a foreigner—what a devil's mess!"

He waved the telegram towards Jean Jacques.

"Did he owe you anything, Louis?" asked old Mere Langlois, whose practical mind was alert to find the material status of things.

"Not a sou. Well, but he was honest, I'll say that for the rogue and seducer."

"Seducer—ah, God choke you with your own tongue!" cried Jean Jacques, turning on Louis Charron with a savage jerk of the whip he held. "She is as pure—"

"It is no marriage, of course!" squeaked a voice from the crowd.

"It'll be all right among the English, won't it, monsieur le juge?" asked the gentle widow of Palass Poucette, whom the scene seemed to rouse out of her natural shyness.

"Most sure, madame, most sure," answered the Judge. "It will be all right among the English, and it is all right among the French so far as the law is concerned. As for the Church, that is another matter. But—but see," he added addressing Louis Charron, "does the station-master say what place they took tickets for?"

"Montreal and Winnipeg," was the reply. "Here it is in the telegram. Winnipeg—that's as English as London."

"Winnipeg—a thousand miles!" moaned Jean Jacques.

With the finality which the tickets for Winnipeg signified, the shrill panic emotion seemed to pass from him. In its mumbling, deadening force it was like a sentence on a prisoner.

As many eyes were on Sebastian Dolores as on Jean Jacques. "It's the bad blood that was in her," said a farmer with a significant gesture towards Sebastian Dolores.

"A little bad blood let out would be a good thing," remarked a truculent river-driver, who had given evidence directly contrary to that given by Sebastian Dolores in the trial just concluded. There was a savage look in his eye.

Sebastian Dolores heard, and he was not the man to invite trouble. He could do no good where he was, and he turned to leave the market-place; but in doing so he sought the eye of Virginie Poucette, who, however, kept her face at an angle from him, as she saw Mere Langlois sharply watching her.

"Grandfather, mother and daughter, all of a piece!" said a spiteful woman, as Sebastian Dolores passed her. The look he gave her was not the same as that he had given to Palass Poucette's widow. If it had been given by a Spanish inquisitor to a heretic, little hope would have remained in the heretic's heart. Yet there was a sad patient look on his face, as though he was a martyr. He had no wish to be a martyr; but he had a feeling that for want of other means of expressing their sympathy with Jean Jacques, these rough people might tar and feather him at least; though it was only his misfortune that those sprung from his loins had such adventurous spirits!

Sebastian Dolores was not without a real instinct regarding things. What was in his mind was also passing through that of the river-driver and a few of his friends, and they carefully watched the route he was taking.

Jean Jacques prepared to depart. He had ever loved to be the centre of a picture, but here was a time when to be in the centre was torture. Eyes of morbid curiosity were looking at the open wounds of his heart-ragged wounds made by the shrapnel of tragedy and treachery, not the clean wounds got in a fair fight, easily healed. For the moment at least the little egoist was a mere suffering soul—an epitome of shame, misery and disappointment. He must straightway flee the place where he was tied to the stake of public curiosity and scorn. He drew the reins tighter, and the horses straightened to depart. Then it was that old Judge Carcasson laid a hand on his knee.

"Come, come," he said to the dejected and broken little man, "where is your philosophy?"

Jean Jacques looked at the Judge, as though with a new-born suspicion that henceforth the world would laugh at him, and that Judge Carcasson was setting the fashion; but seeing a pitying moisture in the other's eyes, he drew himself up, set his jaw, and calling on all the forces at his command, he said:

"Moi je suis philosophe!"

His voice frayed a little on the last word, but his head was up now. The Clerk of the Court would have asked to accompany him to the Manor Cartier, but he was not sure that Jean Jacques would like it. He had a feeling that Jean Jacques would wish to have his dark hour alone. So he remained silent, and Jean Jacques touched his horses with the whip. After starting, however, and having been followed for a hundred yards or so by the pitying murmurs and a few I-told-you-so's and revilings for having married as he did, Jean Jacques stopped the ponies. Standing up in the red wagon he looked round for someone whom, for a moment, he did not see in the slowly shifting crowd.

Philosophy was all very well, and he had courageously given his allegiance to it, or a formula of it, a moment before; but there was something deeper and rarer still in the little man's soul. His heart hungered for the two women who had been the joy and pride of his life, even when he had been lost in the business of the material world. They were more to him than he had ever known; they were parts of himself which had slowly developed, as the features and characteristics of ancestors gradually emerge and are emphasized in a descendant as his years increase. Carmen and Zoe were more a part of himself now than they had ever been.

They were gone, the living spirits of his home. Anything that reminded him of them, despite the pain of the reminder, was dear to him. Love was greater than the vengeful desire of injured human nature. His eyes wandered over the people, over the market. At last he saw what he was looking for. He called. A man turned. Jean Jacques beckoned to him. He came eagerly, he hurried to the red wagon.

"Come home with me," said Jean Jacques.

The words were addressed to Sebastian Dolores, who said to himself that this was a refuge surer than "The Red Eagle," or the home of the widow Poucette. He climbed in beside Jean Jacques with a sigh of content.

"Ah, but that—but that is the end of our philosopher," said Judge Carcasson sadly to the Clerk of the Court, as with amazement he saw this catastrophe.

"Alas! if I had only asked to go with him, as I wished to do!" responded M. Fille. "There, but a minute ago, it was in my mind," he added with a look of pain.

"You missed your chance, falterer," said the Judge severely. "If you have a good thought, act on it—that is the golden rule. You missed your chance. It will never come again. He has taken the wrong turning, our unhappy Jean Jacques."

"Monsieur—oh, monsieur, do not shut the door in the face of God like that!" said the shocked little master of the law. "Those two together—it may be only for a moment."

"Ah, no, my little owl, Jean Jacques will wind the boa-constrictor round his neck like a collar, all for love of those he has lost," answered the Judge with emotion; and he caught M. Fille's arm in the companionship of sorrow.

In silence these two watched the red wagon till it was out of sight.

CHAPTER XVI. MISFORTUNES COME NOT SINGLY

Judge Carcasson was right. For a year after Zoe's flight Jean Jacques wrapped Sebastian Dolores round his neck like a collar, and it choked him like a boaconstrictor. But not Sebastian Dolores alone did that. When things begin to go wrong in the life of a man whose hands have held too many things, the disorder flutters through all the radii of his affairs, and presently they rattle away from the hub of his control.

So it was with Jean Jacques. To take his reprobate father-in-law to his lonely home would have brought him trouble in any case; but as things were, the Spaniard became only the last straw which broke his camel's back. And what a burden his camel carried—flour-mill, saw-mill, ash-factory, farms, a general store, lime-kilns, agency for lightning-rods and insurance, cattle-dealing, the project for the new cheese-factory, and money-lending!

Money-lending? It seemed strange that Jean Jacques should be able to lend money, since he himself had to borrow, and mortgage also, from time to time. When things began to go really wrong with him financially, he mortgaged his farms, his flour-mill, and saw-mill, and then lent money on other mortgages. This he did because he had always lent money, and it was a habit so associated with his prestige, that he tied himself up in borrowing and lending and counter-mortgaging till, as the saying is, "a Philadelphia lawyer" could not have unravelled his affairs without having been born again in the law. That he was able to manipulate his tangled affairs, while keeping the confidence of those from whom he borrowed, and the admiration of those to whom he lent, was evidence of his capacity. "Genius of a kind" was what his biggest creditor called it later.

After a personal visit to St. Saviour's, this biggest creditor and financial potentate—M. Mornay—said that if Jean Jacques had been started right and trained right, he would have been a "general in the financial field, winning big battles."

M. Mornay chanced to be a friend of Judge Carcasson, and when he visited Vilray he remembered that the Judge had spoken often of his humble but learned friend, the Clerk of the Court, and of his sister. So M. Mornay made his way from the office of the firm of avocats whom he had instructed in his affairs with Jean Jacques, to that of M. Fille. Here he was soon engaged in comment on the master-miller and philosopher.

"He has had much trouble, and no doubt his affairs have suffered," remarked M. Fille cautiously, when the ice had been broken and the Big Financier had referred casually to the difficulties among which Jean

Jacques was trying to maintain equilibrium; "but he is a man who can do things too hard for other men."

The Big Financier lighted another cigar and blew away several clouds of smoke before he said in reply, "Yes, I know he has had family trouble again, but that is a year ago, and he has had a chance to get another grip of things."

"He did not sit down and mope," explained M. Fille. "He was at work the next day after his daughter's flight just the same as before. He is a man of great courage. Misfortune does not paralyse him."

M. Mornay's speech was of a kind which came in spurts, with pauses of thought between, and the pause now was longer than usual.

"Paralysis—certainly not," he said at last. "Physical activity is one of the manifestations of mental, moral, and even physical shock and injury. I've seen a man with a bullet in him run a half-mile—anywhere; I've seen a man ripped up by a crosscut-saw hold himself together, and walk—anywhere—till he dropped. Physical and nervous activity is one of the forms which shattered force takes. I expect that your 'M'sieu' Jean Jacques' has been busier this last year than ever before in his life. He'd have to be; for a man who has as many irons in the fire as he has, must keep running from bellows to bellows when misfortune starts to damp him down."

The Clerk of the Court sighed. He realized the significance of what his visitor was saying. Ever Since Zoe had gone, Jean Jacques had been for ever on the move, for ever making hay on which the sun did not shine. Jean Jacques' face these days was lined and changeful. It looked unstable and tired—as though disturbing forces were working up to the surface out of control. The brown eyes, too, were far more restless than they had ever been since the Antoine was wrecked, and their owner returned with Carmen to the Manor Cartier. But the new restlessness of the eyes was different from the old. That was a mobility impelled by an active, inquisitive soul, trying to observe what was going on in the world, and to make sure that its possessor was being seen by the world. This activity was that of a mind essentially concerned to find how many ways it could see for escape from a maze of things; while his vanity was taking new forms. It was always anxious to discover if the world was trying to know how he was taking the blows of fate and fortune. He had been determined that, whatever came, it should not see him paralysed or broken.

As M. Fille only nodded his head in sorrowful assent, the Big Financier became more explicit. He was determined to lose nothing by Jean Jacques, and he was prepared to take instant action when it was required; but he was also interested in the man who might have done really powerful things in the world, had he gone about them in the right way.

"M. Barbille has had some lawsuits this year, is it not so?" he asked.

"Two of importance, monsieur, and one is not yet decided," answered M. Fille.

"He lost those suits of importance?"

"That is so, monsieur."

"And they cost him six thousand dollars—and over?" The Big Financier seemed to be pressing towards a point.

"Something over that amount, monsieur."

"And he may lose the suit now before the Courts?"

"Who can tell, monsieur!" vaguely commented the little learned official.

M. Mornay was not to be evaded. "Yes, yes, but the case as it stands—to you who are wise in experience of legal affairs, does it seem at all a sure thing for him?"

"I wish I could say it was, monsieur," sadly answered the other.

The Big Financier nodded vigorously. "Exactly. Nothing is so unproductive as the law. It is expensive whether you win or lose, and it is murderously expensive when you do lose. You will observe, I know, that your Jean Jacques is a man who can only be killed once—eh?"

"Monsieur?" M. Fille really did not grasp this remark.

M. Mornay's voice became precise. "I will explain. He has never created; he has only developed what has been created. He inherited much of what he has or has had. His designs were always affected by the fact that he had never built from the very bottom. When he goes to pieces—"

"Monsieur—to pieces!" exclaimed the Clerk of the Court painfully.

"Well, put it another way. If he is broken financially, he will never come up again. Not because of his age—I lost a second fortune at fifty, and have a third ready to lose at sixty—but because the primary initiative won't be in him. He'll say he has lost, and that there's an end to it all. His philosophy will come into play—just at the last. It will help him in one way and harm him in another."

"Ah, then you know about his philosophy, monsieur?" queried M. Fille. Was Jean Jacques' philosophy, after all, to be a real concrete asset of his life sooner or later?

The Big Financier smiled, and turned some coins over in his pocket rather loudly. Presently he said: "The first time I ever saw him he treated me to a page of Descartes. It cost him one per cent. I always charge a man for talking sentiment to me in business hours. I had to listen to him, and he had to pay me for listening. I've no doubt his general yearly expenditure has been increased for the same reason—eh, Maitre Fille? He has done it with others—yes?" M. Fille waved a hand in deprecation, and his voice had a little acidity as he replied: "Ah, monsieur, what can we poor provincials do—any of us—in dealing with men like you, philosophy or no philosophy? You get us between the upper and the nether mill stones. You are cosmopolitan; M. Jean Jacques Barbille is a provincial; and you, because he has soul enough to forget business for a moment and to speak of things that matter more than money and business, you grind him into powder."

M. Mornay shook his head and lighted his cigar again. "There you are wrong, Maitre Fille. It is bad policy to grind to powder, or grind at all, men out of whom you are making money. It is better to keep them from between the upper and nether mill-stones.

"I have done so with your Barbille. I could give him such trouble as would bring things crashing down upon him at once, if I wanted to be merely vicious in getting my own; but that would make it impossible for me to meet at dinner my friend Judge Carcasson. So, as long as I can, I will not press him. But I tell you that the margin of safety on which he is moving now is too narrow—scarce a foot-hold. He has too much under construction in the business of his life, and if one stone slips out, down may come the whole pile. He has stopped building the cheese-factory—that represents sheer loss. The ash-factory is to close next week, the saw-mill is only paying its way, and the flour-mill and the farms, which have to sustain the call of his many interests, can't stand the drain. Also, he has several people heavily indebted to him, and if they go down—well, it depends on the soundness of the security he holds. If they listened to him talk philosophy, encouraged him to do it, and told him they liked it, when the bargain was being made, the chances are the security is inadequate."

The Clerk of the Court bridled up. "Monsieur, you are very hard on a man who for twenty-five years has been a figure and a power in this part of the province. You sneer at one who has been a benefactor to the place where he lives; who has given with the right hand and the left; whose enterprise has been a source of profit to many; and who has got a savage reward for the acts of a blameless and generous life. You know his troubles, monsieur, and we who have seen him bear them with fortitude and Christian philosophy, we resent—"

"You need resent nothing, Maitre Fille," interrupted the Big Financier, not unkindly. "What I have said has been said to his friend and the friend of my own great friend, Judge Carcasson; and I am only anxious that he should be warned by someone whose opinions count with him; whom he can trust—"

"But, monsieur, alas!" broke in the Clerk of the Court, "that is the trouble; he does not select those he can trust. He is too confiding. He believes those who flatter him, who impose on his good heart. It has always been so."

"I judge it is so still in the case of Monsieur Dolores, his daughter's grandfather?" the Big Financier asked quizzically.

"It is so, monsieur," replied M. Fille. "The loss of his daughter shook him even more than the flight of his wife; and it is as though he could not live without that scoundrel near him—a vicious man, who makes trouble wherever he goes. He was a cause of loss to M. Barbille years ago when he managed the ash-factory; he is very dangerous to women—even now he is a danger to the future of a young widow" (he meant the widow of Palass Poucette); "and he has caused a scandal by perjury as a witness, and by the consequences—but I need not speak of that here. He will do Jean Jacques great harm in the end, of that I am sure. The very day Mademoiselle Zoe left the Manor Cartier to marry the English actor, Jean Jacques took that Spanish bad-lot to his home; and there he stays, and the old friends go—the old friends go; and he does not seem to miss them."

There was something like a sob in M. Fille's voice. He had loved Zoe in a way that in a mother would have meant martyrdom, if necessary, and in a father would have meant sacrifice when needed; and indeed he had sacrificed both time and money to find Zoe. He had even gone as far as Winnipeg on the chance of finding her, making that first big journey in the world, which was as much to him in all ways as a journey to Bagdad would mean to most people of M. Mornay's world. Also he had spent money since in corresponding with lawyers in the West whom he engaged to search for her; but Zoe had never been found. She had never written but one letter to Jean Jacques since her flight. This letter said, in effect, that she would come back when her husband was no longer "a beggar" as her father had called him, and not till then. It was written en route to Winnipeg, at the dictation of Gerard Fynes, who had a romantic view of life and a mistaken pride, but some courage too—the courage of love.

"He thinks his daughter will come back—yes?" asked M. Mornay. "Once he said to me that he was sorry there was no lady to welcome me at the Manor Cartier, but that he hoped his daughter would yet have the honour. His talk is quite spacious and lofty at times, as you know."

"So—that is so, monsieur... Mademoiselle Zoe's room is always ready for her. At time of Noel he sent cards to all the families of the parish who had been his friends, as from his daughter and himself; and when people came to visit at the Manor on New Year's Day, he said to each and all that his daughter regretted she could not arrive in time from the West to receive them; but that next year she would certainly have the pleasure."

"Like the light in the window for the unreturning sailor," somewhat cynically remarked the Big Financier. "Did many come to the Manor on that New Year's Day?"

"But yes, many, monsieur. Some came from kindness, and some because they were curious—"

"And Monsieur Dolores?"

The lips of the Clerk of the Court curled, "He went about with a manner as soft as that of a young cure. Butter would not melt in his mouth. Some of the women were sorry for him, until they knew he had given one of Jean Jacques' best bear-skin rugs to Madame Palass Poucette for a New Year's gift."

The Big Financier laughed cheerfully. "It's an old way to popularity—being generous with other people's money. That is why I am here. The people that spend your Jean Jacques' money will be spending mine too, if I don't take care."

M. Fille noted the hard look which now settled in M. Mornay's face, and it disturbed him. He rose and leaned over the table towards his visitor anxiously.

"Tell me, if you please, monsieur, is there any real and immediate danger of the financial collapse of Jean Jacques?"

The other regarded M. Fille with a look of consideration. He liked this Clerk of the Court, but he liked Jean Jacques for the matter of that, and away now from the big financial arena where he usually worked, his natural instincts had play. He had come to St. Saviour's with a bigger thing in his mind than Jean Jacques and his affairs; he had come on the matter of a railway, and had taken Jean Jacques on the way, as it were. The scheme for the railway looked very promising to him, and he was in good humour; so that all he said about Jean Jacques was free from that general irritation of spirit which has sacrificed many a small man on a big man's altar. He saw the agitation he had caused, and he almost repented of what he had already said; yet he had acted with a view to getting M. Fille to warn Jean Jacques.

"I repeat what I said," he now replied. "Monsieur Jean Jacques' affairs are too nicely balanced. A little shove one way or another and over goes the whole caboose. If anyone here has influence over him, it would be a kindness to use it. That case before the Court of Appeal, for instance; he'd be better advised to settle it, if there is still time. One or two of the mortgages he holds ought to be foreclosed, so that he may get out of them all the law will let him. He ought to pouch the money that's owing him; he ought to shave away his insurance, his lightning-rod, and his horsedealing business; and he ought to sell his farms and his store, and concentrate on the flour-mill and the saw-mill. He has had his warnings generally from my lawyers, but what he wants most is the gentle hand to lead him; and I should think that yours, M. Fille, is the hand the Almighty would choose if He was concerned with what happens at St. Saviour's and wanted an agent."

The Clerk of the Court blushed greatly. This was a very big man indeed in the great commercial world, and flattery from him had unusual significance; but he threw out his hands with a gesture of helplessness, and said: "Monsieur, if I could be of use I would; but he has ceased to listen to me; he—"

He got no further, for there was a sharp knock at the street door of the outer office, and M. Fille hastened to the other room. After a moment he came back, a familiar voice following him.

"It is Monsieur Barbille, monsieur," M. Fille said quietly, but with apprehensive eyes.

"Well—he wants to see me?" asked M. Mornay. "No, no, monsieur. It would be better if he did not see you. He is in some agitation."

"Fille! Maitre Fille—be quick now," called Jean Jacques' voice from the other room.

"What did I say, monsieur?" asked the Big Financier. "The mind that's received a blow must be moving—moving; the man with the many irons must be flying from bellows to bellows!"

"Come, come, there's no time to lose," came Jean Jacques' voice again, and the handle of the door of their room turned.

M. Fille's hand caught the handle. "Excuse me, Monsieur Barbille,—a minute please," he persisted almost querulously. "Be good enough to keep your manners... monsieur!" he added to the Financier, "if you do not wish to speak with him, there is a door"—he pointed—"which will let you into the side-street."

"What is his trouble?" asked M. Mornay.

M. Fille hesitated, then said reflectively: "He has lost his case in the Appeal Court, monsieur; also, his cousin, Auguste Charron, who has been working the Latouche farm, has flitted, leaving—"

"Leaving Jean Jacques to pay unexpected debts?"

"So, monsieur."

"Then I can be of no use, I fear," remarked M. Mornay dryly.

"Fille! Fille!" came the voice of Jean Jacques insistently from the room.

"And so I will say au revoir, Monsieur Fille," continued the Big Financier.

A moment later the great man was gone, and M. Fille was alone with the philosopher of the Manor Cartier.

"Well, well, why do you keep me waiting! Who was it in there—anyone that's concerned with my affairs?" asked Jean Jacques.

In these days he was sensitive when there was no cause, and he was credulous where he ought to be suspicious. The fact that the little man had held the door against him made him sure that M. Fille had not wished him to see the departed visitor.

"Come, out with it—who was it making fresh trouble for me?" persisted Jean Jacques.

"No one making trouble for you, my friend," answered the Clerk of the Court, "but someone who was trying to do you a good turn."

"He must have been a stranger then," returned Jean Jacques bitterly. "Who was it?"

M. Fille, after an instant's further hesitation, told him.

"Oh, him—M. Momay!" exclaimed Jean Jacques, with a look of relief, his face lighting. "That's a big man with a most capable and far-reaching mind. He takes a thing in as the ocean mouths a river. If I had had men like that to deal with all my life, what a different ledger I'd be balancing now! Descartes, Kant, Voltaire, Rousseau, Hume, Hegel—he has an ear for them all. That is the intellectual side of him; and in business"—he threw up a hand—"there he views the landscape from the mountain-top. He has vision, strategy, executive. He is Napoleon and Anacreon in one. He is of the builders on the one hand, of the Illuminati and the Encyclopedistes on the other."

Even the Clerk of the Court, with his circumscribed range of thought and experience, in that moment saw Jean Jacques as he really was. Here was a man whose house of life was beginning to sway from an earthquake; who had been smitten in several deadly ways, and was about to receive buffetings beyond aught he had yet experienced, philosophizing on the tight-rope—Blondin and Plato in one. Yet sardonically piteous as it was, the incident had shown Jean Jacques with the germ of something big in him. He had recognized in M. Mornay, who could level him to the dust tomorrow financially, a master of the world's affairs, a prospector of life's fields, who would march fearlessly beyond the farthest frontiers into the unknown. Jean Jacques' admiration of the lion who could, and would, slay him was the best tribute to his own character.

M. Fille's eyes moistened as he realized it; and he knew that nothing he could say or do would make this man accommodate his actions to the hard rules of the business of life; he must for ever be applying to them conceptions of a half-developed mind.

"Quite so, quite so, Jean Jacques," M. Fille responded gently, "but"—here came a firmer note to his voice, for he had taken to heart the lesson M. Mornay had taught him, and he was determined to do his duty now when the opportunity was in his hand—"but you have got to deal with things as they are; not as they might have been. If you cannot have the great men you have to deal with the little men like me. You have to prove yourself bigger than the rest of us by doing things better. A man doesn't fail only because of others, but also because of himself. You were warned that the chances were all against you in the case that's just been decided, yet you would go on; you were warned that your cousin, Auguste Charron, was in debt, and that his wife was mad to get away from the farm and go West, yet you would take no notice. Now he has gone, and you have to pay, and your case has gone against you in the Appellate Court besides.... I will tell you the truth, my friend, even if it cuts me to the heart. You have not kept your judgment in hand; you have gone ahead like a bull at a gate; and you pay the price. You listen to those who flatter, and on those who would go through fire and water for you, you turn your back—on those who would help you in your hour of trouble, in your dark day."

Jean Jacques drew himself up with a gesture, impatient, masterful and forbidding. "I have fought my fight alone in the dark day; I have not asked for any one's help," he answered. "I have wept on no man's shoulder. I have been mauled by the claws of injury and shame, and I have not flinched. I have healed my own wounds, and I wear my scars without—"

He stopped, for there came a sharp rat-tat-tat at the door which opened into the street. Somehow the commonplace, trivial interruption produced on both a strange, even startling effect. It suddenly produced in their minds a feeling of apprehension, as though there was whispered in their ears, "Something is going to happen—beware!"

Rat-tat-tat! The two men looked at each other. The same thought was in the mind of both. Jean Jacques clutched at his beard nervously, then with an effort he controlled himself. He took off his hat as though he was about to greet some important person, or to receive sentence in a court. Instinctively he felt the little book of philosophy which he always carried now in his breast-pocket, as a pietist would finger his beads in moments of fear or anxiety. The Clerk of the Court passed his thin hand over his hair, as he was wont to do in court when the Judge began his charge to the Jury, and then with an action more impulsive than was usual with him, he held out his hand, and Jean Jacques grasped it. Something was bringing them together just when it seemed that, in the storm of Jean Jacques' indignation, they were about to fall apart. M. Fille's eyes said as plainly as words could do, "Courage, my friend!"

Rat-tat-tat! Rat-tat-tat! The knocking was sharp and imperative now. The Clerk of the Court went quickly forward and threw open the door.

There stepped inside the widow of Palass Poucette. She had a letter in her hand. "M'sieu', pardon, if I intrude," she said to M. Fille; "but I heard that M'sieu' Jean Jacques was here. I have news for him."

"News!" repeated Jean Jacques, and he looked like a man who was waiting for what he feared to hear. "They told me at the post-office that you were here. I got the letter only a quarter of an hour ago, and I thought I would go at once to the Manor Cartier and tell M'sieu' Jean Jacques what the letter says. I wanted to go to the Manor Cartier for something else as well, but I will speak of that by and by. It is the letter now."

She pulled off first one glove and then the other, still holding the letter, as though she was about to perform some ceremony. "It was a good thing I found out that M'sieu' Jean Jacques was here. It saves a four-mile drive," she remarked.

"The news—ah, nom de Dieu, the slowness of the woman—like a river going uphill!" exclaimed Jean Jacques, who was finding it hard to still the trembling of his limbs.

The widow of Palass Poucette flushed, but she had some sense in her head, and she realized that Jean Jacques was a little unbalanced at the moment. Indeed, Jean Jacques was not so old that she would have found it difficult to take a well-defined and warm interest in him, were circumstances propitious. She held out the letter to him at once. "It is from my sister in the West—at Shilah," she explained. "There is nothing in it you can't read, and most of it concerns you." Jean Jacques took the letter, but he could not bring himself to read it, for Virginie Poucette's manner was not suggestive of happy tidings. After an instant's hesitation he handed the letter to M. Fille, who pressed his lips with an air of determination, and put on his glasses.

Jean Jacques saw the face of the Clerk of the Court flush and then turn pale as he read the letter. "There, be quick!" he said before M. Fille had turned the first page.

Then the widow of Palass Poucette came to him and, in a simple harmless way she had, free from coquetry or guile, stood beside him, took his hand and held it. He seemed almost unconscious of her act, but his fingers convulsively tightened on hers; while she reflected that here was one who needed help sorely; here was a good, warm-hearted man on whom a woman could empty out affection like rain and get a good harvest. She really was as simple as a child, was Virginie Poucette, and even in her acquaintance with Sebastian Dolores, there had only been working in her the natural desire of a primitive woman to have a man saying that which would keep alive in her the things that make her sing as she toils; and certainly Virginie toiled late and early on her farm. She really was concerned for Jean Jacques. Both wife and daughter had taken flight, and he was alone and in trouble. At this moment she felt she would like to be a sister to him—she was young enough to be his daughter almost. Her heart was kind.

"Now!" said Jean Jacques at last, as the Clerk of the Court's eyes reached the end of the last page. "Now, speak! It is—it is my Zoe?"

"It is our Zoe," answered M. Fille.

"Figure de Christ, what do you wait for—she is not dead?" exclaimed Jean Jacques with a courage which made him set his feet squarely.

The Clerk of the Court shook his head and began. "She is alive. Madame Poucette's sister saw her by chance. Zoe was on her way up the Saskatchewan River to the Peace River country with her husband. Her husband's health was bad. He had to leave the stage in the United States where he had gone after Winnipeg. The doctors said he must live the open-air life. He and Zoe were going north, to take a farm somewhere."

"Somewhere! Somewhere!" murmured Jean Jacques. "The farther away from Jean Jacques the better—that is what she thinks."

"No, you are wrong, my friend," rejoined M. Fille. "She said to Madame Poucette's sister"—he held up the letter—"that when they had proved they could live without anybody's help they would come back to see you. Zoe thought that, having taken her life in her own hands, she ought to justify herself before she asked your forgiveness and a place at your table. She felt that you could only love her and be glad of her, if her man was independent of you. It is a proud and sensitive soul—but there it is!"

"It is romance, it is quixotism—ah, heart of God, what quixotism!" exclaimed Jean Jacques.

"She gets her romance and quixotism from Jean Jacques Barbille," retorted the Clerk of the Court. "She does more feeling than thinking—like you."

Jean Jacques' heart was bleeding, but he drew himself up proudly, and caught his hand away from the warm palm of Poucette's widow. As his affairs crumbled his pride grew more insistent. M. Fille had challenged his intellect—his intellect!

"My life has been a procession of practical things," he declared oracularly. "I have been a man of business who designs. I am no dreamer. I think. I act. I suffer. I have been the victim of romance, not its interpreter. Mercy of God, what has broken my life, what but romance—romance, first with one and then with another! More feeling than thinking, Maitre Fille—you say that? Why the Barbilles have ever in the past built up life on a basis of thought and action, and I have added philosophy—the science of thought and act. Jean Jacques Barbille has been the man of design and the man of action also. Don Quixote was a fool, a dreamer, but Jean Jacques is no Don Quixote. He is a man who has done things, but also he is a man who has been broken on the wheel of life. He is a man whose heart-strings have been torn—"

He had worked himself up into a fit of eloquence and revolt. He was touched by the rod of desperation, which makes the soul protest that it is right when it knows that it is wrong.

Suddenly, breaking off his speech, he threw up his hands and made for the door.

"I will fight it out alone!" he declared with rough emotion, and at the door he turned towards them again. He looked at them both as though he would dare them to contradict him. The restless fire of his eyes seemed to dart from one to the other.

"That's the way it is," said the widow of Palass Poucette coming quickly forward to him. "It's always the way. We must fight our battles alone, but we don't have to bear the wounds alone. In the battle you are alone, but the hand to heal the wounds may be another's. You are a philosopher—well, what I speak is true, isn't it?"

Virginie had said the one thing which could have stayed the tide of Jean Jacques' pessimism and broken his cloud of gloom. She appealed to him in the tune of an old song. The years and the curses of years had not dispelled the illusion that he was a philosopher. He stopped with his hand on the door.

"That's so, without doubt that's so," he said. "You have stumbled on a truth of life, madame."

Suddenly there came into his look something of the yearning and hunger which the lonely and forsaken feel when they are not on the full tide of doing. It was as though he must have companionship, in spite of his brave announcement that he must fight his fight alone. He had been wounded in the battle, and here was one who held out the hand of healing to him. Never since his wife had left him the long lonely years ago had a woman meant anything to him except as one of a race; but in this moment here a woman had held his hand, and he could feel still the warm palm which had comforted his own agitated fingers.

Virginie Poucette saw, and she understood what was passing in his mind. Yet she did not see and understand all by any means; and it is hard to tell what further show of fire there might have been, but that the Clerk of the Court was there, saying harshly under his breath, "The huzzy! The crafty huzzy!"

The Clerk of the Court was wrong. Virginie was merely sentimental, not intriguing or deceitful; for Jean Jacques was not a widower—and she was an honest woman and genuinely tender-hearted.

"I'm coming to the Manor Cartier to-morrow," Virginie continued. "I have a rug of yours. By mistake it was left at my house by M'sieu' Dolores."

"You needn't do that. I will call at your place tomorrow for it," replied Jean Jacques almost eagerly. "I told M'sieu' Dolores to-day never to enter my house again. I didn't know it was your rug. It was giving away your property, not his own," she hurriedly explained, and her face flushed.

"That is the Spanish of it," said Jean Jacques bitterly. His eyes were being opened in many directions to-day.

M. Fille was in distress. Jean Jacques had had a warning about Sebastian Dolores, but here was another pit into which he might fall, the pit digged by a widow, who, no doubt, would not hesitate to marry a divorced Catholic philosopher, if he could get a divorce by hook or by crook. Jean Jacques had said that he was going to Virginie Poucette's place the next day. That was as bad as it could be; yet there was this to the good, that it was to-morrow and not to-day; and who could tell what might happen between to-day and to-morrow!

A moment later the three were standing outside the office in the street. As Jean Jacques climbed into his red wagon, Virginie Poucette's eyes were attracted to the northern sky where a reddish glow appeared, and she gave an exclamation of surprise.

"That must be a fire," she said, pointing.

"A bit of pine-land probably," said M. Fille—with anxiety, however, for the red glow lay in the direction of St. Saviour's where were the Manor Cartier and Jean Jacques' mills. Maitre Fille was possessed of a superstition that all the things which threaten a man's life to wreck it, operate awhile in their many fields before they converge like an army in one field to deliver the last attack on their victim. It would not have seemed strange to him, if out of the night a voice of the unseen had said that the glow in the sky came from the Manor Cartier. This very day three things had smitten Jean Jacques, and, if three, why not four or five, or fifty!

With a strange fascination Jean Jacques' eyes were fastened on the glow. He clucked to his horses, and they started jerkily away. M. Fille and the widow Poucette said good-bye to him, but he did not hear, or if he heard, he did not heed. His look was set upon the red reflection which widened in the sky and seemed to grow nearer and nearer. The horses quickened their pace. He touched them with the whip, and they went faster. The glow increased as he left Vilray behind. He gave the horses the whip again sharply, and they broke into a gallop. Yet his eyes scarcely left the sky. The crimson glow drew him, held him, till his brain was afire also. Jean Jacques had a premonition and a conviction which was even deeper than the imagination of M. Fille.

In Vilray, behind him, the telegraph clerk was in the street shouting to someone to summon the local fire-brigade to go to St. Saviour's.

"What is it—what is it?" asked M. Fille of the telegraph clerk in marked agitation.

"It's M'sieu' Jean Jacques' flour-mill," was the reply.

Wagons and buggies and carts began to take the road to the Manor Cartier; and Maitre Fille went also with the widow of Palass Poucette.

CHAPTER XVII. HIS GREATEST ASSET

Jean Jacques did not go to the house of the widow of Palass Poucette "next day" as he had proposed: and she did not expect him. She had seen his flour-mill burned to the ground on the-evening when they met in the office of the Clerk of the evening Court, when Jean Jacques had learned that his Zoe had gone into farther and farther places away from him. Perhaps Virginie Poucette never had shed as many tears in any whole year of her life as she did that night, not excepting the year Palass Poucette died, and left her his farm and seven horses, more or less sound, and a threshing-machine in good condition. The woman had a rare heart and there was that about Jean Jacques which made her want to help him. She had no clear idea as to how that could be done, but she had held his hand at any rate, and he had seemed the better for it. Virginie had only an objective view of things; and if she was not material, still she could best express herself through the medium of the senses.

There were others besides her who shed tears also—those who saw Jean Jacques' chief asset suddenly disappear in flame and smoke and all his other assets become thereby liabilities of a kind; and there were many who would be the poorer in the end because of it. If Jean Jacques went down, he probably would not go alone. Jean Jacques had done a good fire-insurance business over a course of years, but somehow he had not insured himself as heavily as he ought to have done; and in any case the fire-policy for the mill was not in his own hands. It was in the safe-keeping of M. Mornay at Montreal, who had warned M. Fille of the crisis in the money-master's affairs on the very day that the crisis came.

No one ever knew how it was that the mill took fire, but there was one man who had more than a shrewd suspicion, though there was no occasion for mentioning it. This was Sebastian Dolores. He had not set the mill afire. That would have been profitable from no standpoint, and he had no grudge against Jean Jacques. Why should he have a grudge? Jean Jacques' good fortune, as things were, made his own good fortune; for he ate and drank and slept and was clothed at his son-in-law's expense. But he guessed accurately who had set the mill on fire, and that it was done accidentally. He remembered that a man who smoked bad tobacco which had to be lighted over and over again, threw a burning match down after applying it to his pipe. He remembered that there was a heap of flour-bags near where the man stood when the match was thrown down; and that some loose strings for tying were also in a pile beside the bags. So it was easy for the thing to have happened if the man did not turn round after he threw the match down, but went swaying on out of the mill, and over to the Manor Cartier, and up staggering to bed; for he had been drinking potato-brandy, and he had been brought up on the mild wines of Spain! In other words, the man who threw down the lighted match which did the mischief was Sebastian Dolores himself.

He regretted it quite as much as he had ever regretted anything; and on the night of the fire there were tears in his large brown eyes which deceived the New Cure and others; though they did not deceive the widow of Palass Poucette, who had found him out, and who now had no pleasure at all in his aged gallantries. But the regret Dolores experienced would not prevent him from doing Jean Jacques still greater injury if, and when, the chance occurred, should it be to his own advantage.

Jean Jacques shed no tears on the night that his beloved flour-mill became a blackened ruin, and his saw-mill had a narrow escape. He was like one in a dream, scarcely realizing that men were saying kind things to him; that the New Cure held his hand and spoke to him more like a brother than one whose profession it was to be good to those who suffered. In his eyes was the same half-rapt, intense, distant look which came into them when, at Vilray, he saw that red reflection in the sky over against St. Saviour's, and urged his horses onward.

The world knew that the burning of the mill was a blow to Jean Jacques, but it did not know how great and heavy the blow was. First one and then another of his friends said he was insured, and that in another six months the mill-wheel would be turning again. They said so to Jean Jacques when he stood with his eyes fixed on the burning fabric, which nothing could save; but he showed no desire to speak. He only nodded and kept on staring at the fire with that curious underglow in his eyes. Some chemistry of the soul had taken place in him in the hour when he drove to the Manor Cartier from Vilray, and it produced a strange fire, which merged into the reflection of the sky above the burning mill. Later, came things which were strange and eventful in his life, but that under-glow was for ever afterwards in his eyes. It was in singular contrast to the snapping fire which had been theirs all the days of his life till now—the snapping fire of action, will and design. It still was there when they said to him suddenly that the wind had changed, and that the flame and sparks were now blowing toward the saw-mill. Even when he gave orders, and set to work to defend the saw-mill, arranging a line of men with buckets on its roof, and so saving it, this look remained. It was something spiritual and unmaterial, something, maybe, which had to do with the philosophy he had preached, thought and practised over long years. It did not disappear when at last, after midnight, everyone had gone, and the smouldering ruins of his greatest asset lay mournful in the wan light of the moon.

Kind and good friends like the Clerk of the Court and the New Cure had seen him to his bedroom at midnight, leaving him there with a promise that they would come on the morrow; and he had said goodnight evenly, and had shut the door upon them with a sort of smile. But long after they had gone, when Sebastian Dolores and Seraphe Corniche were asleep, he had got up again and left the house, to gaze at the spot where the big white mill with the red roof had been-the mill which had been there in the days of the Baron of Beaugard, and to which time had only added size and adornment. The gold-cock weathervane of the mill, so long the admiration of people living and dead, and indeed the symbol of himself, as he had been told, being so full of life and pride, courage and vigour-it lay among the ruins, a blackened relic of the Barbilles.

He had said in M. Fille's office not many hours before, "I will fight it all out alone," and here in the tragic quiet of the night he made his resolve a reality. In appearance he was not now like the "Seigneur" who sang to the sailors on the Antoine when she was fighting for the shore of Gaspe; nevertheless there was that in him which would keep him much the same man to the end.

Indeed, as he got into bed that fateful night he said aloud: "They shall see that I am not beaten. If they give me time up there in Montreal I'll keep the place till Zoe comes back—till Zoe comes home."

As he lay and tried to sleep, he kept saying over to himself, "Till Zoe comes home."

He thought that if he could but have Zoe back, it all would not matter so much. She would keep looking at him and saying, "There's the man that never flinched when things went wrong; there's the man that was a friend to everyone."

At last a thought came to him—the key to the situation as it seemed, the one thing necessary to meet the financial situation. He would sell the biggest farm he owned, which had been to him in its importance like the flour-mill itself. He had had an offer for it that very day, and a bigger offer still a week before. It was mortgaged to within eight thousand dollars of what it could be sold for but, if he could gain time, that eight thousand dollars would build the mill again. M. Mornay, the Big Financier, would certainly see that this was his due—to get his chance to pull things straight. Yes, he would certainly sell the Barbille farm to-morrow. With this thought in his mind he went to sleep at last, and he did not wake till the sun was high.

It was a sun of the most wonderful brightness and warmth. Yesterday it would have made the Manor Cartier and all around it look like Arcady. But as it shone upon the ruins of the mill, when Jean Jacques went out into the working world again, it made so gaunt and hideous a picture that, in spite of himself, a cry of misery came from his lips.

Through all the misfortunes which had come to him the outward semblance of things had remained, and when he went in and out of the plantation of the Manor Cartier, there was no physical change in the surroundings, which betrayed the troubles and disasters fallen upon its overlord. There it all was just as it had ever been, and seeming to deny that anything had changed in the lives of those who made the place other than a dead or deserted world. When Carmen went, when Zoe fled, when his cousin Auguste Charron took his flight, when defeats at law abashed him, the house and mills, and stores and offices, and goodly trees, and well-kept yards and barns and cattle-sheds all looked the same. Thus it was that he had been fortified. In one sense his miseries had seemed unreal, because all was the same in the outward scene. It was as though it all said to him: "It is a dream that those you love have vanished, that ill-fortune sits by your fireside. One night you will go to bed thinking that wife and child have gone, that your treasury is nearly empty; and in the morning you will wake up and find your loved ones sitting in their accustomed places, and your treasury will be full to overflowing as of old."

So it was while the picture of his home scene remained unbroken and serene; but the hideous mass of last night's holocaust was now before his eyes, with little streams of smoke rising from the cindered pile, and a hundred things with which his eyes had been familiar lay distorted, excoriated and useless. He realized with sudden completeness that a terrible change bad come in his life, that a cyclone had ruined the face of his created world.

This picture did more to open up Jean Jacques' eyes to his real position in life than anything he had experienced, than any sorrow he had suffered. He had been in torment in the past, but he had refused to see that he was in Hades. Now it was as though he had been led through the streets of Hell by some dark spirit, while in vain he looked round for his old friends Kant and Hegel, Voltaire and Rousseau and Rochefoucauld, Plato and Aristotle.

While gazing at the dismal scene, however, and unheeding the idlers who poked about among the ruins, and watched him as one who was the centre of a drama, he suddenly caught sight of the gold Cock of Beaugard, which had stood on the top of the mill, in the very centre of the ruins.

Yes, there it was, the crested golden cock which had typified his own life, as he went head high, body erect, spurs giving warning, and a clarion in his throat ready to blare forth at any moment. There was the golden Cock of Beaugard in the cinders, the ashes and the dust. His chin dropped on his breast, and a cloud like a fog on the coast of Gaspe settled round him. Yet even as his head drooped, something else happened—one of those trivial things which yet may be the pivot of great things. A cock crowed—almost in his very ear, it seemed. He lifted his head quickly, and a superstitious look flashed into his face. His eyes fastened on the burnished head of the Cock among the ruins. To his excited imagination it was as though the ancient symbol of the Barbilles had spoken to him in its own language of good cheer and defiance. Yes, there it was, half covered by the ruins, but its head was erect in the midst of fire and disaster. Brought low, it was still alert above the wreckage. The child, the dreamer, the optimist, the egoist, and the man alive in Jean Jacques sprang into vigour again. It was as though the Cock of Beaugard had really summoned him to action, and the crowing had not been that of a barnyard bantam not a hundred feet away from him. Jean Jacques' head went up too.

"Me—I am what I always was, nothing can change me," he exclaimed defiantly. "I will sell the Barbille farm and build the mill again."

So it was that by hook or by crook, and because the Big Financier had more heart than he even acknowledged to his own wife, Jean Jacques did sell the Barbille farm, and got in cash—in good hard cash-eight thousand dollars after the mortgage was paid. M. Mornay was even willing to take the inadequate indemnity of the insurance policy on the mill, and lose the rest, in order that Jean Jacques should have the eight thousand dollars to rebuild. This he did because Jean Jacques showed such amazing courage after the burning of the mill, and spread himself out in a greater activity than his career had yet shown. He shaved through this financial crisis, in spite of the blow he had received by the loss of his lawsuits, the flitting of his cousin, Auguste Charron, and the farm debts of this same cousin. It all meant a series of manipulations made possible by the apparent confidence reposed in him by M. Mornay.

On the day he sold his farm he was by no means out of danger of absolute insolvency—he was in fact ruined; but he was not yet the victim of those processes which would make him legally insolvent. The vultures were hovering, but they had not yet swooped, and there was the Manor saw-mill going night and day; for by the strangest good luck Jean Jacques received an order for M. Mornay's new railway (Judge Carcasson was behind that) which would keep his saw-mill working twenty-four hours in the day for six months.

"I like his pluck, but still, ten to one, he loses," remarked M. Mornay to Judge Carcasson. "He is an unlucky man, and I agree with Napoleon that you oughtn't to be partner with an unlucky man."

"Yet you have had to do with Monsieur Jean Jacques," responded the aged Judge.

M. Mornay nodded indulgently.

"Yes, without risk, up to the burning of the mill. Now I take my chances, simply because I'm a fool too, in spite of all the wisdom I see in history and in life's experiences. I ought to have closed him up, but I've let him go on, you see."

"You will not regret it," remarked the Judge. "He really is worth it."

"But I think I will regret it financially. I think that this is the last flare of the ambition and energy of your Jean Jacques. That often happens—a man summons up all his reserves for one last effort. It's partly pride, partly the undefeated thing in him, partly the gambling spirit which seizes men when nothing is left but one great spectacular success or else be blotted out. That's the case with your philosopher; and I'm not sure that I won't lose twenty thousand dollars by him yet."

"You've lost more with less justification," retorted the Judge, who, in his ninetieth year, was still as alive as his friend at sixty.

M. Mornay waved a hand in acknowledgment, and rolled his cigar from corner to corner of his mouth. "Oh, I've lost a lot more in my time, Judge, but with a squint in my eye! But I'm doing this with no astigmatism. I've got the focus."

The aged Judge gave a conciliatory murmur-he had a fine persuasive voice. "You would never be sorry for what you have done if you had known his daughter—his Zoe. It's the thought of her that keeps him going. He wants the place to be just as she left it when she comes back."

"Well, well, let's hope it will. I'm giving him a chance," replied M. Mornay with his wineglass raised. "He's got eight thousand dollars in cash to build his mill again; and I hope he'll keep a tight hand on it till the mill is up."

Keep a tight hand on it?

That is what Jean Jacques meant to do; but if a man wants to keep a tight hand on money he should not carry it about in his pocket in cold, hard cash. It was a foolish whim of Jean Jacques that he must have the eight thousand dollars in cash—in hundred-dollar bills—and not in the form of a cheque; but there was something childlike in him. When, as he thought, he had saved himself from complete ruin, he wanted to keep and gloat over the trophy of victory, and his trophy was the eight thousand dollars got from the Barbille farm. He would have to pay out two thousand dollars in cash to the contractors for the rebuilding of the mill at once,—they were more than usually cautious—but he would have six thousand left, which he would put in the bank after he had let people see that he was well fortified with cash.

The child in him liked the idea of pulling out of his pocket a few thousand dollars in hundred-dollar bills. He had always carried a good deal of money loose in his pocket, and now that his resources were so limited he would still make a gallant show. After a week or two he would deposit six thousand dollars in the bank; but he was so eager to begin building the mill, that he paid over the stipulated two thousand dollars to the contractors on the very day he received the eight thousand. A few days later the remaining six thousand were housed in a cupboard with an iron door in the wall of his office at the Manor Cartier.

"There, that will keep me in heart and promise," said Jean Jacques as he turned the key in the lock.

CHAPTER XVIII. JEAN JACQUES HAS AN OFFER

The day after Jean Jacques had got a new lease of life and become his own banker, he treated himself to one of those interludes of pleasure from which he had emerged in the past like a hermit from his cave. He sat on the hill above his lime-kilns, reading the little hand-book of philosophy which had played so big a part in his life. Whatever else had disturbed his mind and diverted him from his course, nothing had weaned him from this obsession. He still interlarded all his conversation with quotations from brilliant poseurs like Chateaubriand and Rochefoucauld, and from missionaries of thought like Hume and Hegel.

His real joy, however, was in withdrawing for what might be called a seance of meditation from the world's business. Some men make celebration in wine, sport and adventure; but Jean Jacques made it in flooding his mind with streams of human thought which often tried to run uphill, which were frequently choked with weeds, but still were like the pool of Siloam to his vain mind. They bathed that vain mind in the illusion that it could see into the secret springs of experience.

So, on as bright a day as ever the New World offered, Jean Jacques sat reciting to himself a spectacular bit of logic from one of his idols, wedged between a piece of Aristotle quartz and Plato marble. The sound of it was good in his ears. He mouthed it as greedily and happily as though he was not sitting on the edge of a volcano instead of the moss-grown limestone on a hill above his own manor.

"The course of events in the life of a man, whatever their gravity or levity, are only to be valued and measured by the value and measure of his own soul. Thus, what in its own intrinsic origin and material should in all outer reason be a tragedy, does not of itself shake the foundations or make a fissure in the superstructure. Again—"

Thus his oracle, but Jean Jacques' voice suddenly died down, for, as he sat there, the face of a woman made a vivid call of recognition. He slowly awakened from his self-hypnotism, to hear a woman speaking to him; to see two dark eyes looking at him from under heavy black brows with bright, intent friendliness.

"They said at the Manor you had come this way, so I thought I'd not have my drive for nothing, and here I am. I wanted to say something to you, M'sieu' Jean Jacques."

It was the widow of Palass Poucette. She looked very fresh and friendly indeed, and she was the very acme of neatness. If she was not handsome, she certainly had a true and sweet comeliness of her own, due to the deep rose-colour of her cheeks, the ivory whiteness round the lustrous brown eyes, the regular shining teeth which showed so much when she smiled, and the look half laughing, half sentimental which dominated all.

Before she had finished speaking Jean Jacques was on his feet with his hat off. Somehow she seemed to be a part of that abstraction, that intoxication, in which he had just been drowning his accumulated anxieties. Not that Virginie Poucette was logical or philosophical, or a child of thought, for she was wholly the opposite-practical, sensuous, emotional, a child of nature and of Eve. But neither was Jean Jacques a real child of thought, though he made unconscious pretence of it. He also was a child of nature—and Adam. He thought he had the courage of his convictions, but it was only the courage of his emotions. His philosophy was but the bent or inclination of a mind with a capacity to feel things rather than to think them. He had feeling, the first essential of the philosopher, but there he stayed, an undeveloped chrysalis.

His look was abstracted still as he took the hand of the widow of Palass Poucette; but he spoke cheerfully. "It is a pleasure, madame, to welcome you among my friends," he said.

He made a little flourish with the book which had so long been his bosom friend, and added: "But I hope you are in no trouble that you come to me—so many come to me in their troubles," he continued with an air of satisfaction.

"Come to you—why, you have enough troubles of your own!" she made answer. "It's because you have your own troubles that I'm here."

"Why you are here," he remarked vaguely.

There was something very direct and childlike in Virginie Poucette. She could not pretend; she wore her heart on her sleeve. She travelled a long distance in a little while.

"I've got no trouble myself," she responded. "But, yes, I have," she added. "I've got one trouble—it's yours. It's that you've been having hard times—the flour-mill, your cousin Auguste Charron, the lawsuits, and all the rest. They say at Vilray that you have all you can do to keep out of the Bankruptcy Court, and that—"

Jean Jacques started, flushed, and seemed about to get angry; but she put things right at once.

"People talk more than they know, but there's always some fire where there's smoke," she hastened to explain. "Besides, your father-in-law babbles more than is good for him or for you. I thought at first that M. Dolores was a first-class kind of man, that he had had hard times too, and I let him come and see me; but I found him out, and that was the end of it, you may be sure. If you like him, I don't want to say anything more, but I'm sure that he's no real friend to you-or to anybody. If that man went to confession—but there, that's not what I've come for. I've come to say to you that I never felt so sorry for anyone in my life as I do for you. I cried all night after your beautiful mill was burned down. You were coming to see me next day—you remember what you said in M. Fille's office—but of course you couldn't. Of course, there was no reason why you should come to see me really—I've 'only got two hundred acres and the house. It's a good house, though—Palass saw to that—and it's insured; but still I know you'd have come just the same if I'd had only two acres. I know. There's hosts of people you've been good to here, and they're sorry for you; and I'm sorrier than any, for I'm alone, and you're alone, too, except for the old Dolores, and he's no good to either of us—mark my words, no good to you! I'm sorry for you, M'sieu' Jean Jacques, and I've come to say that I'm ready to lend you two thousand dollars, if that's any help. I could make it more if I had time; but sometimes money on the spot is worth a lot more than what's just crawling to you—snailing along while you eat your heart out. Two thousand dollars is two thousand dollars—I know what it's worth to me, though it mayn't be much to you; but I didn't earn it. It belonged to a first-class man, and he worked for it, and he died and left it to me. It's not come easy, go easy with me. I like to feel I've got two thousand cash without having to mortgage for it. But it belonged to a number-one man, a man of brains—I've got no brains, only some sense—and I want another good man to use it and make the world easier for himself."

It was a long speech, and she delivered it in little gasps of oratory which were brightened by her wonderfully kind smile and the heart—not to say sentiment—which showed in her face. The sentiment, however, did not prejudice Jean Jacques against her, for he was a sentimentalist himself. His feelings were very quick, and before she had spoken fifty words the underglow of his eyes was flooded by something which might have been mistaken for tears. It was, however, only the moisture of gratitude and the soul's good feeling.

"Well there, well there," he said when she had finished, "I've never had anything like this in my life before. It's the biggest thing in the art of being a neighbour I've ever seen. You've only been in the parish three years, and yet you've shown me a confidence immense, inspiring! It is as the Greek philosopher said, 'To conceive the human mind aright is the greatest gift from the gods.' And to you, who never read a line of philosophy, without doubt, you have done the thing that is greatest. It says, 'I teach neighbourliness and life's exchange.' Madame, your house ought to be called Neighbourhood House. It is the epitome of the spirit, it is the shrine of—"

He was working himself up to a point where he could forget all the things that trouble humanity, in the inebriation of an idealistic soul which had a casing of passion, but the passion of the mind and not of the body; for Jean Jacques had not a sensual drift in his organism. If there had been a sensual drift, probably Carmen would still have been the lady of his manor, and he would still have been a magnate and not a potential bankrupt; for in her way Carmen had been a kind of balance to his judgment in the business of life, in spite of her own material and (at the very last) sensual strain. It was a godsend to Jean Jacques to have such an inspiration as Virginie Poucette had given him. He could not in these days, somehow, get the fires of his soul lighted, as he was wont to do in the old times, and he loved talking—how he loved talking of great things! He was really going hard, galloping strong, when Virginie interrupted him, first by an exclamation, then, as insistently he repeated the words, "It is the epitome of the spirit, the shrine of—"

She put out a hand, interrupting him, and said: "Yes, yes, M'sieu' Jean Jacques, that's as good as Moliere, I s'pose, or the Archbishop at Quebec, but are you going to take it, the two thousand dollars? I made a long speech, I know, but that was to tell you why I come with the money"—she drew out a pocketbook—"with the order on my lawyer to hand the cash over to you. As a woman I had to explain to you, there being lots of ideas about what a woman should do and what she shouldn't do; but there's nothing at all for you to explain, and Mere Langlois and a lot of others would think I'm vain enough now without your compliments. I'm a neighbour if you like, and I offer you a loan. Will you take it—that's all?"

He held out his hand in silence and took the paper from her. Putting his head a little on one side, he read it. At first he seemed hardly to get the formal language clear in his mind; however, or maybe his mind was still away in that abstraction into which he had whisked it when he began his reply to her fine offer; but he read it out aloud, first quickly, then very slowly, and he looked at the signature with a deeply meditative air.

"Virginie Poucette—that's a good name," he remarked; "and also good for two thousand dollars!" He paused to smile contentedly over his own joke. "And good for a great deal more than that too," he added with a nod.

"Yes, ten times as much as that," she responded quickly, her eyes fixed on his face. She scarcely knew herself what she was thinking when she said it; but most people who read this history will think she was hinting that her assets might be united with his, and so enable him to wipe out his liabilities and do a good deal more besides. Yet, how could that be, since Carmen Dolores was still his wife if she was alive; and also they both were Catholics, and Catholics did not recognize divorce!

Truth is, Virginie Poucette's mind did not define her feelings at all clearly, or express exactly what she wanted. Her actions said one thing certainly; but if the question had been put to her, whether she was doing this thing because of a wish to take the place of Carmen Dolores in Jean Jacques' life she would have said no at once. She had not come to that—yet. She was simply moved by a sentiment of pity for Jean Jacques, and as she had no child, or husband, or sister, or brother, or father, or mother, but only relatives who tried to impose upon her, she needed an objective for the emotions of her nature, for the overflow of her unused affection and her unsatisfied maternal spirit. Here, then, was the most obvious opportunity—a man in trouble who had not deserved the bitter bad luck which had come to him. Even old Mere Langlois in the market-place at Vilray had admitted that, and had said the same later on in Virginie's home.

For an instant Jean Jacques was fascinated by the sudden prospect which opened out before him. If he asked her, this woman would probably loan him five thousand dollars—and she had mentioned nothing about security!

"What security do you want?" he asked in a husky voice.

"Security? I don't understand about that," she replied. "I'd not offer you the money if I didn't think you were an honest man, and an honest man would pay me back. A dishonest man wouldn't pay me back, security or no security."

"He'd have to pay you back if the security was right to start with," Jean Jacques insisted. "But you don't want security, because you think I'm an honest man! Well, for sure you're right. I am honest. I never took a cent that wasn't mine; but that's not everything. If you lend you ought to have security. I've lost a good deal from not having enough security at the start. You are willing to lend me money without security—that's enough to make me feel thirty again, and I'm fifty—I'm fifty," he added, as though with an attempt to show her that she could not think of him in any emotional way; though the day when his flour-mill was burned he had felt the touch of her fingers comforting and thrilling.

"You think Jean Jacques Barbille's word as good as his bond?" he continued. "So it is; but I'm going to pull this thing through alone. That's what I said to you and Maitre Fille at his office. I meant it too—help of God, it is the truth!"

He had forgotten that if M. Mornay had not made it easy for him, and had not refrained from insisting on his pound of flesh, he would now be insolvent and with no roof over him. Like many another man Jean Jacques was the occasional slave of formula, and also the victim of phases of his own temperament. In truth he had not realized how big a thing M. Mornay had done for him. He had accepted the chance given him as the tribute to his own courage and enterprise and integrity, and as though it was to the advantage of his greatest creditor to give him another start; though in reality it had made no difference to the Big Financier, who knew his man and, with wide-open eyes, did what he had done.

Virginie was not subtle. She did not understand, was never satisfied with allusions, and she had no gift for catching the drift of things. She could endure no peradventure in her conversation. She wanted plain speaking and to be literally sure.

"Are you going to take it?" she asked abruptly.

He could not bear to be checked in his course. He waved a hand and smiled at her. Then his eyes seemed to travel away into the distance, the look of the dreamer in them; but behind all was that strange, ruddy underglow of revelation which kept emerging from shadows, retreating and emerging, yet always there now, in much or in little, since the burning of the mill.

"I've lent a good deal of money without security in my time," he reflected, "but the only people who ever paid me back were a deaf and dumb man and a flyaway—a woman that was tired of selling herself, and started straight and right with the money I lent her. She had been the wife of a man who studied with me at Laval. She paid me back every penny, too, year by year for five years. The rest I lent money to never paid; but they paid, the dummy and the harlot that was, they paid! But they paid for the rest also! If I had refused these two because of the others, I'd not be fit to visit at Neighbourhood House where Virginie Poucette lives."

He looked closely at the order she had given him again, as though to let it sink in his mind and be registered for ever. "I'm going to do without any further use of your two thousand dollars," he continued cheer fully. "It has done its work. You've lent it to me, I've used it"—he put the hand holding it on his breast—"and I'm paying it back to you, but without interest." He gave the order to her.

"I don't see what you mean," she said helplessly, and she looked at the paper, as though it had undergone some change while it was in his hand.

"That you would lend it me is worth ten times two thousand to me, Virginie Poucette," he explained. "It gives me, not a kick from behind—I've not had much else lately—but it holds a light in front of me. It calls me. It says, 'March on, Jean Jacques—climb the mountain.' It summons me to dispose my forces for the campaign which will restore the Manor Cartier to what it has ever been since the days of the Baron of Beaugard. It quickens the blood at my heart. It restores—"

Virginie would not allow him to go on. "You won't let me help you? Suppose I do lose the money—I didn't earn it; it was earned by Palass Poucette, and he'd understand, if he knew. I can live without the money, if I have to, but you would pay it back, I know. You oughtn't to take any extra risks. If your daughter should come back and not find you here, if she returned to the Manor Cartier, and—"

He made an insistent gesture. "Hush! Be still, my friend—as good a friend as a man could have. If my Zoe came back I'd like to feel—I'd like to feel that I had saved things alone; that no woman's money made me safe. If Zoe or if—"

He was going to say, "If Carmen came back," for his mind was moving in past scenes; but he stopped short and looked around helplessly. Then presently, as though by an effort, he added with a bravura note in his voice:

"The world has been full of trouble for a long time, but there have always been men to say to trouble, 'I am master, I have the mind to get above it all.' Well, I am one of them."

There was no note of vanity or bombast in his voice as he said this, and in his eyes that new underglow deepened and shone. Perhaps in this instant he saw more of his future than he would speak of to anyone on earth. Perhaps prevision was given him, and it was as the Big Financier had said to Maitre Fille, that his philosophy was now, at the last, to be of use to him. When his wife had betrayed him, and his wife and child had left him, he had said, "Moi je suis philosophe!" but he was a man of wealth in those days, and money soothes hurts of that kind in rare degree. Would he still say, whatever was yet to come, that he was a philosopher?

"Well, I've done what I thought would help you, and I can't say more than that," Virginie remarked with a sigh, and there was despondency in her eyes. Her face became flushed, her bosom showed agitation; she looked at him as she had done in Maitre Fille's office, and a wave of feeling passed over him now, as it did then, and he remembered, in response to her look, the thrill of his fingers in her palm. His face now flushed also, and he had an impulse to ask her to sit down beside him. He put it away from him, however, for the present, at any rate-who could tell what to-morrow might bring forth!—and then he held out his hand to her. His voice shook a little when he spoke; but it cleared, and began to ring, before he had said a dozen words.

"I'll never forget what you've said and done this morning, Virginie Poucette," he declared; "and if I break the back of the trouble that's in my way, and come out cock o' the walk again"—the gold Cock of Beaugard in the ruins near and the clarion of the bantam of his barnyard were in his mind and ears—"it'll be partly because of you. I hug that thought to me."

"I could do a good deal more than that," she ventured, with a tremulous voice, and then she took her warm hand from his nervous grasp, and turned sharply into the path which led back towards the Manor. She did not turn around, and she walked quickly away.

There was confusion in her eyes and in her mind. It would take some time to make the confusion into order, and she was now hot, now cold, in all her frame, when at last she climbed into her wagon.

This physical unrest imparted itself to all she did that day. First her horses were driven almost at a gallop; then they were held down to a slow walk; then they were stopped altogether, and she sat in the shade of the trees on the road to her home, pondering—whispering to herself and pondering.

As her horses were at a standstill she saw a wagon approaching. Instantly she touched her pair with the whip, and moved on. Before the approaching wagon came alongside, she knew from the grey and the darkbrown horses who was driving them, and she made a strong effort for composure. She succeeded indifferently, but her friend, Mere Langlois, did not notice this fact as her wagon drew near. There was excitement in Mere Langlois' face.

"There's been a shindy at the 'Red Eagle' tavern," she said. "That father-in-law of M'sieu' Jean Jacques and Rocque Valescure, the landlord, they got at each other's throats. Dolores hit Valescure on the head with a bottle."

"He didn't kill Valescure, did he?"

"Not that—no. But Valescure is hurt bad—as bad. It was six to one and half a dozen to the other—both no good at all. But of course they'll arrest the old man—your great friend! He'll not give you any more fur-robes, that's sure. He got away from the tavern, though, and he's hiding somewhere. M'sieu' Jean Jacques can't protect him now; he isn't what he once was in the parish. He's done for, and old Dolores will have to go to trial. They'll make it hot for him when they catch him. No more fur-robes from your Spanish friend, Virginie! You'll have to look somewhere else for your beaux, though to be sure there are enough that'd be glad to get you with that farm of yours, and your thrifty ways, if you keep your character."

Virginie was quite quiet now. The asperity and suggestiveness of the other's speech produced a cooling effect upon her.

"Better hurry, Mere Langlois, or everybody won't hear your story before sundown. If your throat gets tired, there's Brown's Bronchial Troches—" She pointed to an advertisement on the fence near by. "M. Fille's cook says they cure a rasping throat."

With that shot, Virginie Poucette whipped up her horses and drove on. She did not hear what Mere Langlois called after her, for Mere Langlois had been slow to recover from the unexpected violence dealt by one whom she had always bullied.

"Poor Jean Jacques!" said Virginie Poucette to herself as her horses ate up the ground. "That's another bit of bad luck. He'll not sleep to-night. Ah, the poor Jean Jacques—and all alone—not a hand to hold; no one to rumple that shaggy head of his or pat him on the back! His wife and Ma'm'selle Zoe, they didn't know a good thing when they had it. No, he'll not sleep to-night-ah, my dear Jean Jacques!"

CHAPTER XIX. SEBASTIAN DOLORES DOES NOT SLEEP

But Jean Jacques did sleep well that night; though it would have been better for him if he had not done so. The contractor's workmen had arrived in the early afternoon, he had seen the first ton of debris removed from the ruins of the historic mill, and it was crowned by the gold Cock of Beaugard, all grimy with the fire, but jaunty as of yore. The cheerfulness of the workmen, who sang gaily an old chanson of mill-life as they tugged at the timbers and stones, gave a fillip to the spirits of Jean Jacques, to whom had come a red-letter day.

Like Mirza on the high hill of Bagdad he had had his philosophic meditations; his good talk with Virginie Poucette had followed; and the woman of her lingered in the feeling of his hand all day, as something kind and homelike and true. Also in the evening had come M. Fille, who brought him a message from Judge Carcasson, that he must make the world sing for himself again.

Contrary to what Mere Langlois had thought, he had not been perturbed by the parish noise about the savage incident at "The Red Eagle," and the desperate affair which would cause the arrest of his father-in-law. He was at last well inclined to be rid of Sebastian Dolores, who had ceased to be a comfort to him, and who brought him hateful and not kindly memories of his lost women, and the happy hours of the past they represented.

M. Fille had come to the Manor in much alarm, lest the news of the miserable episode at "The Red Eagle" should bring Jean Jacques down again to the depths. He was infinitely relieved, however, to find that the lord of the Manor Cartier seemed only to be grateful that Sebastian Dolores did not return, and nodded emphatically when M. Fille remarked that perhaps it would be just as well if he never did return.

As M. Fille sat with his host at the table in the sunset light, Jean Jacques seemed quieter and steadier of body and mind than he had been for a long, long time. He even drank three glasses of the cordial which Mere Langlois had left for him, with the idea that it might comfort him when he got the bad news about Sebastian Dolores; and parting with M. Fille at the door, he waved a hand and said: "Well, good-night, master of the laws. Safe journey! I'm off to bed, and I'll sleep without rocking, that's very sure and sweet."

He stood and waved his hand several times to M. Fille—till he was out of sight indeed; and the Clerk of the Court smiled to himself long afterwards, recalling Jean Jacques' cheerful face as he had seen it at their parting in the gathering dusk. As for Jean Jacques, when he locked up the house at ten o'clock, with Dolores still absent, he had the air of a man from whose shoulders great weights had fallen.

"Now I've shut the door on him, it'll stay shut," he said firmly. "Let him go back to work. He's no good here to me, to himself, or to anyone. And that business of the fur-robe and Virginie Poucette—ah, that!"

He shook his head angrily, then seeing the bottle of cordial still uncorked on the sideboard, he poured some out and drank it very slowly, till his eyes were on the ceiling above him and every drop had gone home. Presently, with the bedroom lamp in his hand, he went upstairs, humming to himself the chanson the workmen had sung that afternoon as they raised again the walls of the mill:

"Distaff of flax flowing behind her

Margatton goes to the mill

On the old grey ass she goes,

The flour of love it will blind her

Ah, the grist the devil will grind her,

When Margatton goes to the mill!

On the old grey ass she goes,

And the old grey ass, he knows!"

He liked the sound of his own voice this night of his Reconstruction Period—or such it seemed to him; and he thought that no one heard his singing save himself. There, however, he was mistaken. Someone was hidden in the house—in the big kitchen-bunk which served as a bed or a seat, as needed. This someone had stolen in while Jean Jacques and M. Fille were at supper. His name was Dolores, and he had a horse just over the hill near by, to serve him when his work was done, and he could get away.

The constables of Vilray had twice visited the Manor to arrest him that day, but they had been led in another direction by a clue which he had provided; and afterwards in the dusk he had doubled back and hid himself under Jean Jacques' roof. He had very important business at the Manor Cartier.

Jean Jacques' voice ceased one song, and then, after a silence, it took up another, not so melodious. Sebastian Dolores had impatiently waited for this later "musicale" to begin—he had heard it often before; and when it was at last a regular succession of nasal explosions, he crawled out and began to do the business which had brought him to the Manor Cartier.

He did it all alone and with much skill; for when he was an anarchist in Spain, those long years ago, he had learned how to use tools with expert understanding. Of late, Spain had been much in his mind. He wanted to go back there. Nostalgia had possessed him ever since he had come again to the Manor Cartier after Zoe had left. He thought much of Spain, and but little of his daughter. Memory of her was only poignant, in so far as it was associated with the days preceding the wreck of the Antoine. He had had far more than enough of the respectable working life of the New World; but there never was sufficient money to take him back to Europe, even were it safe to go. Of late, however, he felt sure that he might venture, if he could only get cash for the journey. He wanted to drift back to the idleness and adventure and the "easy money" of the old anarchist days in Cadiz and Madrid. He was sick for the patio and the plaza, for the bull-fight, for the siesta in the sun, for the lazy glamour of the gardens and the red wine of Valladolid, for the redolent cigarette of the roadside tavern. This cold iron land had spoiled him, and he would strive to get himself home again before it was too late. In Spain there would always be some woman whom he could cajole; some comrade whom he could betray; some priest whom he could deceive, whose pocket he could empty by the recital of his troubles. But if, peradventure, he returned to Spain with money to spare in his pocket, how easy indeed it would all be, and how happy he would find himself amid old surroundings and old friends!

The way had suddenly opened up to him when Jean Jacques had brought home in hard cash, and had locked away in the iron-doored cupboard in the officewall, his last, his cherished, eight thousand dollars. Six thousand of that eight were still left, and it was concern for this six thousand which had brought Dolores to the Manor this night when Jean Jacques snored so loudly. The events of the day at "The Red Eagle" had brought things to a crisis in the affairs of Carmen's father. It was a foolish business that at the tavern—so, at any rate, he thought, when it was all over, and he was awake to the fact that he must fly or go to jail. From the time he had, with a bottle of gin, laid Valescure low, Spain was the word which went ringing through his head, and the way to Spain was by the Six Thousand Dollar Route, the New World terminal of which was the cupboard in the wall at the Manor Cartier.

Little cared Sebastian Dolores that the theft of the money would mean the end of all things for Jean Jacques Barbille-for his own daughter's husband. He was thinking of himself, as he had always done.

He worked for two whole hours before he succeeded in quietly forcing open the iron door in the wall; but it was done at last. Curiously enough, Jean Jacques' snoring stopped on the instant that Sebastian Dolores' fingers clutched the money; but it began cheerfully again when the door in the wall closed once more.

Five minutes after Dolores had thrust the six thousand dollars into his pocket, his horse was galloping away over the hills towards the River St. Lawrence. If he had luck, he would reach it by the morning. As it happened, he had the luck. Behind him, in the Manor Cartier, the man who had had no luck and much philosophy, snored on till morning in unconscious content.

It was a whole day before Jean Jacques discovered his loss. When he had finished his lonely supper the next evening, he went to the cupboard in his office to cheer himself with the sight of the six thousand dollars. He felt that he must revive his spirits. They had been drooping all day, he knew not why.

When he saw the empty pigeon-hole in the cupboard, his sight swam. It was some time before it cleared, but, when it did, and he knew beyond peradventure the crushing, everlasting truth, not a sound escaped him. His heart stood still. His face filled with a panic confusion. He seemed like one bereft of understanding.

CHAPTER XX. "AU 'VOIR, M'SIEU' JEAN JACQUES"

It is seldom that Justice travels as swiftly as Crime, and it is also seldom that the luck is more with the law than with the criminal. It took the parish of St. Saviour's so long to make up its mind who stole Jean Jacques' six thousand dollars, that when the hounds got the scent at last the quarry had reached the water—in other words, Sebastian Dolores had achieved the St. Lawrence. The criminal had had near a day's start before a telegram was sent to the police at Montreal, Quebec, and other places to look out for the picaroon who had left his mark on the parish of St. Saviour's. The telegram would not even then have been sent had it not been for M. Fille, who, suspecting Sebastian Dolores, still refrained from instant action. This he did because he thought Jean Jacques would not wish his beloved Zoe's grandfather sent to prison. But when other people at last declared that it must have been Dolores, M. Fille insisted on telegrams being sent by the magistrate at Vilray without Jean Jacques' consent. He had even urged the magistrate to "rush" the wire, because it came home to him with stunning force that, if the money was not recovered, Jean Jacques would be a beggar. It was better to jail the father-in-law, than for the little money-master to take to the road a pauper, or stay on at St. Saviour's as an underling where he had been overlord.

As for Jean Jacques, in his heart of hearts he knew who had robbed him. He realized that it was one of the radii of the comedy-tragedy which began on the Antoine, so many years before; and it had settled in his mind at last that Sebastian Dolores was but part of the dark machinery of fate, and that what was now had to be.

For one whole day after the robbery he was like a man paralysed—dispossessed of active being; but when his creditors began to swarm, when M. Mornay sent his man of business down to foreclose his mortgages before others could take action, Jean Jacques waked from his apathy. He began an imitation of his old restlessness, and made essay again to pull the strings of his affairs. They were, however, so confused that a pull at one string tangled them all.

When the constables and others came to him, and said that they were on the trail of the robber, and that the rogue would be caught, he nodded his head encouragingly; but he was sure in his own mind that the flight of Dolores would be as successful as that of Carmen and Zoe.

This is the way he put it: "That man—we will just miss finding him, as I missed Zoe at the railroad junction when she went away, as I missed catching Carmen at St. Chrisanthine. When you are at the shore, he will be on the river; when you are getting into the train, he will be getting out. It is the custom of the family. At Bordeaux, the Spanish detectives were on the shore gnashing their teeth, when he was a hundred yards away at sea on the Antoine. They missed him like that; and we'll miss him too. What is the good! It was not his fault—that was the way of his bringing up beyond there at Cadiz, where they think more of a toreador than of John the Baptist. It was my fault. I ought to have banked the money. I ought not to have kept it to look at like a gamin with his marbles. There it was in the wall; and there was Dolores a long way from home and wanting to get back. He found the way by a gift of the tools; and I wish I had the same gift now; for I've got no other gift that'll earn anything for me."

These were the last dark or pessimistic words spoken at St. Saviour's by Jean Jacques; and they were said to the Clerk of the Court, who could not deny the truth of them; but he wrung the hand of Jean Jacques nevertheless, and would not leave him night or day. M. Fille was like a little cruiser protecting a fort when gunboats swarm near, not daring to attack till their battleship heaves in sight. The battleship was the Big Financier, who saw that a wreck was now inevitable, and was only concerned that there should be a fair distribution of the assets. That meant, of course, that he should be served first, and then that those below the salt should get a share.

Revelation after revelation had been Jean Jacques' lot of late years, but the final revelation of his own impotence was overwhelming. When he began to stir about among his affairs, he was faced by the fact that the law stood in his way. He realized with inward horror his shattered egotism and natural vanity; he saw that he might just as well be in jail; that he had no freedom; that he could do nothing at all in regard to anything he owned; that he was, in effect, a prisoner of war where he had been the general commanding an army.

Yet the old pride intervened, and it was associated with some innate nobility; for from the hour in which it was known that Sebastian Dolores had escaped in a steamer bound for France, and could not be overhauled, and the chances were that he would never have to yield up the six thousand dollars, Jean Jacques bustled about cheerfully, and as though he had still great affairs of business to order and regulate. It was a make-believe which few treated with scorn. Even the workmen at the mill humoured him, as he came several times every day to inspect the work of rebuilding; and they took his orders, though they did not carry them out. No one really carried out any of his orders except Seraphe Corniche, who, weeping from morning till night, protested that there never was so good a man as M'sieu' Jean Jacques; and she cooked his favourite dishes, giving him no peace until he had eaten them.

The days, the weeks went on, with Jean Jacques growing thinner and thinner, but going about with his head up like the gold Cock of Beaugard, and even crowing now and then, as he had done of yore. He faced the inevitable with something of his old smiling volubility; treating nothing of his disaster as though it really existed; signing off this asset and that; disposing of this thing and that; stripping himself bare of all the properties on his life's stage, in such a manner as might have been his had he been receiving gifts and not yielding up all he owned. He chatted as his belongings were, figuratively speaking, being carried away—as though they were mechanical, formal things to be done as he had done them every day of a fairly long life; as a clerk would check off the boxes or parcels carried past him by the porters. M. Fille could hardly bear to see him in this mood, and the New Cure hovered round him with a mournful and harmlessly deceptive kindness. But the end had to come, and practically all the parish was present when it came. That was on the day when the contents of the Manor were sold at auction by order of the Court. One thing Jean Jacques refused absolutely and irrevocably to do from the first—refused it at last in anger and even with an oath: he would not go through the Bankruptcy Court. No persuasion had any effect. The very suggestion seemed to smirch his honour. His lawyer pleaded with him, said he would be able to save something out of the wreck, and that his creditors would be willing that he should take advantage of the privileges of that court; but he only said in reply:

"Thank you, thank you altogether, monsieur, but it is impossible—'non possumus, non possumus, my son,' as the Pope said to Bonaparte. I owe and I will pay what I can; and what I can't pay now I will try to pay in the future, by the cent, by the dollar, till all is paid to the last copper. It is the way with the Barbilles. They have paid their way and their debts in honour, and it is in the bond with all the Barbilles of the past that I do as they do. If I can't do it, then that I have tried to do it will be endorsed on the foot of the bill."

No one could move him, not even Judge Carcasson, who from his armchair in Montreal wrote a feeble-handed letter begging him to believe that it was "well within his rights as a gentleman"—this he put in at the request of M. Mornay—to take advantage of the privileges of the Bankruptcy Court. Even then Jean Jacques had only a few moments' hesitation. What the Judge said made a deep impression; but he had determined to drink the cup of his misfortune to the dregs. He was set upon complete renunciation; on going forth like a pilgrim from the place of his troubles and sorrows, taking no gifts, no mercies save those which heaven accorded him.

When the day of the auction came everything went. Even his best suit of clothes was sold to a blacksmith, while his fur-coat was bought by a horse-doctor for fifteen dollars. Things that had been part of his life for a generation found their way into hands where he would least have wished them to go—of those who had been envious of him, who had cheated or deceived him, of people with whom he had had nothing in common. The red wagon and the pair of little longtailed stallions, which he had driven for six years, were bought by the owner of a rival flour-mill in the parish of Vilray; but his best sleigh, with its coon-skin robes, was bought by the widow of Palass Poucette, who bought also the famous bearskin which Dolores had given her at Jean Jacques' expense, and had been returned by her to its proper owner. The silver fruitdish, once (it was said) the property of the Baron of Beaugard, which each generation of Barbilles had displayed with as much ceremony as though it was a chalice given by the Pope, went to Virginie Poucette. Virginie also bought the furniture from Zoe's bedroom as it stood, together with the little upright piano on which she used to play. The Cure bought Jean Jacques' writing-desk, and M. Fille purchased his armchair, in which had sat at least six Barbilles as owners of the Manor. The beaver-hat which Jean Jacques wore on state occasions, as his grandfather had done, together with the bonnet rouge of the habitant, donned by him in his younger days—they fell to the nod of Mere Langlois, who declared that, as she was a cousin, she would keep the things in the family. Mere Langlois would have bought the fruit-dish also if she could have afforded to bid against Virginie Poucette; but the latter would have had the dish if it had cost her two hundred dollars. The only time she had broken bread in Jean Jacques' house, she had eaten cake from this fruit-dish; and to her, as to the parish generally, the dish so beautifully shaped, with its graceful depth and its fine-chased handles, was symbol of the social caste of the Barbilles, as the gold Cock of Beaugard was sign of their civic and commercial glory.

Jean Jacques, who had moved about all day with an almost voluble affability, seeming not to realize the tragedy going on, or, if he realized it, rising superior to it, was noticed to stand still suddenly when the auctioneer put up the fruit-dish for sale. Then the smile left his face, and the reddish glow in his eyes, which had been there since the burning of the mill, fled, and a touch of amazement and confusion took its place. All in a moment he was like a fluttered dweller of the wilds to whom comes some tremor of danger.

His mouth opened as though he would forbid the selling of the heirloom; but it closed again, because he knew he had no right to withhold it from the hammer; and he took on a look like that which comes to the eyes of a child when it faces humiliating denial. Quickly as it came, however, it vanished, for he remembered that he could buy the dish himself. He could buy it himself and keep it.... Yet what could he do with it? Even so, he could keep it. It could still be his till better days came.

The auctioneer's voice told off the value of the fruitdish—"As an heirloom, as an antique; as a piece of workmanship impossible of duplication in these days of no handicraft; as good pure silver, bearing the head of Louis Quinze—beautiful, marvellous, historic, honourable," and Jean Jacques made ready to bid. Then he remembered he had no money—he who all his life had been able to take a roll of bills from his pocket as another man took a packet of letters. His glance fell in shame, and the words died on his lips, even as M. Manotel, the auctioneer, was about to add another five-dollar bid to the price, which already was standing at forty dollars.

It was at this moment Jean Jacques heard a woman's voice bidding, then two women's voices. Looking up he saw that one of the women was Mere Langlois and the other was Virginie Poucette, who had made the first bid. For a moment they contended, and then Mere Langlois fell out of the contest, and Virginie continued it with an ambitious farmer from the next county, who was about to become a Member of Parliament. Presently the owner of a river pleasure-steamer entered into the costly emulation also, but he soon fell away; and Virginie Poucette stubbornly raised the bidding by five dollars each time, till the silver symbol of the Barbilles' pride had reached one hundred dollars. Then she raised the price by ten dollars, and her rival, seeing that he was face to face with a woman who would now bid till her last dollar was at stake, withdrew; and Virginie was left triumphant with the heirloom.

At the moment when Virginie turned away with the handsome dish from M. Manotel, and the crowd cheered her gaily, she caught Jean-Jacques' eye, and she came straight towards him. She wanted to give the dish to him then and there; but she knew that this would provide annoying gossip for many a day, and besides, she thought he would refuse. More than that, she had in her mind another alternative which might in the end secure the heirloom to him, in spite of all. As she passed him, she said:

"At least we keep it in the parish. If you don't have it, well, then..."

She paused, for she did not quite know what to say unless she spoke what was really in her mind, and she dared not do that.

"But you ought to have an heirloom," she added, leaving unsaid what was her real thought and hope. With sudden inspiration, for he saw she was trying to make it easy for him, he drew the great silver-watch from his pocket, which the head of the Barbilles had worn for generations, and said:

"I have the only heirloom I could carry about with me. It will keep time for me as long as I'll last. The Manor clock strikes the time for the world, and this watch is set by the Manor clock."

"Well said—well and truly said, M'sieu' Jean Jacques," remarked the lean watchmaker and so-called jeweller of Vilray, who stood near. "It is a watch which couldn't miss the stroke of Judgment Day."

It was at that moment, in the sunset hour, when the sale had drawn to a close, and the people had begun to disperse, that the avocat of Vilray who represented the Big Financier came to Jean Jacques and said:

"M'sieu', I have to say that there is due to you three hundred and fifty dollars from the settlement, excluding this sale, which will just do what was expected of it. I am instructed to give it to you from the creditors. Here it is."

He took out a roll of bills and offered it to Jean Jacques.

"What creditors?" asked Jean Jacques.

"All the creditors," responded the other, and he produced a receipt for Jean Jacques to sign. "A formal statement will be sent you, and if there is any more due to you, it will be added then. But now—well, there it is, the creditors think there is no reason for you to wait."

Jean Jacques did not yet take the roll of bills. "They come from M. Mornay?" he asked with an air of resistance, for he did not wish to be under further obligations to the man who would lose most by him.

The lawyer was prepared. M. Mornay had foreseen the timidity and sensitiveness of Jean Jacques, had anticipated his mistaken chivalry—for how could a man decline to take advantage of the Bankruptcy Court unless he was another Don Quixote! He had therefore arranged with all the creditors for them to take responsibility with 'himself, though he provided the cash which manipulated this settlement.

"No, M'sieu' Jean Jacques," the lawyer replied, "this comes from all the creditors, as the sum due to you from all the transactions, so far as can be seen as yet. Further adjustment may be necessary, but this is the interim settlement."

Jean Jacques was far from being ignorant of business, but so bemused was his judgment and his intelligence now, that he did not see there was no balance which could possibly be his, since his liabilities vastly exceeded his assets. Yet with a wave of the hand he accepted the roll of bills, and signed the receipt with an air which said, "These forms must be observed, I suppose."

What he would have done if the three hundred and fifty dollars had not been given him, it would be hard to say, for with gentle asperity he had declined a loan from his friend M. Fille, and he had but one silver dollar in his pocket, or in the world. Indeed, Jean Jacques was living in a dream in these dark days—a dream of renunciation and sacrifice, and in the spirit of one who gives up all to some great cause. He was not yet even face to face with the fulness of his disaster. Only at moments had the real significance of it all come to him, and then he had shivered as before some terror menacing his path. Also, as M. Mornay had said, his philosophy was now in his bones and marrow rather than in his words. It had, after all, tinctured his blood and impregnated his mind. He had babbled and been the egotist, and played cock o' the walk; and now at last his philosophy was giving some foundation for his feet. Yet at this auction-sale he looked a distracted, if smiling, whimsical, rather bustling figure of misfortune, with a tragic air of exile, of isolation from all by which he was surrounded. A profound and wayworn loneliness showed in his figure, in his face, in his eyes.

The crowd thinned in time, and yet very many lingered to see the last of this drama of lost fortunes. A few of the riff-raff, who invariably attend these public scenes, were now rather the worse for drink, from the indifferent liquor provided by the auctioneer, and they were inclined to horseplay and coarse chaff. More than one ribald reference to Jean Jacques had been checked by his chivalrous fellow-citizens; indeed, M. Fille had almost laid himself open to a charge of assault in his own court by raising his stick at a loafer, who made insulting references to Jean Jacques. But as the sale drew to a close, an air of rollicking humour among the younger men would not be suppressed, and it looked as though Jean Jacques' exit would be attended by the elements of farce and satire.

In this world, however, things do not happen logically, and Jean Jacques made his exit in a wholly unexpected manner. He was going away by the train which left a new railway junction a few miles off, having gently yet firmly declined M. Fille's invitation, and also the invitations of others—including the Cure and Mere Langlois—to spend the night with them and start off the next day. He elected to go on to Montreal that very night, and before the sale was quite finished he prepared to start. His carpet-bag containing a few clothes and necessaries had been sent on to the junction, and he meant to walk to the station in the cool of the evening.

M. Manotel, the auctioneer, hoarse with his heavy day's work, was announcing that there were only a few more things to sell, and no doubt they could be had at a bargain, when Jean Jacques began a tour of the Manor. There was something inexpressibly mournful in this lonely pilgrimage of the dismantled mansion. Yet there was no show of cheap emotion by Jean Jacques; and a wave of the hand prevented any one from following him in his dry-eyed progress to say farewell to these haunts of childhood, manhood, family, and home. There was a strange numbness in his mind and body, and he had a feeling that he moved immense and reflective among material things. Only tragedy can produce that feeling. Happiness makes the universe infinite and stupendous, despair makes it small and even trivial.

It was when he had reached the little office where he had done the business of his life—a kind of neutral place where he had ever isolated himself from the domestic scene—that the final sensation, save one, of his existence at the Manor came to him. Virginie Poucette had divined his purpose when he began the tour of the house, and going by a roundabout way, she had placed herself where she could speak with him alone before he left the place for ever—if that was to be. She was not sure that his exit was really inevitable—not yet.

When Jean Jacques saw Virginie standing beside the table in his office where he lead worked over so many years, now marked Sold, and waiting to be taken away by its new owner, he started and drew back, but she held out her hand and said:

"But one word, M'sieu' Jean Jacques; only one word from a friend—indeed a friend."

"A friend of friends," he answered, still in abstraction, his eyes having that burnished light which belonged to the night of the fire; but yet realizing that she was a sympathetic soul who had offered to lend him money without security.

"Oh, indeed yes, as good a friend as you can ever have!" she added.

Something had waked the bigger part of her, which had never been awake in the days of Palass Poucette. Jean Jacques was much older than she, but what she felt had nothing to do with age, or place or station. It had only to do with understanding, with the call of nature and of a motherhood crying for expression. Her heart ached for him.

"Well, good-bye, my friend," he said, and held out his hand. "I must be going now."

"Wait," she said, and there was something insistent and yet pleading in her voice. "I've got something to say. You must hear it.... Why should you go? There is my farm—it needs to be worked right. It has got good chances. It has water-power and wood and the best flax in the province—they want to start a flax-mill on it—I've had letters from big men in Montreal. Well, why shouldn't you do it instead? There it is, the farm, and there am I a woman alone. I need help. I've got no head. I have to work at a sum of figures all night to get it straight.... Ah, m'sieu', it is a need both sides! You want someone to look after you; you want a chance again to do things; but you want someone to look after you, and it is all waiting there on the farm.

Palass Poucette left behind him seven sound horses, and cows and sheep, and a threshing-machine and a fanning-mill, and no debts, and two thousand dollars in the bank. You will never do anything away from here. You must stay here, where—where I can look after you, Jean Jacques."

The light in his eyes flamed up, died down, flamed up again, and presently it covered all his face, as he grasped what she meant.

"Wonder of God, do you forget?" he asked. "I am married—married still, Virginie Poucette. There is no divorce in the Catholic Church—no, none at all. It is for ever and ever."

"I said nothing about marriage," she said bravely, though her face suffused.

"Hand of Heaven, what do you mean? You mean to say you would do that for me in spite of the Cure and—and everybody and everything?"

"You ought to be taken care of," she protested. "You ought to have your chance again. No one here is free to do it all but me. You are alone. Your wife that was—maybe she is dead. I am alone, and I'm not afraid of what the good God will say. I will settle with Him myself. Well, then, do you think I'd care what—what Mere Langlois or the rest of the world would say?... I can't bear to think of you going away with nothing, with nobody, when here is something and somebody—somebody who would be good to you. Everybody knows that you've been badly used—everybody. I'm young enough to make things bright and warm in your life, and the place is big enough for two, even if it isn't the Manor Cartier."

"Figure de Christ, do you think I'd let you do it—me?" declared Jean Jacques, with lips trembling now and his shoulders heaving. Misfortune and pain and penalty he could stand, but sacrifice like this and—and whatever else it was, were too much for him. They brought him back to the dusty road and everyday life again; they subtracted him from his big dream, in which he had been detached from the details of his catastrophe.

"No, no, no," he added. "You go look another way, Virginie. Turn your face to the young spring, not to the dead winter. To-morrow I'll be gone to find what I've got to find. I've finished here, but there's many a good man waiting for you—men who'll bring you something worth while besides themselves. Make no mistake, I've finished. I've done my term of life. I'm only out on ticket-of-leave now—but there, enough, I shall always want to think of you. I wish I had something to give you—but yes, here is something." He drew from his pocket a silver napkin-ring. "I've had that since I was five years old. My uncle Stefan gave it to me. I've always used it. I don't know why I put it in my pocket this morning, but I did. Take it. It's more than money. It's got something of Jean Jacques about it. You've got the Barbille fruit-dish-that is a thing I'll remember. I'm glad you've got it, and—"

"I meant we should both eat from it," she said helplessly.

"It would cost too much to eat from it with you, Virginie—"

He stopped short, choked, then his face cleared, and his eyes became steady.

"Well then, good-bye, Virginie," he said, holding out his hand.

"You don't think I'd say to any other living man what I've said to you?" she asked.

He nodded understandingly. "That's the best part of it. It was for me of all the world," he answered. "When I look back, I'll see the light in your window—the light you lit for the lost one—for Jean Jacques Barbille."

Suddenly, with eyes that did not see and hands held out before him, he turned, felt for the door and left the room.

She leaned helplessly against the table. "The poor Jean Jacques—the poor Jean Jacques!" she murmured. "Cure or no Cure, I'd have done it," she declared, with a ring to her voice. "Ah, but Jean Jacques, come with me!" she added with a hungry and compassionate gesture, speaking into space. "I could make life worth while for us both."

A moment later Virginie was outside, watching the last act in the career of Jean Jacques in the parish of St. Saviour's.

This was what she saw.

The auctioneer was holding up a bird-cage containing a canary-Carmen's bird-cage, and Zoe's canary which had remained to be a vocal memory of her in her old home.

"Here," said the rhetorical, inflammable auctioneer, "here is the choicest lot left to the last. I put it away in the bakery, meaning to sell it at noon, when everybody was eating-food for the soul and food for the body. I forgot it. But here it is, worth anything you like to anybody that loves the beautiful, the good, and the harmonious. What do I hear for this lovely saffron singer from the Elysian fields? What did the immortal poet of France say of the bird in his garret, in 'L'Oiseau de Mon Crenier'? What did he say:

> 'Sing me a song of the bygone hour,
>
> A song of the stream and the sun;
>
> Sing of my love in her bosky bower,
>
> When my heart it was twenty-one.'

"Come now, who will renew his age or regale her youth with the divine notes of nature's minstrel? Who will make me an offer for this vestal virgin of song—the joy of the morning and the benediction of the evening? What do I hear? The best of the wine to the last of the feast! What do I hear?—five dollars—seven dollars—nine dollars—going at nine dollars—ten dollars— Well, ladies and gentlemen, the bird can sing—ah, voila!"

He stopped short for a moment, for as the evening sun swept its veil of rainbow radiance over the scene, the bird began to sing. Its little throat swelled, it chirruped, it trilled, it called, it soared, it lost itself in a flood of ecstasy. In the applausive silence, the emotional recess of the sale, as it were, the man to whom the bird and the song meant most, pushed his way up to the stand where M. Manotel stood. When the people saw who it was, they fell back, for there was that in his face which needed no interpretation. It filled them with a kind of awe.

He reached up a brown, eager, affectionate hand—it had always been that— fat and small, but rather fine and certainly emotional, though not material or sensual.

"Go on with your bidding," he said.

He was going to buy the thing which had belonged to his daughter, was beloved by her—the living oracle of the morning, the muezzin of his mosque of home. It had been to the girl who had gone as another such a bird had been to the mother of the girl, the voice that sang, "Praise God," in the short summer of that bygone happiness of his. Even this cage and its homebird were not his; they belonged to the creditors.

"Go on. I buy—I bid," Jean Jacques said in a voice that rang. It had no blur of emotion. It had resonance. The hammer that struck the bell of his voice was the hammer of memory, and if it was plaintive it also was clear, and it was also vibrant with the silver of lost hopes.

M. Manotel humoured him, while the bird still sang. "Four dollars—five dollars: do I hear no more than five dollars?—going once, going twice, going three times—gone!" he cried, for no one had made a further bid; and indeed M. Manotel would not have heard another voice than Jean Jacques' if it had been as loud as the falls of the Saguenay. He was a kind of poet in his way, was M. Manotel. He had been married four times, and he would be married again if he had the chance; also he wrote verses for tombstones in the churchyard at St. Saviour's, and couplets for fetes and weddings.

He handed the cage to Jean Jacques, who put it down on the ground at his feet, and in an instant had handed up five dollars for one of the idols of his own altar. Anyone else than M. Manotel, or perhaps M. Fille or the New Cure, would have hesitated to take the five dollars, or, if they had done so, would have handed it back; but they had souls to understand this Jean Jacques, and they would not deny him his insistent independence. And so, in a moment, he was making his way out of the crowd with the cage in his hand, the bird silent now.

As he went, some one touched his arm and slipped a book into his hand. It was M. Fille, and the book was his little compendium of philosophy which his friend had retrieved from his bedroom in the early morning.

"You weren't going to forget it, Jean Jacques?" M. Fille said reproachfully. "It is an old friend. It would not be happy with any one else."

Jean Jacques looked M. Fille in the eyes. "Moi—je suis philosophe," he said without any of the old insistence and pride and egotism, but as one would make an affirmation or repeat a creed.

"Yes, yes, to be sure, always, as of old," answered M. Fille firmly; for, from that formula might come strength, when it was most needed, in a sense other and deeper far than it had been or was now. "You will remember that you will always know where to find us—eh?" added the little Clerk of the Court.

The going of Jean Jacques was inevitable; all persuasion had failed to induce him to stay—even that of Virginie; and M. Fille now treated it as though it was the beginning of a new career for Jean Jacques, whatever that career might be. It might be he would come back some day, but not to things as they were, not ever again, nor as the same man.

"You will move on with the world outside there," continued M. Fille, "but we shall be turning on the same swivel here always; and whenever you come—there, you understand. With us it is semper fidelis, always the same."

Jean Jacques looked at M. Fille again as though to ask him a question, but presently he shook his head in negation to his thought.

"Well, good-bye," he said cheerfully—"A la bonne heure!"

By that M. Fille knew that Jean Jacques did not wish for company as he went—not even the company of his old friend who had loved the bright whimsical emotional Zoe; who had hovered around his life like a protecting spirit.

"A bi'tot," responded M. Fille, declining upon the homely patois.

But as Jean Jacques walked away with his little book of philosophy in his pocket, and the bird-cage in his hand, someone sobbed. M. Fille turned and saw. It was Virginie Poucette. Fortunately for Virginie other women did the same, not for the same reason, but out of a sympathy which was part of the scene.

It had been the intention of some friends of Jean Jacques to give him a cheer when he left, and even his sullen local creditors, now that the worst had come, were disposed to give him a good send-off; but the incident of the canary in its cage gave a turn to the feeling of the crowd which could not be resisted. They were not a people who could cut and dry their sentiments; they were all impulse and simplicity, with an obvious cocksure shrewdness too, like that of Jean Jacques—of the old Jean Jacques. He had been the epitome of all their faults and all their virtues.

No one cheered. Only one person called, "Au 'voir, M'sieu' Jean Jacques!" and no one followed him—a curious, assertive, feebly-brisk, shock-headed figure in the brown velveteen jacket, which he had bought in Paris on his Grand Tour.

"What a ridiculous little man!" said a woman from Chalfonte over the water, who had been buying freely all day for her new "Manor," her husband being a member of the provincial legislature.

The words were no sooner out of her mouth than two women faced her threateningly.

"For two pins I'd slap your face," said old Mere Langlois, her great breast heaving. "Popinjay—you, that ought to be in a cage like his canary."

But Virginie Poucette also was there in front of the offender, and she also had come from Chalfonte—was born in that parish; and she knew what she was facing.

"Better carry a bird-cage and a book than carry swill to swine," she said; and madame from Chalfonte turned white, for it had been said that her father was once a swine-herd, and that she had tried her best to forget it when, with her coarse beauty, she married the well-to-do farmer who was now in the legislature.

"Hold your tongues, all of you, and look at that," said M. Manotel, who had joined the agitated group. He was pointing towards the departing Jean Jacques, who was now away upon his road.

Jean Jacques had raised the cage on a level with his face, and was evidently speaking to the bird in the way birds love—that soft kissing sound to which they reply with song.

Presently there came a chirp or two, and then the bird thrust up its head, and out came the full blessedness of its song, exultant, home-like, intimate.

Jean Jacques walked on, the bird singing by his side; and he did not look back.

CHAPTER XXI. IF SHE HAD KNOWN IN TIME

Nothing stops when we stop for a time, or for all time, except ourselves. Everything else goes on—not in the same way; but it does go on. Life did not stop at St. Saviour's after Jean Jacques made his exit. Slowly the ruined mill rose up again, and very slowly indeed the widow of Palass Poucette recovered her spirits, though she remained a widow in spite of all appeals; but M. Fille and his sister never were the same after they lost their friend. They had great comfort in the dog which Jean Jacques had given to them, and they roused themselves to a malicious pleasure when Bobon, as he had been called by Zoe, rushed out at the heels of an importunate local creditor who had greatly worried Jean Jacques at the last. They waited in vain for a letter from Jean Jacques, but none came; nor did they hear anything from him, or of him, for a long, long time.

Jean Jacques did not mean that they should. When he went away with his book of philosophy and his canary he had but one thing in his mind, and that was to find Zoe and make her understand that he knew he had been in the wrong. He had illusions about starting life again, in which he probably did not believe; but the make-believe was good for him. Long before the crash came, in Zoe's name—not his own—he had bought from the Government three hundred and twenty acres of land out near the Rockies and had spent five hundred dollars in improvements on it.

There it was in the West, one remaining asset still his own—or rather Zoe's—but worth little if he or she did not develop it. As he left St. Saviour's, however, he kept fixing his mind on that "last domain," as he called it to himself. If this was done intentionally, that he might be saved from distraction and despair, it was well done; if it was a real illusion—the old self-deception which had been his bane so often in the past—it still could only do him good at the present. It prevented him from noticing the attention he attracted on the railway journey from St. Saviour's to Montreal, cherishing his canary and his book as he went.

He was not so self-conscious now as in the days when he was surprised that Paris did not stop to say, "Bless us, here is that fine fellow, Jean Jacques Barbille of St. Saviour's!" He could concentrate himself more now on things that did not concern the impression he was making on the world. At present he could only think of Zoe and of her future.

When a patronizing and aggressive commercial traveller in the little hotel on a side-street where he had taken a room in Montreal said to him, "Bien, mon vieux" (which is to say, "Well, old cock"), "aren't you a long way from home?"

something of a new dignity came into Jean Jacques' bearing, very different from the assurance of the old days, and in reply he said:

"Not so far that I need be careless about my company." This made the landlady of the little hotel laugh quite hard, for she did not like the braggart "drummer" who had treated her with great condescension for a number of years. Also Madame Glozel liked Jean Jacques because of his canary. She thought there must be some sentimental reason for a man of fifty or more carrying a bird about with him; and she did not rest until she had drawn from Jean Jacques that he was taking the bird to his daughter in the West. There, however, madame was stayed in her search for information. Jean Jacques closed up, and did but smile when she adroitly set traps for him, and at last asked him outright where his daughter was.

Why he waited in Montreal it would be hard to say, save that it was a kind of middle place between the old life and the new, and also because he must decide what was to be his plan of search. First the West—first Winnipeg, but where after that? He had at last secured information of where Zoe and Gerard Fynes had stayed while in Montreal; and now he followed clues which would bring him in touch with folk who knew them. He came to know one or two people who were with Zoe and Gerard in the last days they spent in the metropolis, and he turned over and over in his mind every word said about his girl, as a child turns a sweetmeat in its mouth. This made him eager to be off; but on the very day he decided to start at once for the West, something strange happened.

It was towards the late afternoon of a Saturday, when the streets were full of people going to and from the shops in a marketing quarter, that Madame Glozel came to him and said:

"M'sieu', I have an idea, and you will not think it strange, for you have a kind heart. There is a woman—look you, it is a sad, sad story hers. She is ill and dying in a room a little way down the street. But yes, I am sure she is dying—of heart disease it is. She came here first when the illness took her, but she could not afford to stay. She went to those cheaper lodgings down the street. She used to be on the stage over in the States, and then she came back here, and there was a man—married to him or not I do not know, and I will not think. Well, the man—the brute—he left her when she got ill—but yes, forsook her absolutely! He was a land-agent or something like that, and all very fine to your face, to promise and to pretend—just make-believe. When her sickness got worse, off he went with 'Au revoir, my dear—I will be back to supper.' Supper! If she'd waited for her supper till he came back, she'd have waited as long as I've done for the fortune the gipsy promised me forty years ago. Away he went, the rogue, without a thought of her, and with another woman. That's what hurt her most of all. Straight from her that could hardly drag herself about—ah, yes, and has been as handsome a woman as ever was!—straight from her he went to a slut. She was a slut, m'sieu'—did I not know her? Did Ma'm'selle Slut not wait at table in this house and lead the men a dance here night and day-day and night till I found it out! Well, off he went with the slut, and left the lady behind.... You men, you treat women so."

Jean Jacques put out a hand as though to argue with her. "Sometimes it is the other way," he retorted. "Most of us have seen it like that."

"Well, for sure, you're right enough there, m'sieu'," was the response. "I've got nothing to say to that, except that it's a man that runs away with a woman, or that gets her to leave her husband when she does go. There's always a man that says, 'Come along, I'm the better chap for you.'"

Jean Jacques wearily turned his head away towards the cage where his canary was beginning to pipe its evening lay.

"It all comes to the same thing in the end," he said pensively; and then he who had been so quiet since he came to the little hotel—Glozel's, it was called—began to move about the room excitedly, running his fingers through his still bushy hair, which, to his credit, was always as clean as could be, burnished and shiny even at his mid-century period. He began murmuring to himself, and a frown settled on his fore head. Mme. Glozel saw that she had perturbed him, and that no doubt she had roused some memories which made sombre the sunny little room where the canary sang; where, to ravish the eyes of the pessimist, was a picture of Louis XVI. going to heaven in the arms of St. Peter.

When started, however, the good woman could no more "slow down" than her French pony would stop when its head was turned homewards from market. So she kept on with the history of the woman down the street.

"Heart disease," she said, nodding with assurance and finality; "and we know what that is—a start, a shock, a fall, a strain, and pht! off the poor thing goes. Yes, heart disease, and sometimes with such awful pain. But so; and yesterday she told me she had only a hundred dollars left. 'Enough to last me through,' she said to me. Poor thing, she lifted up her eyes with a way she has, as if looking for something she couldn't find, and she says, as simple as though she was asking about the price of a bed-tick, 'It won't cost more than fifty dollars to bury me, I s'pose?' Well, that made me squeamish, for the poor dear's plight came home to me so clear, and she young enough yet to get plenty out of life, if she had the chance. So I asked her again about her people—whether I couldn't send for someone belonging to her. 'There's none that belongs to me,' she says, 'and there's no one I belong to.'

"I thought very likely she didn't want to tell me about herself; perhaps because she had done wrong, and her family had not been good to her. Yet it was right I should try and get her folks to come, if she had any folks. So I said to her, 'Where was your home?' And now, what do you think she answered, m'sieu'?' 'Look there,' she said to me, with her big eyes standing out of her head almost—for that's what comes to her sometimes when she is in pain, and she looks more handsome then than at any other time—'Look there,' she said to me, 'it was in heaven, that's where—my home was; but I didn't know it. I hadn't been taught to know the place when I saw it.'

"Well, I felt my skin go goosey, for I saw what was going on in her mind, and how she was remembering what had happened to her some time, somewhere; but there wasn't a tear in her eyes, and I never saw her cry—never once, m'sieu'—well, but as brave as brave. Her eyes are always dry—burning. They're like two furnaces scorching up her face. So I never found out her history, and she won't have the priest. I believe that's because she wants to die unknown, and doesn't want to confess. I never saw a woman I was sorrier for, though I think she wasn't married to the man that left her. But whatever she was, there's good in her—I haven't known hundreds of women and had seven sisters for nothing. Well, there she is—not a friend near her at the last; for it's coming soon, the end—no one to speak to her, except the woman she pays to come in and look after her and nurse her a bit. Of course there's the landlady too, Madame Popincourt, a kind enough little cricket of a woman, but with no sense and no head for business. And so the poor sick thing has not a single pleasure in the world. She can't read, because it makes her head ache, she says; and she never writes to any one. One day she tried to sing a little, but it seemed to hurt her, and she stopped before she had begun almost. Yes, m'sieu', there she is without a single pleasure in the long hours when she doesn't sleep."

"There's my canary—that would cheer her up," eagerly said Jean Jacques, who, as the story of the chirruping landlady continued, became master of his agitation, and listened as though to the tale of some life for which he had concern. "Yes, take my canary to her, madame. It picked me up when I was down. It'll help her—such a bird it is! It's the best singer in the world. It's got in its throat the music of Malibran and Jenny Lind and Grisi, and all the stars in heaven that sang together. Also, to be sure, it doesn't charge anything, but just as long as there's daylight it sings and sings, as you know."

"M'sieu'—oh, m'sieu', it was what I wanted to ask you, and I didn't dare!" gushingly declared madame. "I never heard a bird sing like that—just as if it knew how much good it was doing, and with all the airs of a grand seigneur. It's a prince of birds, that. If you mean it, m'sieu', you'll do as good a thing as you have ever done."

"It would have to be much better, or it wouldn't be any use," remarked Jean Jacques.

The woman made a motion of friendliness with both hands. "I don't believe that. You may be queer, but you've got a kind eye. It won't be for long she'll need the canary, and it will cheer her. There certainly was never a bird so little tied to one note. Now this note, now that, and so amusing. At times it's as though he was laughing at you."

"That's because, with me for his master, he has had good reason to laugh," remarked Jean Jacques, who had come at last to take a despondent view of himself.

"That's bosh," rejoined Mme. Glozel; "I've seen several people odder than you."

She went over to the cage eagerly, and was about to take it away. "Excuse me," interposed Jean Jacques, "I will carry the cage to the house. Then you will go in with the bird, and I'll wait outside and see if the little rascal sings."

"This minute?" asked madame.

"For sure, this very minute. Why should the poor lady wait? It's a lonely time of day, this, the evening, when the long night's ahead."

A moment later the two were walking along the street to the door of Mme. Popincourt's lodgings, and people turned to look at the pair, one carrying something covered with a white cloth, evidently a savoury dish of some kind—the other with a cage in which a handsome canary hopped about, well pleased with the world.

At Mme. Popincourt's door Mme. Glozel took the cage and went upstairs. Jean Jacques, left behind, paced backwards and forwards in front of the house waiting and looking up, for Mme. Glozel had said that behind the front window on the third floor was where the sick woman lived. He had not long to wait. The setting sun shining full on the window had roused the bird, and he began to pour out a flood of delicious melody which flowed on and on, causing the people in the street to stay their steps and look up. Jean Jacques' face, as he listened, had something very like a smile. There was that in the smile belonging to the old pride, which in days gone by had made him say when he looked at his domains at the Manor Cartier—his houses, his mills, his store, his buildings and his lands—"It is all mine. It all belongs to Jean Jacques Barbille."

Suddenly, however, there came a sharp pause in the singing, and after that a cry—a faint, startled cry. Then Mme. Glozel's head was thrust out of the window three floors up, and she called to Jean Jacques to come quickly. As she bade him come, some strange premonition flashed to Jean Jacques, and with thumping heart he hastened up the staircase. Outside a bedroom door, Mme. Glozel met him. She was so excited she could only whisper.

"Be very quiet," she said. "There is something strange. When the bird sang as it did—you heard it—she sat like one in a trance. Then her face took on a look glad and frightened too, and she stared hard at the cage. 'Bring that cage to me,' she said. I brought it. She looked sharp at it, then she gave a cry and fell back. As I took the cage away I saw what she had been looking at—a writing at the bottom of the cage. It was the name Carmen."

With a stifled cry Jean Jacques pushed her aside and entered the room. As he did so, the sick woman in the big armchair, so pale yet so splendid in her death-beauty, raised herself up. With eyes that Francesca might have turned to the vision of her fate, she looked at the opening door, as though to learn if he who came was one she had wished to see through long, relentless days.

"Jean Jacques—ah, my beautiful Jean Jacques!" she cried out presently in a voice like a wisp of sound, for she had little breath; and then with a smile she sank back, too late to hear, but not too late to know, what Jean Jacques said to her.

CHAPTER XXII. BELLS OF MEMORY

However far Jean Jacques went, however long the day since leaving the Manor Cartier, he could not escape the signals from his past. He heard more than once the bells of memory ringing at the touch of the invisible hand of Destiny which accepts no philosophy save its own. At Montreal, for one hallowed instant, he had regained his lost Carmen, but he had turned from her grave—the only mourners being himself, Mme. Glozel and Mme. Popincourt, together with a barber who had coiffed her wonderful hair once a week—with a strange burning at his heart. That iceberg which most mourners carry in their breasts was not his, as he walked down the mountainside from Carmen's grave. Behind him trotted Mme. Glozel and Mme. Popincourt, like little magpies, attendants on this eagle of sorrow whose life-love had been laid to rest, her heart-troubles over. Passion or ennui would no more vex her.

She had had a soul, had Carmen Dolores, though she had never known it till her days closed in on her, and from the dusk she looked out of the casements of life to such a glowing as Jean Jacques had seen when his burning mill beatified the evening sky. She had known passion and vivid life in the days when she went hand-in-hand with Carvillho Gonzales through the gardens of Granada; she had known the smothering home-sickness which does not alone mean being sick for a distant home, but a sickness of the home that is; and she had known what George Masson gave her for one thrilling hour, and then—then the man who left her in her death-year, taking not only the last thread of hope which held her to life. This vulture had taken also little things dear to her daily life, such as the ring Carvillho Gonzales had given her long ago in Cadiz, also another ring, a gift of Jean Jacques, and things less valuable to her, such as money, for which she knew surely she would have no long use.

As she lay waiting for the day when she must go from the garish scene, she unconsciously took stock of life in her own way. There intruded on her sight the stages of the theatres where she had played and danced, and she heard again the music of the paloma and those other Spanish airs which had made the world dance under her girl's feet long ago. At first she kept seeing the faces of thousands looking up at her from the stalls, down at her from the gallery, over at her from the boxes; and the hot breath of that excitement smote her face with a drunken odour that sent her mad. Then, alas! somehow, as disease took hold of her, there were the colder lights, the colder breath from the few who applauded so little. And always the man who had left her in her day of direst need; who had had the last warm fires of her life, the last brief outrush of her soul, eager as it was for a joy which would prove she had not lost all when she fled from the Manor Cartier—a joy which would make her forget!

What she really did feel in this last adventure of passion only made her remember the more when she was alone now, her life at the Manor Cartier. She was wont to wake up suddenly in the morning—the very early morning—with the imagined sound of the gold Cock of Beaugard crowing in her ears. Memory, memory, memory—yet never a word, and never a hearsay of what had happened at the Manor Cartier since she had left it! Then there came a time when she longed intensely to see Jean Jacques before she died, though she could not bring herself to send word to him. She dreaded what the answer might be—not Jean Jacques' answer, but the answer of Life. Jean Jacques and her child, her Zoe—more his than hers in years gone by— one or both might be dead! She dared not write, but she cherished a desire long denied. Then one day she saw everything in her life more clearly than she had ever done. She found an old book of French verse, once belonging to Mme. Popincourt's husband, who had been a professor. Some lines therein opened up a chamber of her being never before unlocked. At first only the feeling of the thing came, then slowly the spiritual meaning possessed her. She learnt it by heart and let it sing to her as she lay half-sleeping and half-waking, half-living and half-dying:

"There is a World; men compass it through tears,

Dare doom for joy of it; it called me o'er the foam;

I found it down the track of sundering years,

Beyond the long island where the sea steals home.

"A land that triumphs over shame and pain,

Penitence and passion and the parting breath,

Over the former and the latter rain,

The birth-morn fire and the frost of death.

"From its safe shores the white boats ride away,

Salving the wreckage of the portless ships

The light desires of the amorous day,

The wayward, wanton wastage of the lips.

"Star-mist and music and the pensive moon

These when I harboured at that perfumed shore;

And then, how soon! the radiance of noon,

And faces of dear children at the door.

"Land of the Greater Love—men call it this;

No light-o'-love sets here an ambuscade;

No tender torture of the secret kiss

Makes sick the spirit and the soul afraid.

"Bright bowers and the anthems of the free,

The lovers absolute—ah, hear the call!

Beyond the long island and the sheltering sea,

That World I found which holds my world in thrall.

"There is a World; men compass it through tears,

Dare doom for joy of it; it called me o'er the foam;

I found it down the track of sundering years,

Beyond the long island where the sea steals home."

At last the inner thought of it got into her heart, and then it was in reply to Mme. Glozel, who asked her where her home was, she said: "In Heaven, but I did not know it!" And thus it was, too, that at the very last, when Jean Jacques followed the singing bird into her death-chamber, she cried out, "Ah, my beautiful Jean Jacques!"

And because Jean Jacques knew that, at the last, she had been his, soul and body, he went down from the mountain-side, the two black magpies fluttering mournfully and yet hopefully behind him, with more warmth at his heart than he had known for years. It never occurred to him that the two elderly magpies would jointly or severally have given the rest of their lives and their scant fortunes to have him with them either as husband, or as one who honourably hires a home at so much a day.

Though Jean Jacques did not know this last fact, when he fared forth again he left behind his canary with Mme. Glozel; also all Carmen's clothes, except the dress she died in, he gave to Mme. Popincourt, on condition that she did not wear them till he had gone. The dress in which Carmen died he wrapped up carefully, with her few jewels and her wedding-ring, and gave the parcel to Mme. Glozel to care for till he should send for it or come again.

"The bird—take him on my birthday to sing at her grave," he said to Mme. Glozel just before he went West. "It is in summer, my birthday, and you shall hear how he will sing there," he added in a low voice at the very door. Then he took out a ten-dollar bill, and would have given it to her to do this thing for him; but she would have none of his money. She only wiped her eyes and deplored his going, and said that if ever he wanted a home, and she was alive, he would know where to find it. It sounded and looked sentimental, yet Jean Jacques was never less sentimental in a very sentimental life. This particular morning he was very quiet and grave, and not in the least agitated; he spoke like one from a friendly, sun-bright distance to Mme. Glozel, and also to Mme. Popincourt as he passed her at the door of her house.

Jean Jacques had no elation as he took the Western trail; there was not much hope in his voice; but there was purpose and there was a little stream of peace flowing through his being—and also, mark, a stream of anger tumbling over rough places. He had read two letters addressed to Carmen by the man—Hugo Stolphe—who had left her to her fate; and there was a grim devouring thing in him which would break loose, if ever the man crossed his path. He would not go hunting him, but if he passed him or met him on the way—! Still he would go hunting—to find his Carmencita, his little Carmen, his Zoe whom he had unwittingly, God knew! driven forth into the far world of the millions of acres—a wide, wide hunting-ground in good sooth.

So he left his beloved province where he no longer had a home, and though no letters came to him from St. Saviour's, from Vilray or the Manor Cartier, yet he heard the bells of memory when the Hand Invisible arrested his footsteps. One day these bells rang so loud that he would have heard them were he sunk in the world's deepest well of shame; but, as it was, he now marched on hills far higher than the passes through the mountains which his patchwork philosophy had ever provided.

It was in the town of Shilah on the Watloon River that the bells boomed out—not because he had encountered one he had ever known far down by the Beau Cheval, or in his glorious province, not because he had found his Zoe, but because a man, the man—not George Masson, but the other—met him in the way.

Shilah was a place to which, almost unconsciously, he had deviated his course, because once Virginie Poucette had read him a letter from there. That was in the office of the little Clerk of the Court at Vilray. The letter was from Virginie's sister at Shilah, and told him that Zoe and her husband had gone away into farther fields of homelessness. Thus it was that Shilah ever seemed to him, as he worked West, a goal in his quest—not the last goal perhaps, but a goal.

He had been far past it by another route, up, up and out into the more scattered settlements, and now at last he had come to it again, having completed a kind of circle. As he entered it, the past crowded on to him with a hundred pictures. Shilah—it was where Virginie Poucette's sister lived; and Virginie had been a part of the great revelation of his life at St. Saviour's.

As he was walking by the riverside at Shilah, a woman spoke to him, touching his arm as she did so. He was in a deep dream as she spoke, but there certainly was a look in her face that reminded him of someone belonging to the old life. For an instant he could not remember. For a moment he did not even realize that he was at Shilah. His meditation had almost been a trance, and it took him time to adjust himself to the knowledge of the conscious mind. His subconsciousness was very powerfully alive in these days. There was not the same ceaselessly active eye, nor the vibration of the impatient body which belonged to the money-master and miller of the Manor Cartier. Yet the eye had more depth and force, and the body was more powerful and vigorous than it had ever been. The long tramping, the everlasting trail on false scents, the mental battling with troubles past and present, had given a fortitude and vigour to the body beyond what it had ever known. In spite of his homelessness and pilgrim equipment he looked as though he had a home—far off. The eyes did not smile; but the lips showed the goodness of his heart—and its hardness too. Hardness had never been there in the old days. It was, however, the hardness of resentment, and not of cruelty. It was not his wife's or his daughter's flight that he resented, nor yet the loss of all he had, nor the injury done him by Sebastian Dolores. No, his resentment was against one he had never seen, but was now soon to see. As his mind came back from the far places where it had been, and his eyes returned to the concrete world, he saw what the woman recalled to him. It was—yes, it was Virginie Poucette—the kind and beautiful Virginie—for her goodness had made him remember her as beautiful, though indeed she was but comely, like this woman who stayed him as he walked by the river.

"You are M'sieu' Jean Jacques Barbille?" she said questioningly.

"How did you know?" he asked.... "Is Virginie Poucette here?"

"Ah, you knew me from her?" she asked.

"There was something about her—and you have it also—and the look in the eyes, and then the lips!" he replied.

Certainly they were quite wonderful, luxurious lips, and so shapely too—like those of Virginie.

"But how did you know I was Jean Jacques Barbille?" he repeated.

"Well, then it is quite easy," she replied with a laugh almost like a giggle, for she was quite as simple and primitive as her sister. "There is a photographer at Vilray, and Virginie got one of your pictures there, and sent, it to me. 'He may come your way,' said Virginie to me, 'and if he does, do not forget that he is my friend.'"

"That she is my friend," corrected Jean Jacques. "And what a friend—merci, what a friend!" Suddenly he caught the woman's arm. "You once wrote to your sister about my Zoe, my daughter, that married and ran away—"

"That ran away and got married," she interrupted.

"Is there any more news—tell me, do you know-?"

But Virginie's sister shook her head. "Only once since I wrote Virginie have I heard, and then the two poor children—but how helpless they were, clinging to each other so! Well, then, once I heard from Faragay, but that was much more than a year ago. Nothing since, and they were going on—on to Fort Providence to spend the winter—for his health—his lungs."

"What to do—on what to live?" moaned Jean Jacques.

"His grandmother sent him a thousand dollars, so your Madame Zoe wrote me."

Jean Jacques raised a hand with a gesture of emotion. "Ah, the blessed woman! May there be no purgatory for her, but Heaven at once and always!"

"Come home with me—where are your things?" she asked.

"I have only a knapsack," he replied. "It is not far from here. But I cannot stay with you. I have no claim. No, I will not, for—"

"As to that, we keep a tavern," she returned. "You can come the same as the rest of the world. The company is mixed, but there it is. You needn't eat off the same plate, as they say in Quebec."

Quebec! He looked at her with the face of one who saw a vision. How like Virginie Poucette—the brave, generous Virginie—how like she was!

In silence now he went with her, and seeing his mood she did not talk to him. People stared as they walked along, for his dress was curious and his head was bare, and his hair like the coat of a young lion. Besides, this woman was, in her way, as brave and as generous as Virginie Poucette. In the very doorway of the tavern by the river a man jostled them. He did not apologize. He only leered. It made his foreign-looking, coarsely handsome face detestable.

"Pig!" exclaimed Virginie Poucette's sister. "That's a man—well, look out! There's trouble brewing for him. If he only knew! If suspicion comes out right and it's proved—well, there, he'll jostle the door-jamb of a jail."

Jean Jacques stared after the man, and somehow every nerve in his body became angry. He had all at once a sense of hatred. He shook the shoulder against which the man had collided. He remembered the leer on the insolent, handsome face.

"I'd like to see him thrown into the river," said Virginie Poucette's sister. "We have a nice girl here—come from Ireland—as good as can be. Well, last night—but there, she oughtn't to have let him speak to her. 'A kiss is nothing,' he said. Well, if he kissed me I would kill him—if I didn't vomit myself to death first. He's a mongrel—a South American mongrel with nigger blood."

Jean Jacques kept looking after the man. "Why don't you turn him out?" he asked sharply.

"He's going away to-morrow anyhow," she replied. "Besides, the girl, she's so ashamed—and she doesn't want anyone to know. 'Who'd want to kiss me after him' she said, and so he stays till to-morrow. He's not in the tavern itself, but in the little annex next door-there, where he's going now. He's only had his meals here, though the annex belongs to us as well. He's alone there on his dung-hill."

She brought Jean Jacques into a room that overlooked the river—which, indeed, hung on its very brink. From the steps at its river-door, a little ferry-boat took people to the other side of the Watloon, and very near—just a few hand-breadths away—was the annex where was the man who had jostled Jean Jacques.

CHAPTER XXIII. JEAN JACQUES HAS WORK TO DO

A single lighted lamp, turned low, was suspended from the ceiling of the raftered room, and through the open doorway which gave on to a little wooden piazza with a slight railing and small, shaky gate came the swish of the Watloon River. No moon was visible, but the stars were radiant and alive—trembling with life. There was something soothing, something endlessly soothing in the sound of the river. It suggested the ceaseless movement of life to the final fulness thereof.

So still was the room that it might have seemed to be without life, were it not for a faint sound of breathing. The bed, however, was empty, and no chair was occupied; but on a settle in a corner beside an unused fireplace sat a man, now with hands clasped between his knees, again with arms folded across his breast; but with his head always in a listening attitude. The whole figure suggested suspense, vigilance and preparedness. The man had taken off his boots and stockings, and his bare feet seemed to grip the floor; also the sleeves of his jacket were rolled up a little. It was not a figure you would wish to see in your room at midnight unasked. Once or twice he sighed heavily, as he listened to the river slishing past and looked out to the sparkle of the skies. It was as though the infinite had drawn near to the man, or else that the man had drawn near to the infinite. Now and again he brought his fists down on his knees with a savage, though noiseless, force. The peace of the river and the night could not contend successfully against a dark spirit working in him. When, during his vigil, he shook his shaggy head and his lips opened on his set teeth, he seemed like one who would take toll at a gateway of forbidden things.

He started to his feet at last, hearing footsteps outside upon the stairs. Then he settled back again, drawing near to the chimney-wall, so that he should not be easily seen by anyone entering. Presently there was the click of a latch, then the door opened and shut, and cigar-smoke invaded the room. An instant later a hand went up to the suspended oil-lamp and twisted the wick into brighter flame. As it did so, there was a slight noise, then the click of a lock. Turning sharply, the man under the lamp saw at the door the man who had been sitting in the corner. The man had a key in his hand. Exit now could only be had through the door opening on to the river.

"Who are you? What the hell do you want here?" asked the fellow under the lamp, his swarthy face drawn with fear and yet frowning with anger.

"Me—I am Jean Jacques Barbille," said the other in French, putting the key of the door in his pocket. The other replied in French, with a Spanish-

English accent. "Barbille—Carmen's husband! Well, who would have thought—!"

He ended with a laugh not pleasant to hear, for it was coarse with sardonic mirth; yet it had also an unreasonable apprehension; for why should he fear the husband of the woman who had done that husband such an injury!

"She treated you pretty bad, didn't she—not much heart, had Carmen!" he added.

"Sit down. I want to talk to you," said Jean Jacques, motioning to two chairs by a table at the side of the room. This table was in the middle of the room when the man under the lamp-Hugo Stolphe was his name—had left it last. Why had the table been moved?

"Why should I sit down, and what are you doing here?—I want to know that," Stolphe demanded. Jean Jacques' hands were opening and shutting. "Because I want to talk to you. If you don't sit down, I'll give you no chance at all.... Sit down!" Jean Jacques was smaller than Stolphe, but he was all whipcord and leather; the other was sleek and soft, but powerful too; and he had one of those savage natures which go blind with hatred, and which fight like beasts. He glanced swiftly round the room.

"There is no weapon here," said Jean Jacques, nodding. "I have put everything away—so you could not hurt me if you wanted.... Sit down!"

To gain time Stolphe sat down, for he had a fear that Jean Jacques was armed, and might be a madman armed—there were his feet bare on the brown painted boards. They looked so strange, so uncanny. He surely must be a madman if he wanted to do harm to Hugo Stolphe; for Hugo Stolphe had only "kept" the woman who had left her husband, not because of himself, but because of another man altogether—one George Masson. Had not Carmen herself told him that before she and he lived together? What grudge could Carmen's husband have against Hugo Stolphe?

Jean Jacques sat down also, and, leaning on the table said: "Once I was a fool and let the other man escape-George Masson it was. Because of what he did, my wife left me."

His voice became husky, but he shook his throat, as it were, cleared it, and went on. "I won't let you go. I was going to kill George Masson—I had him like that!" He opened and shut his hand with a gesture of fierce possession. "But I did not kill him. I let him go. He was so clever—cleverer than you will know how to be. She said to me—my wife said to me, when she thought I had killed him, 'Why did you not fight him? Any man would have fought him.' That was her view. She was right—not to kill without fighting. That is why I did not kill you at once when I knew."

"When you knew what?" Stolphe was staring at the madman.

"When I knew you were you. First I saw that ring—that ring on your hand. It was my wife's. I gave it to her the first New Year after we married. I saw it on your hand when you were drinking at the bar next door. Then I asked them your name. I knew it. I had read your letters to my wife—"

"Your wife once on a time!"

Jean Jacques' eyes swam red. "My wife always and always—and at the last there in my arms." Stolphe temporized. "I never knew you. She did not leave you because of me. She came to me because—because I was there for her to come to, and you weren't there. Why do you want to do me any harm?" He still must be careful, for undoubtedly the man was mad—his eyes were too bright.

"You were the death of her," answered Jean Jacques, leaning forward. "She was most ill-ah, who would not have been sorry for her! She was poor. She had been to you—but to live with a woman day by day, but to be by her side when the days are done, and then one morning to say, 'Au revoir till supper' and then go and never come back, and to take money and rings that belonged to her!... That was her death—that was the end of Carmen Barbille; and it was your fault."

"You would do me harm and not hurt her! Look how she treated you—and others."

Jean Jacques half rose from his seat in sudden rage, but he restrained himself, and sat down again. "She had one husband—only one. It was Jean Jacques Barbille. She could only treat one as she treated me—me, her husband. But you, what had you to do with that! You used her—so!" He made a motion as though to stamp out an insect with his foot. "Beautiful, a genius, sick and alone—no husband, no child, and you used her so! That is why I shall kill you to-night. We will fight for it."

Yes, but surely the man was mad, and the thing to do was to humour him, to gain time. To humour a madman—that is what one always advised, therefore Stolphe would make the pourparler, as the French say.

"Well, that's all right," he rejoined, "but how is it going to be done? Have you got a pistol?" He thought he was very clever, and that he would now see whether Jean Jacques Barbille was armed. If he was not armed, well, then, there would be the chances in his favour; it wasn't easy to kill with hands alone.

Jean Jacques ignored the question, however. He waved a hand impatiently, as though to dismiss it. "She was beautiful and splendid; she had been a queen down there in Quebec. You lied to her, and she was blind at first—I can see it all. She believed so easily—but yes, always! There she was what she was, and you were what you are, not a Frenchman, not Catholic, and an American—no, not an American—a South American. But no, not quite a South American, for there was the Portuguese nigger in you—Sit down!"

Jean Jacques was on his feet bending over the enraged mongrel. He had spoken the truth, and Carmen's last lover had been stung as though a serpent's tooth was in his flesh. Of all things that could be said about him, that which Jean Jacques said was the worst—that he was not all white, that he had nigger blood! Yet it was true; and he realized that Jean Jacques must have got his information in Shilah itself where he had been charged with it. Yet, raging as he was, and ready to take the Johnny Crapaud—that is the name by which he had always called Carmen's husband—by the throat, he was not yet sure that Jean Jacques was unarmed. He sat still under an anger greater than his own, for there was in it that fanaticism which only the love or hate of a woman could breed in a man's mind.

Suddenly Stolphe laughed outright, a crackling, mirthless, ironical laugh; for it really was absurdity made sublime that this man, who had been abandoned by his wife, should now want to kill one who had abandoned her! This outdid Don Quixote over and over.

"Well, what do you want?" he asked.

"I want you to fight," said Jean Jacques. "That is the way. That was Carmen's view. You shall have your chance to live, but I shall throw you in the river, and you can then fight the river. The current is swift, the banks are steep and high as a house down below there. Now, I am ready...!"

He had need to be, for Stolphe was quick, kicking the chair from beneath him, and throwing himself heavily on Jean Jacques. He had had his day at that in South America, and as Jean Jacques Barbille had said, the water was swift and deep, and the banks of the Watloon high and steep!

But Jean Jacques was unconscious of everything save a debt to be collected for a woman he had loved, a compensation which must be taken in flesh and blood. Perhaps at the moment, as Stolphe had said to himself, he was a little mad, for all his past, all his plundered, squandered, spoiled life was crying out at him like a hundred ghosts, and he was fighting with beasts at Ephesus. An exaltation possessed him. Not since the day when his hand was on the lever of the flume with George Masson below; not since the day he had turned his back for ever on the Manor Cartier had he been so young and so much his old self-an egotist, with all the blind confidence of his kind; a dreamer inflamed into action with all a mad dreamer's wild power. He was not fifty-two years of age, but thirty-two at this moment, and all the knowledge got of the wrestling river-drivers of his boyhood, when he had spent hours by the river struggling with river-champions, came back to him. It was a relief to his sick soul to wrench and strain, and propel and twist and force onward, step by step, to the door opening on the river, this creature who had left his Carmen to die alone.

"No, you don't—not yet. The jail before the river!" called a cool, sharp, sour voice; and on the edge of the trembling platform overhanging the river, Hugo Stolphe was dragged back from the plunge downward he was about to take, with Jean Jacques' hand at his throat.

Stolphe had heard the door of the bedroom forced, but Jean Jacques had not heard it; he was only conscious of hands dragging him back just at the moment of Stolphe's deadly peril.

"What is it?" asked Jean Jacques, seeing Stolphe in the hands of two men, and hearing the snap of steel. "Wanted for firing a house for insurance—wanted for falsifying the accounts of a Land Company—wanted for his own good, Mr. Hugo Stolphe, C.O.D.—collect on delivery!" said the officer of the law. "And collected just in time!"

"We didn't mean to take him till to-morrow," the officer added, "but out on the river one of us saw this gladiator business here in the red-light zone, and there wasn't any time to lose.... I don't know what your business with him was," the long-moustached detective said to Jean Jacques, "but whatever the grudge is, if you don't want to appear in court in the morning, the walking's good out of town night or day—so long!"

He hustled his prisoner out.

Jean Jacques did not want to appear in court, and as the walking was officially good at dawn, he said good-bye to Virginie Poucette's sister through the crack of a door, and was gone before she could restrain him.

"Well, things happen that way," he said, as he turned back to look at Shilah before it disappeared from view.

"Ah, the poor, handsome vaurien!" the woman at the tavern kept saying to her husband all that day; and she could not rest till she had written to Virginie how Jean Jacques came to Shilah in the evening, and went with the dawn.

CHAPTER XXIV. JEAN JACQUES ENCAMPED

The Young Doctor of Askatoon had a good heart, and he was exercising it honourably one winter's day near three years after Jean Jacques had left St. Saviour's.

"There are many French Canadians working on the railway now, and a good many habitant farmers live hereabouts, and they have plenty of children—why not stay here and teach school? You are a Catholic, of course, monsieur?"

This is what the Young Doctor said to one who had been under his anxious care for a few, vivid days. The little brown-bearded man with the grey-brown hair nodded in reply, but his gaze was on the billowing waste of snow, which stretched as far as eye could see to the pine-hills in the far distance. He nodded assent, but it was plain to be seen that the Young Doctor's suggestion was not in tune with his thought. His nod only acknowledged the reasonableness of the proposal. In his eyes, however, was the wanderlust which had possessed him for three long years, in which he had been searching for what to him was more than Eldorado, for it was hope and home. Hope was all he had left of the assets which had made him so great a figure—as he once thought—in his native parish of St. Saviour's. It was his fixed idea—une idee fixe, as he himself said. Lands, mills, manor, lime-kilns, factories, store, all were gone, and his wife Carmen also was gone. He had buried her with simple magnificence in Montreal—Mme. Glozel had said to her neighbours afterwards that the funeral cost over seventy-five dollars—and had set up a stone to her memory on which was carved, "Chez nous autrefois, et chez Dieu maintenant"—which was to say, "Our home once, and God's Home now."

That done, with a sorrow which still had the peace of finality in his mind, he had turned his face to the West. His long, long sojourning had brought him to Shilah where a new chapter of his life was closed, and at last to Askatoon, where another chapter still closed an epoch in his life, and gave finality to all. There he had been taken down with congestion of the lungs, and, fainting at the door of a drug-store, had been taken possession of by the Young Doctor, who would not send him to the hospital. He would not send him there because he found inside the waistcoat of this cleanest tramp—if he was a tramp—that he had ever seen, a book of philosophy, the daguerreotype photo of a beautiful foreign-looking woman, and some verses in a child's handwriting. The book of philosophy was underlined and interlined on every page, and every margin had comment which showed a mind of the most singular simplicity, searching wisdom, and hopeless confusion, all in one.

The Young Doctor was a man of decision, and he had whisked the little brown-grey sufferer to his own home, and tended him there like a brother till the danger disappeared; and behold he was rewarded for his humanity by as quaint an experience as he had ever known. He had not succeeded—though he tried hard—in getting at the history of his patient's life; but he did succeed in reading the fascinating story of a mind; for Jean Jacques, if not so voluble as of yore, had still moments when he seemed to hypnotize himself, and his thoughts were alive in an atmosphere of intellectual passion ill in accord with his condition.

Presently the little brown man withdrew his eyes from the window of the Young Doctor's office and the snowy waste beyond. They had a curious red underglow which had first come to them an evening long ago, when they caught from the sky the reflection of a burning mill. There was distance and the far thing in that underglow of his eyes. It had to do with the horizon, not with the place where his feet were. It said, "Out there, beyond, is what I go to seek, what I must find, what will be home to me."

"Well, I must be getting on," he said in a low voice to the Young Doctor, ignoring the question which had been asked.

"If you want work, there's work to be had here, as I said," responded the Young Doctor. "You are a man of education—"

"How do you know that?" asked Jean Jacques.

"I hear you speak," answered the other, and then Jean Jacques drew himself up and threw back his head. He had ever loved appreciation, not to say flattery, and he had had very little of it lately.

"I was at Laval," he remarked with a flash of pride. "No degree, but a year there, and travel abroad—the Grand Tour, and in good style, with plenty to do it with. Oh, certainly, no thought for sous, hardly for francs! It was gold louis abroad and silver dollars at home—that was the standard."

"The dollars are much scarcer now, eh?" asked the Young Doctor quizzically.

"I should think I had just enough to pay you," said the other, bridling up suddenly; for it seemed to him the Young Doctor had become ironical and mocking; and though he had been mocked much in his day, there were times when it was not easy to endure it.

The truth is the Young Doctor was somewhat of an expert in human nature, and he deeply wanted to know the history of this wandering habitant, because he had a great compassionate liking for him. If he could get the little man excited, he might be able to find out what he wanted. During the days in which the wanderer had been in his house, he had been far from silent, for he joked at his own suffering and kept the housekeeper laughing at his whimsical remarks; while he won her heart by the extraordinary cleanliness of his threadbare clothes, and the perfect order of his scantily-furnished knapsack. It had the exactness of one who was set upon a far course and would carry it out on scientific calculation. He had been full of mocking quips and sallies at himself, but from first to last he never talked. The things he said were nothing more than surface sounds, as it were—the ejaculations of a mind, not its language or its meanings.

"He's had some strange history, this queer little man," said the housekeeper to the Young Doctor; "and I'd like to know what it is. Why, we don't even know his name."

"So would I," rejoined the Young Doctor, "and I'll have a good try for it."

He had had his try more than once, but it had not succeeded. Perhaps a little torture would do it, he thought; and so he had made the rather tactless remark about the scarcity of dollars. Also his look was incredulous when Jean Jacques protested that he had enough to pay the fee.

"When you searched me you forgot to look in the right place," continued Jean Jacques; and he drew from the lining of the hat he held in his hand a little bundle of ten-dollar bills. "Here—take your pay from them," he said, and held out the roll of bills. "I suppose it won't be more than four dollars a day; and there's enough, I think. I can't pay you for your kindness to me, and I don't want to. I'd like to owe you that; and it's a good thing for a man himself to be owed kindness. He remembers it when he gets older. It helps him to forgive himself more or less for what he's sorry for in life. I've enough in this bunch to pay for board and professional attendance, or else the price has gone up since I had a doctor before."

He laughed now, and the laugh was half-ironical, half-protesting. It seemed to come from the well of a hidden past; and no past that is hidden has ever been a happy past.

The Young Doctor took the bills, looked at them as though they were curios, and then returned them with the remark that they were of a kind and denomination of no use to him. There was a twinkle in his eye as he said it. Then he added:

"I agree with you that it's a good thing for a man to lay up a little credit of kindness here and there for his old age. Well, anything I did for you was meant for kindness and nothing else. You weren't a bit of trouble, and it was simply your good constitution and a warm room and a few fly-blisters that pulled you through. It wasn't any skill of mine. Go and thank my housekeeper if you like. She did it all."

"I did my best to thank her," answered Jean Jacques. "I said she reminded me of Virginie Palass Poucette, and I could say nothing better than that, except one thing; and I'm not saying that to anybody."

The Young Doctor had a thrill. Here was a very unusual man, with mystery and tragedy, and yet something above both, in his eyes.

"Who was Virginie Palass Poucette?" he asked. Jean Jacques threw out a hand as though to say, "Attend—here is a great thing," and he began, "Virginie Poucette—ah, there...!"

Then he paused, for suddenly there spread out before him that past, now so far away, in which he had lived—and died. Strange that when he had mentioned Virginie's name to the housekeeper he had no such feeling as possessed him now. It had been on the surface, and he had used her name without any deep stir of the waters far down in his soul. But the Young Doctor was fingering the doors of his inner life—all at once this conviction came to him—and the past rushed upon him with all its disarray and ignominy, its sorrow, joy, elation and loss. Not since he had left the scene of his defeat, not since the farewell to his dead Carmen, that sweet summer day when he had put the lovely, ruined being away with her words, "Jean Jacques—ah, my beautiful Jean Jacques," ringing in his ears, had he ever told anyone his story. He had had a feeling that, as Carmen had been restored to him without his crying out, or vexing others with his sad history, so would Zoe also come back to him. Patience and silence was his motto.

Yet how was it that here and now there came an overpowering feeling, that he must tell this healer of sick bodies the story of an invalid soul? This man with the piercing dark-blue eyes before him, who looked so resolute, who had the air of one who could say,

"This is the way to go," because he knew and was sure; he was not to be denied.

"Who was Virginie Poucette?" repeated the Young Doctor insistently, yet ever so gently. "Was she such a prize among women? What did she do?"

A flood of feeling passed over Jean Jacques' face. He looked at his hat and his knapsack lying in a chair, with a desire to seize them and fly from the inquisitor; then a sense of fatalism came upon him. As though he had received an order from within his soul, he said helplessly:

"Well, if it must be, it must."

Then he swept the knapsack and his hat from the chair to the floor, and sat down.

"I will begin at the beginning," he said with his eyes fixed on those of the Young Doctor, yet looking beyond him to far-off things. "I will start from the time when I used to watch the gold Cock of Beaugard turning on the mill, when I sat in the doorway of the Manor Cartier in my pinafore. I don't know why I tell you, but maybe it was meant I should. I obey conviction. While you are able to keep logic and conviction hand in hand then everything is all right. I have found that out. Logic, philosophy are the props of life, but still you must obey the impulse of the soul—oh, absolutely! You must—"

He stopped short. "But it will seem strange to you," he added after a moment, in which the Young Doctor gestured to him to proceed, "to hear me talk like this—a wayfarer—a vagabond you may think. But in other days I was in places—"

The Young Doctor interjected with abrupt friendliness that there was no need to say he had been in high places. It would still be apparent, if he were in rags.

"Then, there, I will speak freely," rejoined Jean Jacques, and he took the cherry-brandy which the other offered him, and drank it off with gusto.

"Ah, that—that," he said, "is like the cordials Mere Langlois used to sell at Vilray. She and Virginie Poucette had a place together on the market—none better than Mere Langlois except Virginie Poucette, and she was like a drink of water in the desert.... Well, there, I will begin. Now my father was—"

It was lucky there were no calls for the Young Doctor that particular early morning, else the course of Jean Jacques' life might have been greatly different from what it became. He was able to tell his story from the very first to the last. Had it been interrupted or unfinished one name might not have been mentioned. When Jean Jacques used it, the Young Doctor sat up and leaned forward eagerly, while a light came into his face-a light of surprise, of revelation and understanding.

When Jean Jacques came to that portion of his life when manifest tragedy began—it began of course on the Antoine, but then it was not manifest—when his Carmen left him after the terrible scene with George Masson, he paused and said: "I don't know why I tell you this, for it is not easy to tell; but you saved my life, and you have a right to know what it is you have saved, no matter how hard it is to put it all before you."

It was at this point that he mentioned Zoe's name—he had hitherto only spoken of her as "my daughter"; and here it was the Young Doctor showed startled interest, and repeated the name after Jean Jacques. "Zoe! Zoe!—ah!" he said, and became silent again.

Jean Jacques had not noticed the Young Doctor's pregnant interruption, he was so busy with his own memories of the past; and he brought the tale to the day when he turned his face to the West to look for Zoe. Then he paused.

"And then?" the Young Doctor asked. "There is more—there is the search for Zoe ever since."

"What is there to say?" continued Jean Jacques. "I have searched till now, and have not found."

"How have you lived?" asked the other.

"Keeping books in shops and factories, collecting accounts for storekeepers, when they saw they could trust me, working at threshings and harvests, teaching school here and there. Once I made fifty dollars at a railway camp telling French Canadian tales and singing chansons Canadiennes. I have been insurance agent, sold lightning-rods, and been foreman of a gang building a mill—but I could not bear that. Every time I looked up I could see the Cock of Beaugard where the roof should be. And so on, so on, first one thing and then another till now—till I came to Askatoon and fell down by the drug-store, and you played the good Samaritan. So it goes, and I step on from here again, looking—looking."

"Wait till spring," said the Young Doctor. "What is the good of going on now! You can only tramp to the next town, and—"

"And the next," interposed Jean Jacques. "But so it is my orders." He put his hand on his heart, and gathered up his hat and knapsack.

"But you haven't searched here at Askatoon."

"Ah?... Ah-well, surely that is so," answered Jean Jacques wistfully. "I had forgotten that. Perhaps you can tell me, you who know all. Have you any news about my Zoe for me? Do you know—was she ever here? Madame Gerard Fynes would be her name. My name is Jean Jacques Barbille."

"Madame Zoe was here, but she has gone," quietly answered the Young Doctor.

Jean Jacques dropped the hat and the knapsack. His eyes had a glad, yet staring and frightened look, for the Young Doctor's face was not the bearer of good tidings.

"Zoe—my Zoe! You are sure?... When was she here?" he added huskily.

"A month ago."

"When did she go?" Jean Jacques' voice was almost a whisper.

"A month ago."

"Where did she go?" asked Jean Jacques, holding himself steady, for he had a strange dreadful premonition.

"Out of all care at last," answered the Young Doctor, and took a step towards the little man, who staggered, then recovered himself.

"She—my Zoe is dead! How?" questioned Jean Jacques in a ghostly sort of voice, but there was a steadiness and control unlike what he had shown in other tragic moments.

"It was a blizzard. She was bringing her husband's body in a sleigh to the railway here. He had died of consumption. She and the driver of the sleigh went down in the blizzard. Her body covered the child and saved it. The driver was lost also."

"Her child—Zoe's child?" quavered Jean Jacques. "A little girl—Zoe. The name was on her clothes. There were letters. One to her father—to you. Your name is Jean Jacques Barbille, is it not? I have that letter to you. We buried her and her husband in the graveyard yonder." He pointed. "Everybody was there—even when they knew it was to be a Catholic funeral."

"Ah! she was buried a Catholic?" Jean Jacques' voice was not quite so blurred now.

"Yes. Her husband had become Catholic too. A priest who had met them in the Peace River Country was here at the time."

At that, with a moan, Jean Jacques collapsed. He shed no tears, but he sat with his hands between his knees, whispering his child's name.

The Young Doctor laid a hand on his shoulder gently, but presently went out, shutting the door after him. As he left the room, however, he turned and said, "Courage, Monsieur Jean Jacques! Courage!"

When the Young Doctor came back a half-hour later he had in his hand the letters found in Zoe's pocket. "Monsieur Jean Jacques," he said gently to the bowed figure still sitting as he left him.

Jean Jacques got up slowly and looked at him as though scarce understanding where he was.

"The child—the child—where is my Zoe's child? Where is Zoe's Zoe?" he asked in agitation. His whole body seemed to palpitate. His eyes were all red fire.

CHAPTER XXV. WHAT WOULD YOU HAVE DONE?

The Young Doctor did not answer Jean Jacques at once. As he looked at this wayworn fugitive he knew that another, and perhaps the final crisis of his life, was come to Jean Jacques Barbille, and the human pity in him shrank from the possible end to it all. It was an old-world figure this, with the face of a peasant troubadour and the carriage of an aboriginal—or an aristocrat. Indeed, the ruin, the lonely wandering which had been Jean Jacques' portion, had given him that dignity which often comes to those who defy destiny and the blows of angry fate. Once there had been in his carriage something jaunty. This was merely life and energy and a little vain confidence; now there was the look of courage which awaits the worst the world can do. The life which, according to the world's logic, should have made Jean Jacques a miserable figure, an ill-nourished vagabond, had given him a physical grace never before possessed by him. The face, however, showed the ravages which loss and sorrow had made. It was lined and shadowed with dark reflection, yet the forehead had a strange smoothness and serenity little in accord with the rest of the countenance. It was like the snow-summit of a mountain below which are the ragged escarpments of trees and rocks, making a look of storm and warfare.

"Where is she—the child of my Zoe?" Jean Jacques repeated with an almost angry emphasis; as though the Young Doctor were hiding her from him.

"She is with the wife of Nolan Doyle, my partner in horse-breeding, not very far from here. Norah Doyle was married five years, and she had no child. This was a grief to her, even more than to Nolan, who, like her, came of a stock that was prolific. It was Nolan who found your daughter on the prairie—the driver dead, but she just alive when found. To give her ease of mind, Nolan said he would make the child his own. When he said that, she smiled and tried to speak, but it was too late, and she was gone."

In sudden agony Jean Jacques threw up his hands. "So young and so soon to be gone!" he exclaimed. "But a child she was and had scarce tasted the world. The mercy of God—what is it!"

"You can't take time as the measure of life," rejoined the Young Doctor with a compassionate gesture. "Perhaps she had her share of happiness—as much as most of us get, maybe, in a longer course."

"Share! She was worth a hundred years of happiness!" bitterly retorted Jean Jacques.

"Perhaps she knew her child would have it?" gently remarked the Young Doctor.

"Ah, that—that!... Do you think that possible, m'sieu'? Tell me, do you think that was in her mind—to have loved, and been a mother, and given her life for the child, and then the bosom of God. Answer that to me, m'sieu'?"

There was intense, poignant inquiry in Jean Jacques' face, and a light seemed to play over it. The Young Doctor heeded the look and all that was in the face. It was his mission to heal, and he knew that to heal the mind was often more necessary than to heal the body. Here he would try to heal the mind, if only in a little.

"That might well have been in her thought," he answered. "I saw her face. It had a wonderful look of peace, and a smile that would reconcile anyone she loved to her going. I thought of that when I looked at her. I recall it now. It was the smile of understanding."

He had said the only thing which could have comforted Jean Jacques at that moment. Perhaps it was meant to be that Zoe's child should represent to him all that he had lost—home, fortune, place, Carmen and Zoe. Perhaps she would be home again for him and all that home should mean—be the promise of a day when home would again include that fled from Carmen, and himself, and Carmen's child. Maybe it was sentiment in him, maybe it was sentimentality—and maybe it was not.

"Come, m'sieu'," Jean Jacques said impatiently: "let us go to the house of that M'sieu' Doyle. But first, mark this: I have in the West here some land—three hundred and twenty acres. It may yet be to me a home, where I shall begin once more with my Zoe's child—with my Zoe of Zoe—the home-life I lost down by the Beau Cheval.... Let us go at once."

"Yes, at once," answered the Young Doctor. Yet his feet were laggard, for he was not so sure that there would be another home for Jean Jacques with his grandchild as its star. He was thinking of Norah, to whom a waif of the prairie had made home what home should be for herself and Nolan Doyle.

"Read these letters first," he said, and he put the letters found on Zoe in Jean Jacques' eager hands.

A half-hour later, at the horse-breeding ranch, the Young Doctor introduced Jean Jacques to Norah Doyle, and instantly left the house. He had no wish to hear the interview which must take place between the two. Nolan Doyle was not at home, but in the room where they were shown to Norah was a cradle. Norah was rocking it with one foot while, standing by the table, she busied herself with sewing.

The introduction was of the briefest. "Monsieur Barbille wishes a word with you, Mrs. Doyle," said the Young Doctor. "It's a matter that doesn't need me. Monsieur has been in my care, as you know.... Well, there, I hope Nolan is all right. Tell him I'd like to see him to-morrow about the bay stallion and the roans. I've had an offer for them. Good-bye—good-bye, Mrs. Doyle"—he was at the door—"I hope you and Monsieur Barbille will decide what's best for the child without difficulty."

The door opened quickly and shut again, and Jean Jacques was alone with the woman and the child. "What's best for the child!"

That was what the Young Doctor had said. Norah stopped rocking the cradle and stared at the closed door. What had this man before her, this tramp habitant of whom she had heard, of course, to do with little Zoe in the cradle—her little Zoe who had come just when she was most needed; who had brought her man and herself close together again after an estrangement which neither had seemed able to prevent.

"What's best for the child!" How did the child in the cradle concern this man? Then suddenly his name almost shrieked in her brain. Barbille—that was the name on the letter found on the body of the woman who died and left Zoe behind—M. Jean Jacques Barbille.

Yes, that was the name. What was going to happen? Did the man intend to try and take Zoe from her?

"What is your name—all of it?" she asked sharply. She had a very fine set of teeth, as Jean Jacques saw mechanically; and subconsciously he said to himself that they seemed cruel, they were so white and regular—and cruel. The cruelty was evident to him as she bit in two the thread for the waistcoat she was mending, and then plied her needle again. Also the needle in her fingers might have been intended to sew up his shroud, so angry did it appear at the moment. But her teeth had something almost savage about them. If he had seen them when she was smiling, he would have thought them merely beautiful and rare, atoning for her plain face and flat breast— not so flat as it had been; for since the child had come into her life, her figure, strangely enough, had rounded out, and lines never before seen in her contour appeared.

He braced himself for the contest he knew was at hand, and replied to her. "My name is Jean Jacques Barbille. I was of the Manor Cartier, in St. Saviour's parish, Quebec. The mother of the child Zoe, there, was born at the Manor Cartier. I was her father. I am the grandfather of this Zoe." He motioned towards the cradle.

Then, with an impulse he could not check and did not seek to check—why should he? was not the child his own by every right?—he went to the cradle and looked down at the tiny face on its white pillow. There could be no mistake about it; here was the face of his lost Zoe, with something, too, of Carmen, and also the forehead of the Barbilles. As though the child knew, it opened its eyes wide-big, brown eyes like those of Carmen Dolores.

"Ah, the beautiful, beloved thing!" he exclaimed in a low-voice, ere Norah stepped between and almost pushed him back. An outstretched arm in front of her prevented him from stooping to kiss the child. "Stand back. The child must not be waked," she said. "It must sleep another hour. It has its milk at twelve o'clock. Stand aside. I won't have my child disturbed."

"Have my child disturbed"—that was what she had said, and Jean Jacques realized what he had to overbear. Here was the thing which must be fought out at once.

"The child is not yours, but mine," he declared. "Here is proof—the letter found on my Zoe when she died—addressed to me. The doctor knew. There is no mistake."

He held out the letter for her to see. "As you can read here, my daughter was on her way back to the Manor Cartier, to her old home at St. Saviour's. She was on her way back when she died. If she had lived I should have had them both; but one is left, according to the will of God. And so I will take her—this flower of the prairie—and begin life again."

The face Norah turned on him had that look which is in the face of an animal, when its young is being forced from it—fierce, hungering, furtive, vicious.

"The child is mine," she exclaimed—"mine and no other's. The prairie gave it to me. It came to me out of the storm. 'Tis mine-mine only. I was barren and wantin', and my man was slippin' from me, because there was only two of us in our home. I was older than him, and yonder was a girl with hair like a sheaf of wheat in the sun, and she kept lookin' at him, and he kept goin' to her. 'Twas a man she wanted, 'twas a child he wanted, and there they were wantin', and me atin' my heart out with passion and pride and shame and sorrow. There was he wantin' a child, and the girl wantin' a man, and I only wantin' what God should grant all women that give themselves to a man's arms after the priest has blessed them. And whin all was at the worst, and it looked as if he was away with her—the girl yonder—then two things happened. A man—he was me own brother and a millionaire if I do say it—he took her and married her; and then, too, Heaven's will sent this child's mother to her last end and the child itself to my Nolan's arms. To my husband's arms first it came, you understand; and he give the child to me, as it should be, and said he, 'We'll make believe it is our own.' But I said to him, 'There's no make-believe. 'Tis mine. 'Tis mine. It came to me out of the storm from the hand of God.' And so it was and is; and all's well here in the home, praise be to God. And listen to me: you'll not come here to take the child away from me. It can't be done. I'll not have it. Yes, you can let that sink down into you—I'll not have it."

During her passionate and defiant appeal Jean Jacques was restless with the old unrest of years ago, and his face twitched with emotion; but before she had finished he had himself in some sort of control.

"You—madame, you are only thinking of yourself in this. You are only thinking what you want, what you and your man need. But it's not to be looked at that way only, and—"

"Well, then it isn't to be looked at that way only," she interrupted. "As you say, it isn't Nolan and me alone to be considered. There's—"

"There's me," he interrupted sharply. "The child is bone of my bone. It is bone of all the Barbilles back to the time of Louis XI."—he had said that long ago to Zoe first, and it was now becoming a fact in his mind. "It is linked up in the chain of the history of the Barbilles. It is one with the generations of noblesse and honour and virtue. It is—"

"It's one with Abel the son of Adam, if it comes to that, and so am I," Norah bitingly interjected, while her eyes flashed fire, and she rocked the cradle more swiftly than was good for the child's sleep.

Jean Jacques flared up. "There were sons and daughters of the family of Adam that had names, but there were plenty others you whistled to as you would to a four-footer, and they'd come. The Barbilles had names—always names of their own back to Adam. The child is a Barbille—Don't rock the cradle so fast," he suddenly added with an irritable gesture, breaking off from his argument. "Don't you know better than that when a child's asleep? Do you want it to wake up and cry?"

She flushed to the roots of her hair, for he had said something for which she had no reply. She had undoubtedly disturbed the child. It stirred in its sleep, then opened its eyes, and at once began to cry.

"There," said Jean Jacques, "what did I tell you? Any one that had ever had children would know better than that."

Norah paid no attention to his mocking words, to the undoubted-truth of his complaint. Stooping over, she gently lifted the child up. With hungry tenderness she laid it against her breast and pressed its cheek to her own, murmuring and crooning to it.

"Acushla! Acushla! Ah, the pretty bird—mother's sweet—mother's angel!" she said softly.

She rocked backwards and forwards. Her eyes, though looking at Jean Jacques as she crooned and coaxed and made lullaby, apparently did not see him. She was as concentrated as though it were a matter of life and death. She was like some ancient nurse of a sovereign-child, plainly dressed, while the dainty white clothes of the babe in her arms—ah, hadn't she raided the hoard she had begun when first married, in the hope of a child of her own, to provide this orphan with clothes good enough for a royal princess!

The flow of the long, white dress of the waif on the dark blue of Norah's gown, which so matched the deep sapphire of her eyes, caught Jean Jacques' glance, allured his mind. It was the symbol of youth and innocence and home. Suddenly he had a vision of the day when his own Zoe had been given to the cradle for the first time, and he had done exactly what Norah had done—rocked too fast and too hard, and waked his little one; and Carmen had taken her up in her long white draperies, and had rocked to and fro, just like this, singing a lullaby. That lullaby he had himself sung often afterwards; and now, with his grandchild in Norah's arms there before him—with this other Zoe—the refrain of it kept lilting in his brain. In the pause ensuing, when Norah stooped to put the pacified child again in its nest, he also stooped over the cradle and began to hum the words of the lullaby:

"Sing, little bird, of the whispering leaves,

Sing a song of the harvest sheaves;

Sing a song to my Fanchonette,

Sing a song to my Fanchonette!

Over her eyes, over her eyes, over her eyes of violet,

See the web that the weaver weaves,

The web of sleep that the weaver weaves—

Weaves, weaves, weaves!

Over those eyes of violet,

Over those eyes of my Fanchonette,

Weaves, weaves, weaves—

See the web that the weaver weaves!"

For quite two minutes Jean Jacques and Norah Doyle stooped over the cradle, looking at Zoe's rosy, healthy, pretty face, as though unconscious of each other, and only conscious of the child. When Jean Jacques had finished the long first verse of the chanson, and would have begun another, Norah made a protesting gesture.

"She's asleep, and there's no more need," she said. "Wasn't it a good lullaby, madame?" Jean Jacques asked.

"So, so," she replied, on her defence again.

"It was good enough for her mother," he replied, pointing to the cradle.

"It's French and fanciful," she retorted—"both music and words."

"The child's French—what would you have?" asked Jean Jacques indignantly.

"The child's father was English, and she's goin' to be English, the darlin', from now on and on and on. That's settled. There's manny an English and Irish lullaby that'll be sung to her hence and onward; and there's manny an English song she'll sing when she's got her voice, and is big enough. Well, I think she'll sing like a canary."

"Do the birds sing in English?" exclaimed Jean Jacques, with anger in his face now. Was there ever any vanity like the vanity of these people who had made the conquest of Quebec, when sixteen Barbilles lost their lives, one of them being aide-de-camp to M. Vaudreuil, the governor!

"All the canaries I ever heard sung in English," she returned stubbornly.

"How do Frenchmen understand their singing, then?" irritably questioned Jean Jacques.

"Well, in translation only," she retorted, and with her sharp white teeth she again bit the black thread of her needle, tied the end into a little knot, and began to mend the waistcoat which she had laid down in the first moments of the interview.

"I want the child," Jean Jacques insisted abruptly. "I'll wait till she wakes, and then I'll wrap her up and take her away."

"Didn't you hear me say she was to be brought up English?" asked Norah, with a slowness which clothed her fiercest impulses.

"Name of God, do you think I'll let you have her!" returned Jean Jacques with asperity and decision. "You say you are alone, you and your M'sieu' Nolan. Well, I am alone—all alone in the world, and I need her—Mother of God, I need her more than I ever needed anything in my life! You have each other, but I have only myself, and it is not good company. Besides, the child is mine, a Barbille of Barbilles, une legitime—a rightful child of marriage. But if it was a love-child only it would still be mine, being my daughter's child. Look you, it is no such thing. It is of those who can claim inheritance back to Louis XI. She will be to me the gift of God in return for the robbery of death."

He leaned over the cradle, and his look was like that of one who had found a treasure in the earth.

Now she struck hard. Yet very subtly too did she attack him. "You—you are thinking of yourself, m'sieu', only of yourself. Aren't you going to think of the child at all? It isn't yourself that counts so much. You've had your day, or the part of it that matters most. But her time is not yet even begun. It's all—all—before her. You say you'll take her away—well, to what? To what will you take her? What have you got to give her? What—"

"I have the three hundred and twenty acres out there"—he pointed westward—"and I will make a home and begin again with her."

"Three hundred and twenty acres—'out there'!" she exclaimed in scorn. "Any one can have a farm here for the askin'. What is that? Is it a home? What have you got to start a home with? Do you deny you are no better than a tramp? Have you got a hundred dollars in the world? Have you got a roof over your head? Have you got a trade? You'll take her where—to what? Even if you had a home, what then? You would have to get someone to look after her—some old crone, a wench maybe, who'd be as fit to bring up a child as I would be to—" she paused and looked round in helpless quest for a simile, when, in despair, she caught sight of Jean Jacques' watch-chain—"as I would be to make a watch!" she added.

Instinctively Jean Jacques drew out the ancient timepiece he had worn on the Grand Tour; which had gone down with the Antoine and come up with himself. It gave him courage to make the fight for his own.

"The good God would see that—" he began.

"The good God doesn't interfere in bringing up babies," she retorted. "That's the work for the fathers and mothers, or godfathers and godmothers."

"You are neither," exclaimed Jean Jacques. "You have no rights at all."

"I have no rights—eh? I have no rights! Look at the child. Look at the way she's clothed. Look at the cradle in which it lies. It cost fifteen dollars; and the clothes—what they cost would keep a family half a year. I have no rights, is it?—I who stepped in and took the child without question, without bein' asked, and made it my own, and treated it as if it was me own. No, by the love of God, I treated it far, far better than if it had been me own. Because a child was denied me, the hunger of the years made me love the child as a mother would on a desert island with one child at her knees."

"You can get another-one not your own, as this isn't," argued Jean Jacques fiercely.

She was not to be forced to answer his arguments directly. She chose her own course to convince. "Nolan loves this child as if it was his," she declared, her eyes all afire, "but he mightn't love another—men are queer creatures. Then where would I be? and what would the home be but what it was before—as cold, as cold and bitter! It was the hand of God brought the child to the door of two people who had no child and who prayed for one. Do you deny it was the hand of God that brought your daughter here away, that put the child in my arms? Not its mother, am I not? But I love her better than twenty mothers could. It's the hunger—the hunger—the hunger in me. She's made a woman of me. She has a home where everything is hers—everything. To see Nolan play with her, tossin' her up and down in his arms as if he'd done it all his life—as natural as natural! To take her away from that—all the comfort here where she can have anything she wants! With my old mother to care for her, if so be I was away to market or whereabouts—one that brought up six children, a millionaire among them, praise be to God as my mother did—to take this delicate little thing away from here, what a sin and crime 'twould be! She herself 'd never forgive you for it, if ever she grew up—though that's not likely, things bein' as they are with you, and you bein' what you are. Ah, there—there she is awake and smilin', and kickin' up her pretty toes this minute! There she is, the lovely little Zoe, with eyes like black pearls.... See now—see now which she'll come to—to you or me, m'sieu'. There, put out your arms to her, and I'll put out mine, and see which she'll take. I'll stand by that—I'll stand by that. Let the child decide. Hold out your arms, and so will I."

With an impassioned word Jean Jacques reached down his arms to the child, which lay laughing up at them and kicking its pink toes into the air, and Norah Doyle did the same, murmuring an Irish love-name for a child. Jean Jacques was silent, but in his face was the longing of a soul sick for home, of one who desires the end of a toilsome road.

The laughing child crooned and spluttered and shook its head, as though it was playing some happy game. It looked first at Norah, then at Jean Jacques, then at Norah again, and then, with a little gurgle of pleasure, stretched out its arms to her and half-raised itself from the pillow. With a glad cry Norah gathered it to her bosom, and triumph shone in her face.

"Ah, there, you see!" she said, as she lifted her face from the blossom at her breast.

"There it is," said Jean Jacques with shaking voice.

"You have nothing to give her—I have everything," she urged. "My rights are that I would die for the child—oh, fifty times!... What are you going to do, m'sieu'?"

Jean Jacques slowly turned and picked up his hat. He moved with the dignity of a hero who marches towards a wall to meet the bullets of a firing-squad.

"You are going?" Norah whispered, and in her eyes was a great relief and the light of victory. The golden link binding Nolan and herself was in her arms, over her heart.

Jean Jacques did not speak a word in reply, though his lips moved. She held out the little one to him for a good-bye, but he shook his head. If he did that—if he once held her in his arms—he would not be able to give her up. Gravely and solemnly, however, he stooped over and kissed the lips of the child lying against Norah's breast. As he did so, with a quick, mothering instinct Norah impulsively kissed his shaggy head, and her eyes filled with tears. She smiled too, and Jean Jacques saw how beautiful her teeth were—cruel no longer.

He moved away slowly. At the door he turned, and looked back at the two—a long, lingering look he gave. Then he faced away from them again.

"Moi je suis philosophe," he said gently, and opened the door and stepped out and away into the frozen world.

EPILOGUE.

Change might lay its hand on the parish of St. Saviour's, and it did so on the beautiful sentient living thing, as on the thing material and man-made; but there was no change in the sheltering friendship of Mont Violet or the flow of the illustrious Beau Cheval. The autumns also changed not at all. They cast their pensive canopies over the home-scene which Jean Jacques loved so well, before he was exhaled from its bosom.

One autumn when the hillsides were in those colours which none but a rainbow of the moon ever had, so delicately sad, so tenderly assuring, a traveller came back to St. Saviour's after a long journey. He came by boat to the landing at the Manor Cartier, rather than by train to the railway-station, from which there was a drive of several miles to Vilray. At the landing he was met by a woman, as much a miniature of the days of Orleanist France as himself. She wore lace mits which covered the hands but not the fingers, and her gown showed the outline of a meek crinoline.

"Ah, Fille—ah, dear Fille!" said the little fragment of an antique day, as the Clerk of the Court—rather, he that had been for so many years Clerk of the Court—stepped from the boat. "I can scarce believe that you are here once more. Have you good news?"

"It was to come back with good news that I went," her brother answered smiling, his face lighted by an inner exaltation.

"Dear, dear Fille!" She always called him that now, and not by his Christian name, as though he was a peer. She had done so ever since the Government had made him a magistrate, and Laval University had honoured him with the degree of doctor of laws.

She was leading him to the pony-carriage in which she had come to meet him, when he said:

"Do you think you could walk the distance, my dear?... It would be like old times," he added gently.

"I could walk twice as far to-day," she answered, and at once gave directions for the young coachman to put "His Honour's" bag into the carriage. In spite of Fille's reproofs she insisted in calling him that to the servants. They had two servants now, thanks to the legacy left them by the late Judge Carcasson. Presently M. Fille took her by the hand. "Before we start—one look yonder," he murmured, pointing towards the mill which had once belonged to Jean Jacques, now rebuilt and looking almost as of old. "I promised Jean Jacques that I would come and salute it in his name, before I did aught else, and so now I do salute it."

He waved a hand and made a bow to the gold Cock of Beaugard, the pride of all the vanished Barbilles. "Jean Jacques Barbille says that his head is up like yours, M. le Coq, and he wishes you many, many winds to come," he recited quite seriously, and as though it was not out of tune with the modern world.

The gold Cock of Beaugard seemed to understand, for it swung to the left, and now a little to the right, and then stood still, as if looking at the little pair of exiles from an ancient world—of which the only vestiges remaining may be found in old Quebec.

This ceremony over, they walked towards Mont Violet, averting their heads as they passed the Manor Cartier, in a kind of tribute to its departed master—as a Stuart Legitimist might pass the big palace at the end of the Mall in London. In the wood-path, Fille took his sister's hand.

"I will tell you what you are so trembling to hear," he said. "There they are at peace, Jean Jacques and Virginie—that best of best women."

"To think—married to Virginie Poucette—to think of that!" His sister's voice fluttered as she spoke. "But entirely. There was nothing in the way—and she meant to have him, the dear soul! I do not blame her, for at bottom he is as good a man as lives. Our Judge called him 'That dear fool, Jean Jacques, a man of men in his way, after all,' and our Judge was always right—but yes, nearly always right."

After a moment of contented meditation he resumed. "Well, when Virginie sold her place here and went to live with her sister out at Shilah in the West, she said, 'If Jean Jacques is alive, he will be on the land which was Zoe's, which he bought for her. If he is alive—then!' So it was, and by one of the strange accidents which chance or women like Virginie, who have plenty of courage in their simpleness, arrange, they met on that three hundred and sixty acres. It was like the genius of Jean Jacques to have done that one right thing which would save him in the end—a thing which came out of his love for his child—the emotion of an hour. Indeed, that three hundred and sixty acres was his salvation after he learned of Zoe's death, and the other little Zoe, his grandchild, was denied to him—to close his heart against what seemed that last hope, was it not courage? And so, and so he has the reward of his own soul—a home at last once more."

"With Virginie Poucette—Fille, Fille, how things come round!" exclaimed the little lady in the tiny bonnet with the mauve strings.

"More than Virginie came round," he replied almost oracularly. "Who, think you, brought him the news that coal was found on his acres—who but the husband of Virginie's sister! Then came Virginie. On the day Jean Jacques saw her again, he said to her, 'What you would have given me at such cost, now let me pay for with the rest of my life. It is the great thought which was in your heart that I will pay for with the days left to me.'"

A flickering smile brightened the sensitive ascetic face, and humour was in the eyes. "What do you think Virginie said to that? Her sister told me. Virginie said to that, 'You will have more days left, Jean Jacques, if you have a better cook. What do you like best for supper?' And Jean Jacques laughed much at that. Years ago he would have made a speech at it!"

"Then he is no more a philosopher?"

"Oh always, always, but in his heart, and not with his tongue. I cried, and so did he, when we met and when we parted. I think I am getting old, for indeed I could not help it: yet there was peace in his eyes—peace."

"His eyes used to rustle so."

"Rustle—that is the word. Now, that is what, he has learned in life—the way to peace. When I left him, it was with Virginie close beside him, and when I said to him, 'Will you come back to us one day, Jean Jacques?' he said, 'But no, Fille, my friend; it is too far. I see it—it is a million miles away—too great a journey to go with the feet, but with the soul I will visit it. The soul is a great traveller. I see it always—the clouds and the burnings and the pitfalls gone—out of sight—in memory as it was when I was a child. Well, there it is, everything has changed, except the child-memory. I have had, and I have had not; and there it is. I am not the same man—but yes, in my love just the same, with all the rest—' He did not go on, so I said, 'If not the same, then what are you, Jean Jacques?'"

"Ah, Fille, in the old days he would have said that he was a philosopher"—said his sister interrupting. "Yes, yes, one knows—he said it often enough and had need enough to say it. Well, said he to me, 'Me, I am a'—then he stopped, shook his head, and so I could scarcely hear him, murmured, 'Me—I am a man who has been a long journey with a pack on his back, and has got home again.' Then he took Virginie's hand in his."

The old man's fingers touched the corner of his eye as though to find something there; then continued. "'Ah, a pedlar!' said I to him, to hear what he would answer. 'Follies to sell for sous of wisdom,' he answered. Then he put his arm around Virginie, and she gave him his pipe."

"I wish M. Carcasson knew," the little grey lady remarked.

"But of course he knows," said the Clerk of the Court, with his face turned to the sunset.

Milton Keynes UK
Ingram Content Group UK Ltd.
UKHW051046190424
441445UK00011B/415

9 781835 915196